Anguished hearts…

"Any woman I married would rightfully expect to come first in my life, before my family. But that's not possible, Mattie, not for me. I knew full well what I was promising my father."

"But Joe—"

"So, rather than hurt someone else, or get hurt myself, I decided that it's best that I never marry." His gaze met hers, his eyes dark and very determined. "And it's not something I ever expect to change my mind about."

Mattie merely stared at him in the darkness, her heart aching in a way that left her wanting to weep.

She'd fallen hopelessly, helplessly in love with Joe.

She'd fallen in love with yet another man who didn't want a wife or a family. No matter what the reasons, the reality didn't change. She'd made the same mistake once again….

Dear Reader,

It's that time of year again…for decking the halls, trimming the tree…and sitting by the crackling fire with a good book. And we at Silhouette have just the one to start you off—Joan Elliott Pickart's *The Marrying MacAllister,* the next offering in her series, THE BABY BET: MACALLISTER'S GIFTS. When a prospective single mother out to adopt one baby finds herself unable to choose between two orphaned sisters, she is distressed, until the perfect solution appears: marry handsome fellow traveler and renowned single guy Matt MacAllister! Your heart will melt along with his resolve.

MONTANA MAVERICKS: THE KINGSLEYS concludes with *Sweet Talk* by Jackie Merritt. When the beloved town veterinarian—and trauma survivor—is captivated by the town's fire chief, she tries to suppress her feelings. But the rugged hero is determined to make her his. Reader favorite Annette Broadrick continues her SECRET SISTERS series with *Too Tough To Tame.* A woman out to avenge the harm done to her family paints a portrait of her nemesis—which only serves to bring the two of them together. In *His Defender,* Stella Bagwell offers another MEN OF THE WEST book, in which a lawyer hired to defend a ranch owner winds up under his roof…and falling for her newest client! In *Make-Believe Mistletoe* by Gina Wilkins, a single female professor who has wished for an eligible bachelor for Christmas hardly thinks the grumpy but handsome man who's reluctantly offered her shelter from a storm is the answer to her prayers—at least not at first. And speaking of Christmas wishes—five-year-old twin boys have made theirs—and it all revolves around a new daddy. The candidate they have in mind? The handsome town sheriff, in *Daddy Patrol* by Sharon DeVita.

As you can see, no matter what romantic read you have in mind this holiday season, we have the book for you. Happy holidays, happy reading—and come back next month, for six new wonderful offerings from Silhouette Special Edition!

Sincerely,

Gail Chasan
Senior Editor

Please address questions and book requests to:
Silhouette Reader Service
U.S.: 3010 Walden Ave., P.O. Box 1325, Buffalo, NY 14269
Canadian: P.O. Box 609, Fort Erie, Ont. L2A 5X3

Daddy Patrol

SHARON DE VITA

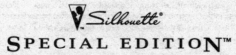

SPECIAL EDITION™

Published by Silhouette Books

America's Publisher of Contemporary Romance

To my mother-in-law, Frances Lillian Cushing. At eighty-four you
continue to be a source of inspiration, courage and grace to me.
You've taught me so very much in this year since we both lost our
sons. And I am so very grateful, not just for your continued love
and support, but also for your kindness, your unconditional
acceptance and your graciousness—even in grief.

And of course for my husband, the Colonel, without whom
life would simply have no meaning.

SILHOUETTE BOOKS

ISBN 0-373-24584-X

DADDY PATROL

Copyright © 2003 by Sharon De Vita

All rights reserved. Except for use in any review, the reproduction
or utilization of this work in whole or in part in any form by any
electronic, mechanical or other means, now known or hereafter
invented, including xerography, photocopying and recording, or in
any information storage or retrieval system, is forbidden without
the written permission of the editorial office, Silhouette Books,
233 Broadway, New York, NY 10279 U.S.A.

All characters in this book have no existence outside the imagination of
the author and have no relation whatsoever to anyone bearing the same
name or names. They are not even distantly inspired by any individual
known or unknown to the author, and all incidents are pure invention.

This edition published by arrangement with Harlequin Books S.A.

® and TM are trademarks of Harlequin Books S.A., used under license.
Trademarks indicated with ® are registered in the United States Patent
and Trademark Office, the Canadian Trade Marks Office and in other
countries.

Visit Silhouette at www.eHarlequin.com

Printed in U.S.A.

SHARON DE VITA,

a former adjunct professor of literature and communications, is a *USA TODAY* bestselling, award-winning author of numerous works of fiction and nonfiction. Her first novel won a national writing competition for Best Unpublished Romance Novel of 1985. This award-winning book, *Heavenly Match*, was subsequently published by Silhouette in 1985. With over two million copies of her novels in print, Sharon's professional credentials have earned her a place in *Who's Who in American Authors, Editors and Poets* as well as the *International Who's Who of Authors*. In 1987, Sharon was the proud recipient of the *Romantic Times* Lifetime Achievement Award for Excellence in Writing.

A newlywed, Sharon met her husband while doing research for one of her books. The widowed, recently retired military officer was so wonderful, Sharon decided to marry him after she interviewed him! Sharon and her new husband have seven grown children, five grandchildren, and currently reside in Arizona.

Deer Offisir Frendlee

When you was at skool you said if we was ever in trubull or had a problum to tell a poleece man cuz you was our frend. Well we got a problum. A big one. Culd you help?

Love,

Cody and Connor Maguire

Chapter One

"Mom! Mom! We're home." The boys' voices echoed through the house, nearly reaching the rafters as the back door slammed soundly.

By the time Mattie Maguire got to the kitchen, Cody and Connor, her beloved five-year-old nearly identical twin sons were shedding their school clothes and their backpacks—in the middle of the kitchen floor.

"Hi, guys," she said with a smile, reaching out to shut the back door and scooping up both backpacks, setting them on the kitchen counter so no one would trip over them. "Did you have a good day?" Mattie bent and gave each twin a loud, smacking kiss on the cheek as she gathered up Cody's school sweater off the floor.

"I got a gold star on my art paper," Connor said proudly, waving the red paper that was now wrinkled in his fist.

"You did?" Mattie retrieved the paper, smoothed it out, then placed it on the refrigerator with one of the many magnets she kept there to display the boys' schoolwork. "My hero." She bent and kissed him again.

"And I got an A on my vocabulary quiz," Cody announced, toeing off his school shoes and wiggling his toes. "I can spell *dog* and *car*."

"You can? I'm very impressed." She pretended to look behind him, next to him and in his hair, making him giggle. "So where's your quiz?"

"Backpack," Cody said with a shrug.

Mattie reached over and unzipped the blue backpack, knowing she'd find Cody's quiz crumbled in a heap. Neatness was not high on the list of her sons' strong suits. With a grin, she retrieved the crumpled paper, smoothed it out, then hung it up on the refrigerator. "Good job, boys." She kissed Cody. "I'm very proud of both of you."

"Guess what Amy Bartlett did in school today?" Connor asked, blue eyes shining in excitement behind his oversize glasses as his gaze traveled from his mother to the snack waiting for him on the counter, obviously torn between his big news and his even bigger hunger.

Connor was two minutes older and twice as serious as his younger, more mischievous brother. Although nearly identical from the tops of their strawberry-blond hair to the freckles on their small, upturned noses, only Connor's glasses enabled others to tell the boys apart.

"What did Amy Bartlett do, honey?" she asked, handing him a glass of milk and a peanut-butter-filled cracker she'd prepared and set out on the counter.

"She barfed," Cody announced with a giggle as he reached for his own glass of milk. He was bouncing from foot to foot, a clear indication he was really excited about something.

Or had to go to the bathroom.

His milk almost splashed over the rim of the glass until Mattie reached out and gave him a hand to steady it. He grinned, took a big gulp, then swiped his mouth on the sleeve of his school shirt, giving her a sheepish shrug at the look she shot him.

"Yeah," Connor confirmed, shoving his glasses up his freckled nose with one fist. "Amy barfed in music class. All over Miss Wilson's—"

"Singing carpet," Cody finished with a delighted grin. "It was so gross." Cody wrinkled his nose and continued bouncing up and down.

Like most twins, her boys had a habit of finishing each other's sentences. They'd been doing it since they'd learned to talk, so she was used to it, but it usually unnerved others who weren't.

"Was Amy sick?" Mattie asked, concerned, as she juggled Connor's glass of milk in order to help him off with his school sweater.

"Dunno," Cody announced with a shrug of his slender shoulders.

"Miss Wilson took Amy to the nurse's office." Connor scratched his head. "I think she went home."

"Sounds like you had an exciting day," Mattie said, cocking her head. "Anything else happen I should know about?"

"Nah," Cody said. "It was a pretty boring day."

"'Cept Bobby Dawson's a pooper head." Connor interjected solemnly, a frown tugging his mouth down. Mattie didn't miss the secretive look the boys exchanged. It immediately set off her mother's early-warning alarm system.

"That's not a very nice thing to call someone, Connor," she scolded gently, reaching out to ruffle his hair and push up his glasses. She knew when they'd moved here to Healing Harbor, Wisconsin, three months ago that the boys might have a hard time adjusting to a new school, and new kids.

For the past couple of days she'd had a feeling something was going on, something they had yet to confide in her, and it was beginning to worry her.

Since her husband had abandoned her when she found out she was expecting and then had been killed two months before the twins were born—and before she'd had a chance to finalize their divorce—she'd been mother and father to the boys their whole life, and they'd always been exceptionally close. The boys knew there wasn't anything they couldn't talk to her about.

Mattie bent down so she was eye level with Connor. "Honey, did Bobby Dawson do or say something to make you mad or upset you?'' She brushed a lock of hair off his forehead as the twins exchanged glances. Mattie sighed. ''Okay, fess up, what's going on?'' She looked from one innocent freckled face to the other as she stood up. ''Ever since you came back from your grandparents last weekend, you two munchkins have been acting pretty darn strange.''

Mattie's gaze shifted from one twin to the other again as another faint warning bell went off inside her. Her relationship with her former in-laws was fragile and fractious—and that was on the best of days.

Her former in-laws had made no secret of the fact that they disapproved of her as both their son's wife, and now, their grandchildren's mother.

''Are you guys in trouble?'' she asked suspiciously, trying not to jump to conclusions. Just because the boys had been acting strange since their return from their grandparents' didn't mean there was anything wrong, she scolded herself. But whenever the boys began communicating with each other by looks and sighs, it usually meant something was up.

They were great kids, and rarely gave her a moment of real worry, thankfully, but they *were* boys, and she had to admit they had a tendency to be a bit…mischievous as well as a bit overzealous at times.

And if she threw her late husband's parents into the mix, well then, Mattie thought with a weary sigh, that alone could mean a whole lot of trouble. Especially for her since her former in-laws were so vocal and obvious in their dislike and disapproval of her.

''We're not in trouble,'' Connor protested, eyes wide and blinking innocently behind his glasses. ''Honest, Ma.'' He poked his brother with his elbow for confirmation. ''Are we?''

''Nah,'' Cody said, swiping his fist against his nose, then reaching for a peanut-butter-filled cracker. ''And nuthin' happened today 'cept all the girls started screeching when Amy puked.'' Cody began mimicking a high-wailed screech, holding his stomach with one hand and his milk glass in the other as he did a mock reprise of Amy's afternoon antics.

''I get the picture,'' Mattie said with a smile, covering her ears for protection. Whatever was going on, the boys weren't ready to talk about it yet. In the years since she'd been a woefully naive new mother, terrified at being totally responsible for two helpless babies, she'd learned when to push and when not to. Generally, if something was bothering the boys, one or the other would come talk to her eventually. She'd learned long ago to be patient.

"Cody, do you have to go to the bathroom?" she asked with a knowing lift of her eyebrow as she watched him bounce around the room.

In answer, he slammed his milk glass onto the kitchen table and made a mad dash out of the kitchen. "Be right back," he called over his shoulder, making her laugh.

"Girls are stupid," Connor said without heat, licking the peanut butter off his cracker.

"I'm a girl," Mattie pointed out with a smile.

Connor's face registered horror at the thought. "Nah," he finally said in relief, shaking his head. "You're a mom."

"True," Mattie said, catching him around the waist and hauling him up in her arms to hug him, loving his little-boy smell. He started giggling as she tickled his belly, making him squirm and squeal with laughter. "But I was a girl before I was a mom," she said. "And girls are not stupid. They're just...different," she said, grateful that she wouldn't be required to have the boy-girl talk with her twins for at least a few more years.

The doorbell rang, and still holding a squirming, giggling Connor in her arms, Mattie headed into the living room to answer the door.

"I'll get it," Cody said, pounding down the stairs, still struggling with the zipper on his pants.

"No, you won't," Mattie said calmly, setting Connor on his feet and turning to Cody. "You know the rules about answering the door, honey. You can finish zipping your pants while *I* get the door. And it might be easier if you stood still," she added with a smile, pointing at his unzipped zipper.

Admittedly a bit overprotective when it came to her boys, she'd lived in the caustic, concrete jungle of the city of Chicago far too long to ignore any dangers, including letting her five-year-old sons open the door to just anyone.

Even though she'd fallen in love with this incredibly wonderful small town the moment she and the twins had moved here, she still felt it necessary to exercise caution, especially where her beloved boys where concerned.

The bell pealed again just as Mattie pulled open the door. For a moment, she simply stared, too stunned to do anything else.

Two things hit her at once.

There was an armed cop at her door.

And he was one of the most gorgeous men she'd ever seen.

Tall, he towered over her five-foot-three frame, and she'd put him somewhere close to six-four or -five. He wore a beige uniform shirt and tight jeans. The shirt had to stretch far and wide to cover his enormously broad shoulders. There was a metal badge right over his heart, and the long sleeves of his shirt had been rolled up, no doubt in deference to the warm spring day, revealing tanned, muscular forearms. His long legs were encased in brown jeans that seemed to hug his muscular legs and go on forever. The scuffed, scarred cowboy boots he had on gave him an additional height advantage he certainly didn't need.

His thick, black hair was swept back from a face that could have been carved by one of the Masters. Olive-skinned, he had rich brown eyes, an aquiline nose that clearly had been broken once or twice, and full lips that were, at the moment, curved into what could only be described as a surprised smile.

"Ms. Maguire?" His voice was deep, smooth and resonated with authority. In spite of the spring-day heat, Mattie had the urge to shiver.

"Y-yes," Mattie said as soon as she managed to find her voice. Embarrassed by her own reaction to him, she shifted her weight, trying to garner some composure. She was a twenty-five-year old mother of two, far too old to be gaping like a guppy at a gorgeous man.

"I'm Joe Marino, sheriff of Healing Harbor." He held out his hand, and for a moment Mattie simply looked at it.

Giving herself a mental shake, she reached for his hand and immediately had her own engulfed in the warmth and softness of his, sending her nerves into silent alarm.

Her gaze shot to his, and she couldn't seem to draw her gaze away from those big brown eyes. It frightened her that she was still capable of reacting and responding to a man this way.

Her disastrous marriage to a selfish, irresponsible *gorgeous* man had taught her to guard her heart to all men, especially men who could set her pulse scrambling with just a look.

She'd learned a lot in the years since she'd been a naive, young, college freshman, reeling from her parents' deaths in a car accident on their way home from visiting her, when she'd fallen head over heels for Gary.

But no lesson had been more important than the knowledge that she would never risk her heart or her children's security for love or a man again.

"It's him, it's him," Connor whispered, bouncing up and down and elbowing Cody, who forgot his zipper long enough to tilt his head back to stare in openmouthed awe. "It's Officer Friendly," Connor whispered.

"Ohmygosh," Cody whispered back, his own mouth dropping open. "He really came," he said. "He really, really came."

Aware that the boys were whispering something behind her, Mattie glanced back at them for a moment, her mother's antennae going almost haywire now. But at the moment, she had a more pressing problem.

"Sheriff, it's very nice to meet you," she said coolly, still stunned and embarrassed by her reaction to him. "I'm Mattie Maguire. Is there something I can do for you?"

"Actually, I'm here to see your boys," he said, wondering what he'd done to warrant her icy greeting.

"My…*boys?*" Puzzled and just a bit frightened, Mattie turned. The twins were gazing up at the sheriff with a look that could be called nothing less than adoration. "Boys?" she said with a lift of her eyebrow. "What on earth is going on?" They merely continued to stare at the sheriff, openmouthed.

"Boys!" she said again in a voice guaranteed to get their attention. "Why is the sheriff here to see you?" Her gaze shifted from one of her sons to the other, vividly aware of the man standing just a few steps behind her.

Her pulse was scrambling and her heart thrumming so loudly she feared he might hear it. She wasn't certain if the reaction was the result of fear from learning the sheriff was here to see her sons or from the man's intense masculinity.

And it irritated her to no end. She wasn't interested in responding to a man purely as a female. Knowing she still could annoyed and frightened her.

"He's our friend, Ma," Connor said by way of explanation, taking a step forward and grinning from ear to ear.

"Yeah, Ma. It's Officer Friendly and he's our friend, right?" Cody took a step closer to his brother, gazing up at the sheriff, waiting for confirmation.

"That's right, son," Joe confirmed when Mattie turned back to face him, total confusion etched in her features. Joe met her gaze, then shifted his weight a bit, trying to get his bearings. He couldn't figure out if this woman was suspicious of him because he was a cop or just suspicious of men in general.

He had to admit, though, his deputy, Clarence—also known as the town's resident gossip—had been right on the money this time. Mattie Maguire would be considered a looker in any guy's book. A *real* looker.

What else had Clarence told him? Joe tried to remember, wishing he'd paid more attention. Clarence had said she was a single mom, widowed, he'd thought, and had moved to town a few months ago. He believed Clarence had also told him that Mattie Maguire was attending the local university part-time in the mornings, and running her aunt Maureen's art gallery part-time in the afternoons.

Now that he was face-to-face with the gorgeous Mattie Maguire, Joe wished he'd paid more attention to Clarence's ramblings.

He hadn't, simply because, quite frankly, he really wasn't interested. He wasn't about to ever put his heart at risk again. He'd been down that road once before, and in fact, had almost made it to the altar, but when his fiancée had objected to his dedication to his twin brother, Johnny, whose guardianship he'd assumed when their father died, telling him his responsibility was to her not to Johnny, Joe knew he'd made a mistake and called off the wedding.

As the eldest of eight in a large, close-knit Italian family, he'd made a deathbed promise to his dad to always look out for his twin brother, Johnny, and Joe was a man who never went back on a promise. Ever.

But that escapade with his fiancée had taught him a lot about women, and although he felt honored that his father had asked him to be Johnny's caretaker, women wouldn't always see it as an honor but simply a responsibility, one that would last a lifetime. And asking a woman to accept his responsibility wasn't something he'd ever ask again.

Looking at Mattie, he realized that it had been a long, long time since he'd had such a gut-level physical reaction to a woman. But, he concluded, the last thing he needed was another woman from the big city with fancy dreams and ideas, not to mention a family and responsibilities of her own.

So, it was a good thing he only allowed himself to look, Joe thought, because a woman like Mattie Maguire was exactly the kind of woman who could tie a man like him into tiny little knots.

Deliberately, Joe shifted his gaze to the boys and felt his resistance melt. They were absolutely adorable. Miniature male versions of their mother right down to the freckles on their noses. They reminded him of him and Johnny at that age.

"The sheriff is your *friend?*" Mattie repeated in surprise, still staring at her sons. She pressed her fingers to her temple, trying to forestall a headache she was almost certain was forthcoming. Most of the boys' friends were about three feet tall, generally missing a few front teeth, and couldn't stand still for longer than ten seconds. Clearly this man didn't fit the usual bill.

"Ma." Cody, always the braver one, stepped forward. "This is Officer Friendly. He came to school and said he was our friend and that if we was ever in trouble to tell a police-man.''

"Or if we had a problem, to tell him, and he would help us,'' Connor added.

"I see,'' Mattie said carefully, trying to follow the maze of her five-year-old sons' minds. "So if you're not in trouble, then I'm assuming you have a problem, one you thought the sheriff could help you with?'' she asked, totally confused and just a bit hurt that her sons would go to a stranger for help instead of coming to her.

Identical strawberry-blond heads bobbed in perfect unison.

"Okay,'' Mattie said with a heavy sigh. "Time for a family conference.'' She glanced up at Joe again, surprised to find him watching her intently. She wished he'd make himself scarce so she could talk to the boys privately, but apparently she was stuck with him—for the moment anyway. "Sher-iff—''

"Joe, please,'' he insisted with another smile that made Mattie frown.

"Joe,'' she said stiffly, wishing he'd quit smiling at her like that. It made her nerves skitter. "Apparently whatever this problem is involves you, so why don't you come in.'' She stepped back to allow him to enter, not certain she was entirely comfortable having this large, gorgeous man in her home. The once-spacious living room suddenly seemed short of air with him in it. "Can I get you anything? Something to drink per-haps?''

"We got milk and juice,'' Cody offered helpfully.

Joe shook his head. "No, thanks, I'm fine.''

Mattie nodded, out of small talk. "Okay, well then, boys, what's this about?''

Connor glanced at Cody, who turned to his mother. "Well, Ma, last weekend when we was at Grandma and Grandpa's we heard Grandma and Grandpa talking—''

"Yeah, they thought we was asleep,'' Connor injected, blinking owlishly behind his glasses. "They always talk about us when they think we're sleeping.''

Mattie wanted to groan. Feeling her headache come on full

force, Mattie cautioned herself to hear the boys out and stay calm. But the amount of grief Gary's family had given her from the moment she'd married him had been never-ending and was difficult to face calmly.

As an only child born to his well-to-do parents late in life, Gary had been spoiled and indulged his whole life, his parents bailing him out of one scrape after another, never forcing him to face up to any responsibility.

When she'd unexpectedly gotten pregnant right after their wedding, Gary had panicked at the prospect and gone to his parents and told them he couldn't handle parenthood. His parents had stepped in, and as they'd done for Gary's whole life, decided to *handle* the situation for him.

Pleading their son's case, the Maguires had basically asked, then demanded she terminate her pregnancy, explaining that forcing Gary to become a father at such a young age when he didn't really want a child was nothing short of cruel.

Cruel was what they'd put her through when she refused to do what they asked. Gary, with his parents' support and blessing, basically abandoned her, moving in with them and resuming his old life as a carefree bachelor while she struggled to support herself and take care of her unborn children.

His parents had been certain that faced with the prospect of giving birth alone she'd come to her senses and do what they'd asked.

As far as Mattie was concerned, it wasn't *her* senses that had ever been in question. From the moment she'd become pregnant she had loved her unborn child—or rather children as it turned out—with everything inside her, and Mattie knew she would never do anything to harm them. They were the miracles of her life.

When Gary was killed two months before the twins' birth and before their divorce could become final, his parents had had a sudden change of heart and had done everything in their power to try to convince her to let *them* raise her precious babies, claiming the twins were the only part of their son they had left.

They'd even offered her money to make her life easier, to

finish her education, to establish herself in business. All she had to do was relinquish her beloved children to Gary's parents.

Their offer had simply horrified her, for she felt as if they'd been trying to *buy* her children from her.

She'd adamantly refused to take a penny from Gary's parents. Not once during all the lean years when she'd struggled to support herself and her sons, living on Gary's life insurance proceeds, monthly Social Security payments for the boys, and then filling in the financial gaps with part-time work she could do at home so she could be with her babies.

It had been hard at times, definitely, but she wasn't about to ask or accept any help from the Maguires, fearing it would give them reason to think that they had some claim to her boys.

She'd have willingly died before giving up her precious sons—to anyone, but especially Gary's parents. The thought of her in-laws raising her children, especially after the way they'd raised their own son, was so ludicrous, she never even considered it. The last thing she wanted was her boys growing up spoiled, selfish and totally self-involved like their irresponsible father.

But the older the twins got, the more her in-laws' pressure and criticism of her increased.

The Maguires claimed they weren't getting any younger and wanted a chance to have the twins in their life full-time. Which, for the boys' own protection, was exactly what Mattie wanted to avoid at all costs, and in fact was one of the main reasons for leaving Chicago and moving here before the twins began school. She was hoping they'd all have a fresh start in this wonderful little town without constant pressure.

She bore Gary's parents no bitterness, and in fact felt sorry for them. She couldn't even imagine losing one of her children, and so she'd allowed her former in-laws to have a relationship with the boys—as long as they did nothing to hurt her children.

But judging from the fear shadowing her sons' faces, the

pressure hadn't stopped, it had merely shifted to her poor innocent sons.

Her stomach muscles clenched along with her fists and Mattie found she had to take a slow, deep breath to rein in her temper. Not wanting to prejudice her sons against Gary's parents, she'd carefully and deliberately kept her feelings and opinions about them to herself.

"Sweetheart," she said gently, laying shaking hands on Cody's slender shoulders and forcing herself to speak calmly. "Did Grandma or Grandpa say something to upset you?"

"Grandma said…Grandma said…" Cody hesitated, looking down, before bringing his gaze back to hers. "Well, we was telling Grandma about how neat our new school was and about the big end-of-school parade—"

"And how we wanted to play in the kindergarten father-son baseball game at the end of the year," Connor added, shoving his glasses up his nose, then frowning again. "But Bobby Dawson said we couldn't 'cuz we don't got a dad—"

"And 'cuz we don't know how to play baseball," Cody added with a scowl of his own.

"We heard Grandma tell Grandpa that we should come to live with them, so Grandpa could be our dad and teach us how to play baseball."

"But Grandpa's too old to play baseball," Cody complained. "He's got 'rthritis or something and he can't catch or run. And we don't want to move from here—"

"'Cuz we like it here, Ma." Connor shoved his glasses up to rub his fists against his eyes.

"Lots," Cody added for emphasis, crossing his arms stubbornly across his skinny chest.

"And we don't want to leave you." Connor's voice trembled at the thought. "So we wrote to Officer Friendly. To see if he could find us our own dad—"

"One who doesn't have 'rthritis, and knows how to play baseball—"

"So then he could teach us, and we could play in the father-son baseball game—"

"And then Bobby Dawson will stop teasing us," Cody finished glumly.

"Yeah, then we won't have to leave you to go live with Grandma and Grandpa." Connor slowly blinked up at her, eyes wide, watching her carefully, and Mattie felt her thundering heart constrict into a tight little ache. "Are you mad at us, Ma?" he asked abruptly, tears suddenly glistening.

"Oh, sweetheart." Emotions swamped her, and Mattie bit her lower lip, trying to contain her own tears. Her poor babies! Her protective instincts went into overdrive and the thought that her boys had been scared and hurting both hurt and infuriated her.

The need to soothe, to protect, was so strong she would have gladly throttled her former in-laws for scaring her children and making them feel less than secure, to say nothing of what she'd like to do to Bobby Dawson for teasing her sons.

"Come here, you two." She reached out and encircled her boys in an enormous hug, holding them tight. As a single parent, she'd tried hard to make certain her boys always felt totally secure and loved, never wanting them to fear *anything.* But now because of a few careless words, her in-laws had shaken the safe, secure world she'd spent years trying to build for her children.

There were so many issues she had to deal with at the moment, she didn't even know where to start. She had to calm the boys' fears about the overheard conversation from their grandparents, and assure them they weren't moving anywhere. Or leaving her.

She had to address the twins' feelings about getting teased at school by the other kids. And she had to talk to them—again—about the "daddy" issue as she referred to it. Then there was the matter of dealing with the baseball issue, her sons' latest, greatest passion.

But Mattie knew at the moment, the only issue that was important was letting her sons know how much she loved them, that she wasn't mad at them, and more important, that they weren't going anywhere, at least not without her.

"Of course I'm not mad at you," she said gently, forcing

a smile she didn't feel and drawing back so she could see their faces. "First of all, you don't have to go live with Grandma or Grandpa or anyone else. Ever," she added firmly. "I'm your mom—"

"And we're a family, right?" Cody said, repeating her often-recited refrain to them.

She smiled at him. "That's right, sweetheart. We are a family, and family sticks together." Mattie hesitated, aware that Joe was watching her intently. But she couldn't worry about him right at the moment. "Now, I know how hard it is to be the new kids at school and how hard it is not to have a daddy like the other kids." Mattie hesitated again. "Do you remember when we talked about this?" she asked, and they both nodded solemnly.

She'd been as honest as possible about their father, and they'd seemingly accepted the fact that their daddy was in heaven. But at times like this, her anger at Gary for his immaturity rankled more than she could ever say.

"I'm sorry that you've been worried that you won't be able to play in the baseball game, but I seem to recall telling you I'd be happy to teach you how to play baseball."

The boys looked at each other, then back up at Joe. Some kind of male look passed between them, the kind of look that spoke only in a language males understood.

"What?" she asked, her gaze going from her sons' faces to Joe's. In spite of the difference in sizes and ages, all three wore those identical male looks. "What? What!" she finally demanded.

"Uh, Mattie," Joe began, trying to smother a smile. "Can I uh…see your hands?"

"My hands?" Mattie frowned. "Why do you want to see my hands?" she asked, confused and annoyed. She was in the middle of a family crisis with the boys, and the man wanted to inspect her hands? Irritated, she laid her hand in his much larger one, merely to appease him, hoping he had a point to this.

"Nice," he said with a smile, lifting her hand in the air. His touch sent her pulse scrambling even further. His hand was warm, tanned and unbelievably masculine. The kind of hand that looked capable of both soothing and arousing a woman. Mattie swallowed hard, shifting her gaze from their joined hands, to somewhere over his head, wondering where on earth that thought had come from.

"Very nice," Joe continued, letting his gaze go over her hand with the slender fingers and the perfectly manicured long nails painted a delicate shade of beige. "You have beautiful hands and nails—"

"Thank you," she snapped. Having him compliment her made her pulse jump like a frightened frog.

"But hardly equipped to catch grounders or fly balls," he said pointedly. "Right, boys?" When the boys nodded in agreement, Mattie felt her spirits droop.

"Oh." Now she understood. Mattie stood up, staring at her hand, remembering the last time she'd played ball with the boys. She'd heard Cody muttering to his brother that she ran like a…girl. Hard to be insulted when it was true.

Watching her, Joe decided it was time he jumped into this since the boys had come to him for help. He went down on his haunches so he was eye level with the twins, casually draping an arm around each slender shoulder, drawing the boys close. "Let me ask you something, boys. When Bobby Dawson was teasing you, did he happen to mention that his dad is a surgeon and can't play baseball because he can't hurt his hands?"

Cody frowned for a moment, then giggled. "You mean, kinda like a girl?"

"Or our *mom?*" Connor added with a giggle of his own.

"Kinda," Joe admitted with a smile. He glanced up at Mattie, surprised to find a faint blush shadowing her cheeks. At least she had a sense of humor about her…shortcomings, he thought in amusement. Not all women did.

His gaze caught hers and he had to draw a quick intake of breath. She was definitely having an impact on him, one he wasn't entirely comfortable with, but he had to admit, Mattie Maguire had impressed the hell out of him.

And she was much more than just a pretty face. She'd handled a very delicate situation with patience, calm and humor. Obviously there were some family problems or issues here, but she seemed to be focusing on the one thing—the only thing that mattered at the moment—her sons' feelings. Clearly, this was one woman who understood about putting family first.

Shifting his gaze, Joe smiled at the boys. "And did Bobby Dawson also happen to mention that you don't need a dad to learn how to play baseball?"

Connor and Cody exchanged glances, then shrugged, their shoulders moving almost in unison. Clearly this was not a thought that had occurred to them.

"Nah," Connor said, eyes wide as he looked at his brother with a "who knew" expression and another shrug.

"You don't?" Cody asked, scratching his head and looking at Joe for confirmation.

"Nope," he said with a grin, drawing the boys even closer. "No dad required." He grinned at the look on the boys' faces. "And uh…did Bobby ever mention that it wasn't *his* dad who taught him how to play baseball?"

Mattie didn't have a clue where the man was going with this, but she didn't care. She could have thrown her arms around him and kissed him simply for making her boys feel better about themselves and their situation.

Scowling, and thinking, Connor scratched his head. "If Bobby's dad didn't teach him how to play baseball, then who did?"

"Yeah, who did?" Cody mimicked, scratching his own head again.

Joe grinned. "The manager and head coach of the Healing Harbor Little League." At the boys' twin frowns, he explained. "The manager is the man who is in charge of all the different baseball teams, including the T-ball league. And as head coach of the entire league, he coaches everyone, including the other coaches and especially the kids."

Both boys' eyes widened in awe. "So he's gotta know lots and lots about baseball, right?" Cody asked, excitement building in his expression.

"That's right," Joe confirmed. "He probably knows more about baseball than anyone else in town."

"Maybe in the world," Cody said, grinning widely.

Touched beyond measure by his kindness, and especially his understanding of the delicate situation she was facing, Mattie managed to smile at Joe, grateful in spite of her own feelings about the man. "Sheriff, do you—"

"It's Joe," he corrected with a patient sigh, wondering why she refused to use his name.

"Joe," she began hesitantly. "Do you think if I talked to this coach he might be willing to teach my boys how to play baseball?" Mattie asked hopefully, making Joe grin.

"Would he?" Cody asked, bouncing up and down in excitement and not giving Joe a chance to answer.

"Could he?" Connor asked, grabbing Joe's arm and bouncing up and down as well, nearly knocking Joe, still on his haunches, off balance.

"I think that can be arranged," Joe said with a wink. Mattie stared at him for a moment, then realization hit her and she felt a sinking feeling in her stomach.

"*You're* the head coach?" she asked, dumbfounded. She stared at him for a moment as all the implications of having her boys interact so closely with this man—whom they clearly already had a bad case of hero worship for—set in.

The twins had had very little interaction with adult males. She was the only child of two only children. Other than her great-aunt Maureen she had no other family to interact with the boys.

And she'd certainly not dated or introduced any men into her sons' lives, so other than their male teachers and their grandfather, Cody and Connor didn't even know any adult males.

The last thing she wanted was for her children to get too attached to *any* male who wouldn't be a permanent part of their lives, especially one they already apparently worshiped. It would be far too easy for the boys to be hurt, something she simply couldn't and wouldn't allow.

"Guilty as charged," Joe admitted. "And I've been playing

baseball with my brothers since I was just about your age,"
he added, glancing at the boys.

"You have brothers?" Connor asked in awe.

"Yep. I've got three brothers." Joe grinned at the twins'
expressions. "And four sisters, all of whom can play baseball
almost as well as I can."

"Sisters are *girls*," Cody said in dawning horror, making
the word girls sound like a terribly fatal disease.

"Girls can't play baseball," Connor announced smugly.

Joe laughed, ruffling Connor's hair. "I don't suggest you
say that within earshot of any of my sisters, since they can
play baseball better than most boys."

"Will you teach us to play, huh, will you?" Connor all but
begged, tilting his head back to meet Joe's gaze.

"*Pul-lease?*" Cody pressed his hands together as if in
prayer.

"We learn real good," Connor assured him. "Honest."

"We got A's on our papers at school today 'cuz we're good
learners." Cody poked his brother with his elbow. "Right,
Connor?"

"Right."

Joe laughed at their enthusiasm. They really were adorable.
"As long as it's okay with your mom," Joe added, glancing
at Mattie. He felt that familiar tightening in his gut every time
he looked at her. It was just physical attraction, he told himself. Nothing to worry about.

He was an adult, he could handle it. It certainly wasn't the
first time he found himself attracted to a beautiful woman. Just
as long as he kept things in perspective, acknowledged his
feelings, and then ignored them, he'd be fine.

But Lord, she was definitely a looker. She was slender and
petite, her long, tanned legs as sexily bare as her feet. The
pair of ragged jean shorts she wore hit her right about her
shapely thighs, only emphasizing the curves of her gorgeous
legs. A pullover top in a shade of melon that caressed the
curve of her breasts and highlighted her ivory complexion
nearly had him tripping over his tongue.

A riot of apricot curls, her hair tumbled down to brush her

shoulders. Her eyes were huge, and a deep, rich blue fringed by thick, inky-black lashes. Her nose was small, upturned and dusted with freckles. A sweetheart bow, bare, her mouth glistened with some kind of shiny, wet stuff that his sisters always told him was designed to make a guy wonder what a woman tasted like.

Well, it worked, he thought, letting his gaze settle on her mouth for a moment. He was wondering all right and it scared the daylights out of him. Looking was fine, he told himself again. But anything else was out of bounds.

"Mom?" Two sets of crystal-blue eyes filled with hope and happiness beseeched her and Mattie sighed at all the implications of involving this man in their lives might bring. She didn't know him, not really, and sheriff or not, she needed to know a great deal more about him before allowing him to interact with her children. Overprotective she might be, but it came with the territory.

"I think this is something the sheriff and I need to discuss in private," she said carefully, aware the boys were waiting for her answer with baited breath. When Joe's eyebrows went up in surprise, she rushed on. "I'm sure the sheriff is a very busy man and we want to make sure we don't impose on his time."

"It's no imposition," Joe said, cocking his head to study her. From the suspicion shadowing her eyes, and her comments, he had a feeling she didn't give one whit about his time.

Something more was at stake here. Clearly, this was a woman who didn't particularly like or trust men. Or maybe it was just him.

"And I'd love to do it," Joe added pointedly. "I've taught a lot of kids in town to play ball." He shrugged. "I consider it part of my job as head coach."

Her eyes cooled and she basically ignored his offer as she dropped a hand to each twin's shoulder in a clearly protective gesture. "This is a big commitment, boys, not just of your time, but also a commitment of responsibility. I just think there're some…things we need to be clear on before we commit to something this…involved.'' Her gaze shifted to Joe, her message clear. She wasn't about to give this stranger, no matter how kind he'd been to the boys, carte blanche, not where her sons were concerned.

''I understand,'' Joe said. ''And I think it's a good idea to consider the idea carefully, particularly since it requires parental involvement as well.'' Her eyebrows went up and he rushed on. ''In a T-ball league, we rely heavily on parental involvement and participation. You'll be required to not only participate, but also to attend practices and games and help out as much as possible.''

Mattie stared at him coolly. She didn't want to be involved with this man on any level.

He scared the blasted daylights out of her.

Having her sons spend time with him was one kettle of fish, but having to spend time with him herself was quite another, and frankly, Mattie knew herself well enough to know she was just plain…terrified by the way he made her feel, something she hadn't done in so long she was surprised she was still capable of feeling.

Terrific, Mattie thought glumly. If she refused now, it would seem as if she wasn't willing to support her boys. So he'd think she wasn't just a chicken, but a nonsupportive chicken!

Unfazed by the absolute panic that flashed across her face, Joe glanced at his watch. ''Since it's almost dinnertime, why don't we discuss the details over a pizza?''

Perhaps if she got to know him better, got to see him as a part of the community, and see him as part of a family, since a person couldn't go anywhere in town without tripping over someone in his family, maybe she wouldn't be quite so suspicious of him, Joe mused, and would know he was not only the kind of man to trust, but also had only her kids' best interests at heart. It was worth a try, Joe decided, for the boys' sake.

''If this is something you'd like to proceed with, there's a lot we need to discuss and we don't have a lot of time,'' he went on. ''I have to give you a practice schedule, arrange for uniform pickups and then have you sign all the permission and insurance forms. We have our first parents' meeting on Thursday evening…it's mandatory,'' he added, sensing she was just about to tell him she couldn't attend. ''And our first team meeting is on Friday evening.'' He smiled at the boys. ''Also mandatory.''

At the cloud of confusion that filled the boys' eyes at the strange word, Joe bent down on his haunches again to speak directly to them.

''Mandatory just means you have to be there if you want to play and be part of the team.''

Cody's and Connor's faces brightened immediately. ''Kinda like school,'' Cody offered with a grin. ''We gotta go even if we don't want to.''

''Exactly,'' Joe agreed with a chuckle. ''We start practice on Tuesday of next week, and our first official game is the following Saturday morning.'' His gaze shifted to Mattie. ''So you see, this is something you need to make a decision about rather quickly.''

Quickly. Mattie swallowed hard and wanted to groan. Rarely did she ever make a decision regarding her boys—or anything else—quickly. But perhaps in this case she would have to make an exception.

''Now, Mattie, what about that pizza?'' Joe watched her, trying not to be amused by the sheer fear on her face. He could understand that look if he'd asked her to…maybe forsake her firstborn child, but all he'd asked was for her to share a pizza with him so they could discuss the boys joining the baseball team, surely a harmless endeavor meant merely to give them a chance to talk in private. So why on earth was she so frightened?

Mattie wanted to give him a quick, definitive answer. A resounding no! The idea of having to spend time with this man alone, without the barrier of her sons or anything else between them was totally intimidating, and not something she really wanted or was really willing to do. But she couldn't very well discuss her concerns about the boys in front of the boys—which meant she'd have to be alone with Joe.

And the thought terrified her. She couldn't even remember

the last time she'd been alone with a man, and she wasn't certain she even remembered how to handle herself with a man.

She glanced up at him and felt a familiar tightening in her gut. She certainly didn't need to be reminded of the fact that she was still a normal, healthy young woman with normal needs and desires, and being in Joe's presence seemed to be a constant reminder, one she wasn't at all comfortable with.

She had to remember, she may be a healthy young woman, but she was first and foremost a mother. That was her primary responsibility and took precedence over everything. Including her own feelings.

"I don't think—"

"*Pul-lease, Ma, pul-lease?*" Cody begged, grabbing her hand and tugging on it.

"We want to get started right away," Connor said, grabbing her other hand.

"'Cuz the first game is next Saturday, and that's only a week away."

"And we only got two more months of school," Cody added with urgency. "So we gotta learn quick so we can play in the big game at the end of the year."

Looking at the twins' faces, Mattie's spirits sunk. She knew in spite of her own reservations and fears, she couldn't refuse to at least consider and discuss this for the boys' sake. This meant far too much to them. She'd simply have to handle the situation and her own fears and check Joe and the situation out, like it or not.

"Okay," she finally said reluctantly, earning a whoop from her sons and praying her knees would stop knocking at the thought of being alone with this man. "But I have an early class in the morning and need to get home early," she added pointedly, looking at Joe and making it clear this was not a social situation. *Definitely not a social situation.*

But a parental situation.

She'd merely think of this as just another meeting, like…a PTA meeting. She could handle that. The mere thought lightened her mood and her pulse finally calmed down.

She'd go with Joe, learn a little bit more about him, at least enough to calm some of her fears about having her boys interact so closely with him, discuss the situation and her concerns about her sons and then come straight home. It would also give her time to consider all the ramifications. Hopefully this would be the last time she had to deal one-on-one with him.

"Great," Joe said with a smile. The twins' mother might not care for him, he thought, but he wasn't going to let that stop him from doing something that would make the boys so happy. He remembered what it was like to lose his dad when he was so young. Remembered too how keenly he'd felt the loss of his dad, and how different he felt from all the other kids who had fathers.

If he could do something—one small thing—to help the Maguire twins fit in and feel less vulnerable and more confident in themselves, not to mention stop them from getting teased at school, then he was going to do his best to help. He'd been where they are, and so had his brothers…he knew how important fitting in at school and just being one of the guys meant.

"I promise to get you home by eight," he said, flashing her a smile that made Mattie highly suspicious again. "And since it's a school night, we'll even have a pizza delivered for the boys."

"Fine," she said stiffly, shoving her hair back off her face and trying to ignore what that megawatt smile did to her pulse. "But I'll have to ask my aunt Maureen to watch the boys." She glanced down at herself again. "And I'll have to change. I can't—"

"You look fine," Joe said, his eyes glittering as they went over her again. He felt almost punchy every time he looked at her. She had to be one of the most beautiful women he'd ever encountered, with the kind of looks that tangled a man's brain. "Beautiful, in fact."

Mattie wanted to shiver at the tone of his voice. It was far too personal, making her feel his words as if they were a warm caress slithering over her skin, warming her. It would be a mite embarrassing to have her heart come right through her chest, she figured, but if he didn't quit looking at her like that—talking to her like that, that's exactly what she feared was going to happen.

What was it about this man that made her respond so foolishly? she wondered, studying him for a moment. Okay, he was the proverbial tall, dark and handsome, but she'd met a lot of good-looking men over the years, and just as easily and quickly dismissed them without thought.

She had a sneaky feeling this man was different; that she couldn't dismiss him quite so easily. Probably because there was something else here, something far more important, at least to her: he was kind. To her children. Mattie sighed. She always was a sucker for a man who could be kind to children. Especially her children.

But that was no reason to have her swooning at this guy's feet. She had to get a grip. She was an adult, the mother of two, she didn't have time to be acting or responding like a lovesick schoolgirl because of some gorgeous guy who'd had a kind word for her boys.

But, in all honesty, she couldn't remember the last time a man had complimented her, and she realized it was nice. A wonderful ego boost to know that a man still found her attractive, even when she was dressed in old clothes without a drop of makeup on.

Her pulse sped up at the look in his eyes. It was pure masculine appreciation and made her wonder just how long it had been since this guy had *seen* a woman. If the way he was looking at her was any indication, it had been a while.

She couldn't imagine he looked at every woman with that raw male hunger in his eyes. He was just going to have to stop looking at her like that, she decided. That was all there was to it.

She glanced at her boys and felt her resolve harden. Joe Marino was only a man, nothing more or less. Surely she could handle him and those dark, smoldering looks of his for a few hours alone. Mattie swallowed hard, swiping her damp hands down her shorts.

She hoped.

Chapter Two

Thirty-three minutes later, Mattie pulled up right in front of Mama Marino's Pizzeria, grateful that even during what would be considered the hours of rush hour, Healing Harbor had very little street traffic. She was able to find a parking spot right in front of the restaurant.

She'd insisted on driving herself to the pizzeria. This was a small town and if she was seen riding around town in the sheriff's car, no doubt small-town tongues would start wagging. She wanted to stay below the resident gossips' radar, at least for the time being.

As Mattie stepped out of the car, she took a deep breath, then ran a shaky hand down her jeans, then through her hair, which curled madly down and across her shoulders.

She'd changed into a pale yellow cotton sweater and a pair of old, comfortable jeans. Her feet were ensconced in a pair of espadrilles that gave her an additional inch of height. Right now, she was feeling so off balance she didn't want to have to worry about her appearance, so she'd deliberately chosen comfort over fashion.

She'd refused to allow herself to fuss over her appearance, firmly telling herself this was not a date and she was not in the least bit interested in impressing Sheriff Joe Marino.

She was here to discuss her children. Nothing more. Nothing less. And she certainly didn't need to look like a fashion plate in order to do so.

Swinging her purse strap over her shoulder, Mattie crossed around the front of her old, rather beat-up car, heading toward the pizzeria. A car was on the list of necessities she'd been hoping to buy this year, but with all the expenses of moving, she'd had to put it off for a few months. She only hoped her old beater would last until she could afford to replace it.

The sun was just setting, casting long, golden shadows across the pavement, basking everything in a soft warm glow. The sweet scent of lilacs hung in the air from a bush flowering wildly in the small patch of budding grass in the parkway. A bed of spring azaleas struggling to bloom lined the walkway all the way up and down Main Street.

For a moment, Mattie just stood there, glancing up and down the street, feeling a sense of peace and contentment that surprised her.

Until she'd actually moved to Healing Harbor, she would never have believed a peaceful little town like this actually existed.

The small pizzeria, the old-fashioned movie house that charges less than two dollars admission and offered real butter on the popcorn, free refills on soda and Saturday-afternoon cartoon matinees. The small diner on the corner with daily lunch and dinner blue-plate specials, where it seemed everyone in town congregated at some time during the day.

Smiling, Mattie waved to a group of men sitting outside the town's only barbershop, drinking coffee and arguing good-naturedly over a checkers game. Down the block, and directly across the street from the sheriff's office, she could see the town librarian sweeping down the steps before closing for the evening.

A dog barked somewhere in the distance, and a church bell pealed, signaling the beginning of evening services. Mattie stood there, taking it all in, breathing deeply of the clean spring air. This was the kind of town she'd always dreamed of living in. The kind of place where it was perfect to raise a family.

Glancing around, Mattie realized that she was content; she'd finally found that sense of peace and tranquillity that had eluded her for so long.

Here, in Healing Harbor, she'd finally begun to feel that she and the boys had come home. Here, she and the boys could have a real future.

With a happy sigh, Mattie blew out a long breath, grateful once again she'd decided to make the move. It had been a big step—a huge change and commitment, both financially and emotionally, accompanied by fear, doubt and a lot of plain old-fashioned worrying, and even though she knew that right now the move might be hard on the boys, what with meeting new people, going to a new school, trying to fit in and adjust, she was certain, in the long run this was the place they belonged.

The thought made her smile again as she headed toward the door of the pizzeria. Heavenly aromas assaulted her, and her empty stomach grumbled, reminding her she'd been so busy today, she hadn't bothered to eat.

She pushed through the front door of the little pizzeria and hesitated for a moment, letting her eyes adjust to the sudden darkness.

She heard a squeal and glanced up just in time to see a beautiful, pint-size brunette with a mane of black gypsy curls launch herself into Joe's arms.

Stunned, Mattie's mouth nearly fell open as the door slammed shut soundly behind her.

"Hey, handsome, you're late," the brunette complained, planting loud, wet kisses across Joe's cheeks as she wrapped her slender arms and legs around him and hung on. "Where were you last night?"

Startled and more than a bit embarrassed, Mattie merely stood there, gaping at the two of them, feeling ridiculously like an unwelcome voyeur.

"I got hung up," Joe explained, wrapping his arms around the petite brunette to hold her in place. "You know how it goes. I got busy and—"

"Excuses, excuses," the brunette said with a saucy grin.

Annoyed with herself, as well as the situation she suddenly found herself in, Mattie glanced away, embarrassed for all of them. She should have figured that a man who looked like Joe would have a whole cartel of women throwing themselves at him.

But why on earth had he invited her here to witness this scene? she wondered in annoyance. She didn't know, but she didn't intend to stick around and find out.

Mattie started to turn on her heel, but Joe caught her arm before she could push the door back open.

"Hey, Mattie, where you going?" he asked with a frown, reaching out to snag her while still juggling the brunette in his arms. "Come here." Ignoring her reluctance, Joe reined her in, shifting the brunette and dropping an arm around Mattie's waist to prevent her from leaving.

She resisted the urge to shift and move away from him, refusing to be intimidated either by him or the feelings he aroused.

"I want you to meet my kid sister."

Mattie merely gaped at Joe, a wild sense of relief rushing through her. "K-kid sister?" she repeated weakly, letting her gaze drift from Joe to the woman, then back again.

Heat crept up her face as she studied the other woman. Looking carefully now, she could clearly see the family resemblance. And felt ridiculously foolish about her initial reaction.

"Yeah, well, at least one of them," Joe admitted with a laugh, setting his sister back down on her feet. "Mattie, this is Gina. Gina, this is Mattie Maguire." He tugged Mattie still closer. The whole purpose in coming here was so that Mattie could meet his sister and see him interact with his family and some of the townspeople.

"Mattie and her twin sons are new in town," Joe explained.

"Hopefully they're going to be playing on our T-ball team, so I thought I'd bring her in for a Marino special."

"Great." Gina wiped her hands down the white apron Mattie hadn't noticed before. "The more the merrier." Gina grinned, extending her hand toward Mattie. "It's nice to meet you, Mattie. Mama Marino's sponsors a few of the teams and my own kids play as well."

"Great," Mattie said as Gina gave her brother a sidelong glance.

"As for you, Joe, I'm going to be thirty on my next birthday, and have a husband and three babies of my own, so when are you going to stop calling me a kid?" Gina asked.

"Probably never," Joe admitted with a laugh.

"Men." Gina shook her head and rolled her eyes at Mattie in a gesture of female solidarity before turning her attention back to her brother. "So how come you didn't come in for dinner last night?" Her eyebrows drew together. "I was worried about you."

"Hey, worrying is *my* job, Gina," Joe laid a gentle hand to his sister's cheek in a move so tender it had Mattie's eyes widening in surprise. "You've got more than enough to worry about."

Any man who was so openly devoted to his sister couldn't be too bad, Mattie decided, observing them carefully. Love and devotion shimmered between them. Watching him interact with his sister made him seem far less intimidating and far more human and Mattie found some of the tension leaving her.

"Did you even have dinner last night?" Gina asked with a knowing lift of her eyebrow.

"Nope," Joe admitted with a sigh, rubbing a hand across his stubbled chin. "I really did get tied up at the office. A few weeks ago I gave Mrs. Petrie another ticket for speeding through town. And you know how she gets. She came in to pay her fine last night and felt it necessary to give me a lecture on respecting my elders—"

"She's not still driving?" Gina asked, eyes wide.

"Any chance she gets." Joe turned to Mattie to explain, his

arm still comfortably around her waist. He liked having her so close to him, he realized. It sent an awareness tingling through him, a distinct *male* awareness he hadn't felt in a long, long time. One that would have normally alarmed him and sent him packing. "Mrs. Petrie, she's, uh…one of the town's matriarchs. Unfortunately, Mrs. Petrie is also half-blind, deaf as a fence post and has two lead feet that she likes to keep pressed to the gas pedal."

"Isn't that a tad dangerous?" Mattie asked with a slight frown. The feel of his hard, warm masculine body so close to her was wreaking havoc with her pulse, to say nothing of her concentration level.

"That would be an understatement," Joe admitted.

"She also has a stubborn streak a mile wide," Gina added.

"And a history of temper tantrums that would put a two-year-old to shame," Joe added, trying not to grin. "But since she's the widow of the town's longtime former mayor, she refuses to believe that laws were meant to apply to her. Especially traffic laws. She tears through town in this pristine '53 Cadillac as if the hounds of hell were after her."

"But usually it's just my brother," Gina confided with a laugh. "When he can catch her." Gina muffled her smile at the look her brother shot her. "What I can't understand, Joe, is why she's still driving. She must be eighty-five if she's a day."

"Eighty-eight if her driver's license is to be believed. And my ears are still ringing from the tongue-lashing she gave me last night in a decibel guaranteed to shatter glass."

Gina cocked her head, looking at her brother with concern. "Joe, I thought after the last ticket you gave her you were going to talk to her son about getting her to stop driving."

"I did." Wincing, he shook his dark head. "Big mistake. Mrs. Petrie did *not* take too kindly to what she referred to as the 'interference of a young whippersnapper not old enough to be dry behind the ears.' It's a good thing I'm fast, or I would have lost a couple of toes to Mrs. Petrie's cane." He chuckled suddenly, glancing down at Mattie. Something about her was distracting him, he realized. Probably that seductively sweet feminine scent she'd put on. It was one of those kind that snuck up on an unsuspecting man, then just lapped at the corner of his senses, teasing him, and leaving him wanting—aching for more.

"You poor thing." Gina gave him a soothing pat on the shoulder while trying to muffle a laugh.

"Yeah, well, I plan to make up for it tonight." Joe glanced around the dimly lit restaurant that had started to fill up with the dinner crowd. "You got a booth for us?"

"In the back, Joe. I set up the family booth after you called. You should be able to hide out there without getting bothered, at least through dinner. Oh, and the pizza you ordered should be delivered just about now," Gina added, glancing at the large black-and-white clock behind the small bar that wound through the middle of the restaurant.

"Thanks." Joe looked at Mattie. He hadn't realized quite how small and petite she really was until this moment. She barely reached his shoulder and yet seemed to fit him perfectly. "I called ahead and had a pizza delivered to your aunt and the boys. I know how wound up they were, I figured a pizza in front of the TV might be just the trick to calm them down."

"T-thank you," Mattie stammered. The man thought of everything, apparently.

"Gina, why don't you send over some appetizers and maybe a pitcher of soft drinks?" He glanced at Mattie. "I hope you don't mind, but I'm still on duty."

"No, soft drinks are fine," Mattie said. "Besides, I'm driving, and I'm a driver who likes to stay on the good side of the sheriff."

"Good point." Their eyes locked for a moment, then he reached for her hand and gave it a squeeze. "Come on, let's go sit down before someone corners me."

Leading the way, Joe hustled her through the restaurant, around several small tables, waving and greeting people as he wound his way to the back of the room to their booth. It was tucked into a corner and partially hidden from most of the rest of the diners, affording some quiet and privacy.

"Have a seat," he said, ushering her into the booth. She slid in, grateful he was no longer touching her or standing so blasted close to her.

The man was definitely a toucher, she decided after watching him interact with his sister. But she wasn't accustomed to being…touched. Especially by a man. Let alone a man she barely knew who could start her heart two-stepping just by one quick brush of him—any part of him—against her skin. It was easier to think when he was safely ensconced in the seat across from her.

"This is a very nice place," Mattie said, glancing around and wondering what on earth she should say to him. Small talk wasn't high on her list of necessities in life. "I didn't make the connection before. Mama Marino's as in Joe Marino? Is this your family business?"

"Yes and no." Joe hesitated, waiting while a waiter set down a pitcher of soft drinks, then filled their water glasses and set down a basket of fresh-baked bread. He gave a nod of thanks before continuing.

"It's Gina and her husband Paul's," Joe said, taking a sip of his water. "After my mom died, Gina took over all the cooking for the family. She always was a fabulous cook, even as a kid, so opening up a restaurant just seemed natural. Fortunately, her husband loved the idea and they opened this place together about six years ago." He glanced around, his face beaming with pride. "I guess you can say it's also become the official Marino family hangout since we all usually end up here sometime during the day."

Fascinated by the changes in his face, Mattie leaned forward, watching him. That face, she thought with a little sigh, was gorgeous. It was the little crook in his nose, she decided, that had saved him. Otherwise he might have been just too pretty.

Listening to him talk about his family, his features softened and his eyes lit with unabashed love. He seemed far less threatening and intimidating.

This was a man who clearly valued family and all it entailed and wasn't afraid to openly show it. His behavior was both surprising and endearing and lowered her defenses several notches.

"Gina and Paul have really made a success of the place." Joe looked around the restaurant as he relaxed against the booth, stretching his long legs out under the table. "Of course, considering it's the only Italian restaurant and pizzeria in town, it would be hard to do otherwise. But the food really is spectacular," he reiterated just as Gina approached, holding a tray laden with overflowing platters of food.

"Here's some appetizers to get you going." Gina expertly juggled the heavy platter. "We've got some homemade minestrone to start." She set a steaming bowl of rich, red broth simmering with vegetables and pasta in front of Mattie.

"It smells heavenly," she said, inhaling deeply. Her stomach rumbled again, making Joe smile.

"And some toasted raviolis with a little marinara on the side, some baked mozzarella and some fresh tomato and garlic bruschetta. I picked the tomatoes fresh myself this morning right from my garden." Satisfied, Gina frowned as she wiped a splash of sauce off the table with the corner of her apron. "Your pizza will be ready in a few minutes." She turned to go, then hesitated. "Oh, Joe? Don't forget Angie has a doctor's appointment tomorrow afternoon at one."

"I know." Joe patted his shirt pocket. "I've got it marked down in my pocket planner so I wouldn't forget, and Clarence has already agreed to cover for me so I can take her."

"I figured as much," Gina said with a smile, giving them a little wave before heading back toward the kitchen.

"Angie's my youngest sister," Joe explained as he picked up a piece of baked mozzarella from the appetizer platter and popped it into his mouth. "She's expecting her first baby in a few months, but since last fall she's been going it alone. Her husband, Jeff, is a navy pilot and he was shipped overseas."

"I'll bet that's been hard on her," Mattie said. As she knew all too well. Being alone and pregnant was not something she'd ever want to do again. Nor would she wish it on any other expectant mother.

Picking up her spoon, Mattie blew on her steaming soup to

cool it before sipping it carefully. She nearly swooned in pleasure as the flavors and textures exploded in her mouth.

"Yeah, it is hard," Joe admitted, chewing thoughtfully. He picked up his napkin, wiped his hands, then surveyed the appetizer platter again, trying to decide what to choose next. He dabbed at his mouth with his napkin before continuing. "I remember when Gina was expecting the first time. She was a nervous wreck, too, and Paul was right here. Angie's pretty much the same nervous wreck, but even more so because her husband's not here. So, we're all just pitching in, trying to take her mind off things and make life a bit easier for her."

Still holding his napkin aloft, Joe leaned across the table to wipe a bit of soup from Mattie's chin. Her eyes went wide and she jerked back as if he were about to strike her.

Surprised by her reaction, Joe stopped midmove, the napkin still in the air. "You…uh…have some soup on your chin," he said quietly, gesturing toward her with his napkin. "I was just going to wipe it off," he explained as she self-consciously took the offered napkin and wiped her chin.

"T-thank you," she stammered, handing him back his napkin and feeling utterly ridiculous. She'd embarrassed both of them, and worse, judging from the look on his face, she'd hurt his feelings. And her reaction was totally uncalled for. He'd been nothing but kind and pleasant from the moment she'd opened her front door to him. "I'm sorry, Joe," she said quietly, glancing down at her soup as remorse rolled over her. "I…I didn't…mean to do that."

"Yes, you did," he countered smoothly, smiling at her. "You can't seem to help it. You jolt or jerk every time I get near you." He studied her for a moment. "Mattie, is there something about me that makes you uncomfortable? Were you perhaps frightened by a tall, dark-haired Italian man as a young child?"

She tried not to laugh. Truly. But she couldn't help it. The way he'd phrased the question made her laugh.

"Ah, so that isn't it," he said, clearly pleased. "Perhaps then it was a cop who frightened you, and ever since you've been terrified of a man wearing a badge."

"No." Still chuckling, Mattie shook her head. "That's not it, Joe. Honestly." Blowing out a breath, Mattie realized he'd successfully diffused her self-conscious nervousness by making a joke out of her reaction. It was a terribly endearing quality, she thought.

"I'm sorry. I…I…guess I'm just…just…" Her voice trailed off helplessly. She was not accustomed to responding so wildly when a man touched her, which was why she kept jumping every time he came near her. It scared her to know she could respond so easily and so quickly, never mind so strongly, to this man. But this was certainly not something she was going to admit to him.

"I guess I've been dealing with kids so long I'm a bit rusty when it comes to dealing one-on-one with…adults."

"I can understand that. My sister Sophie, she's a kindergarten teacher." His face brightened. "In fact, she's probably the boys' kindergarten teacher—"

"I don't think so," Mattie said with a shake of her head. "The boys' teacher's name is Mrs. O'Malley."

Joe laughed. "Yep, that's Sophie. She married Tommy O'Malley right out of college. They were high-school sweethearts. Anyway, for the first few years after Sophie started teaching, she talked to everyone as if they were five years old." Shaking his head, he chuckled softly. "When she started cutting up my meat and offering to tie my shoes, the family figured we'd better have a talk with her."

Mattie laughed. "I know the feeling. So did you? Have a talk with her?"

"I did, indeed," he said. "She listened calmly, nodding all the while. Then she patted me on the cheek in a motherly fashion and told me to make sure I washed my hands before dinner."

Mattie laughed again. "Sounds like you and your family are very close."

"We are," he admitted softly. "There are eight of us kids. I'm the oldest of the boys and Gina's the oldest of the girls. Even though my parents are gone and we're all grown and have lives and families of our own, we're still extremely close.''

''You're very lucky,'' Mattie said almost wistfully, setting her spoon down and wondering what it would be like to have such a big, loving, supportive family. *Supportive* being the key word, she thought dismally.

She was still shaken from what she'd learned about her in-laws' latest antics today, knowing that she'd have to handle the situation soon if she was going to prevent it from happening again. She couldn't risk letting them frighten the boys again.

''I take it you don't have much family,'' Joe said, cocking his head to study her.

Mattie shook her head, then managed a smile. ''Other than my great-aunt Maureen, and the boys, I don't have any family. I was an only child and my parents were killed in a car accident during my freshman year of college.'' She shrugged. ''I'm all that's left.''

''I'm sorry. It's very hard to lose your parents. At least it was on us. My dad went first, then my mom had a fatal heart attack three years ago.'' He shook his head, his eyes sad. ''I don't think my mom really wanted to go on after Dad was gone.''

''Were they married long?'' Mattie couldn't even imagine the kind of love it took to not want to go on after your partner was gone. It must have been something incredibly wonderful, the kind of magic that fanciful authors wrote about in fairy tales.

''Almost forty years.''

''Wow.'' She blew out a breath and pushed her near-empty soup bowl away. The mere thought that love could be that strong and enduring was mind-boggling and just a little awe-inspiring.

Her marriage had barely survived six months and the love had lasted less than that, replaced by disappointment and disillusionment.

Joe was thoughtful for a moment. ''From the conversation you and the boys had back at the house, I take it you've pretty much been a single parent their whole lives.'' He sipped his water, glancing at her hands. She didn't wear a wedding ring.

''I've been a single parent since *before* they were born. Their father was killed in an accident two months before their birth.''

''It had to be terribly difficult for you to go through your husband's death and the twins' birth on your own.''

No wonder she was so skittish around men. She'd been alone for a very long time and never had the privilege of sharing parental or apparently much marital responsibilities with anyone. Especially a man. That explained a lot. He shook his head. ''I can't even imagine it.''

The fact that she'd managed to single-handedly raise not one but two babies all on her own after being suddenly widowed while pregnant was nothing short of amazing. He had to admit he felt a growing admiration for her.

''No,'' Mattie admitted. ''It wasn't easy to go through alone.'' She managed a smile. With her great-aunt Maureen in Europe, there'd been no one for her. Absolutely no one.

Pride had her chin lifting. ''But sometimes we're not given choices in life. You make the best of whatever situation life throws at you. My boys were a blessing from the moment I found out I was expecting.'' Her face lit with unabashed joy and love. ''It wasn't a question of whether I could handle it or not. I just did. Those boys were worth going through anything and everything. I'd do it again in a heartbeat.''

It was clear she was passionate about her sons and about motherhood, Joe realized. Passionate and protective, so why was there a hint of defiance as well as sadness underlying her tone?

''Surely the grandparents the boys mentioned earlier must have been some help and support to you,'' he said as he reached for another toasted ravioli off the appetizer platter.

He glanced up just in time to see her stiffen slightly. She smiled in that coolly pleasant way, but he saw her defenses tidily snap down, deliberately closing off all emotion to him. There was something there, he realized, watching her carefully. Something she obviously wasn't comfortable discussing.

"No, not really," she said, trying to make her voice neutral. "I'm not…particularly close to my former in-laws. I don't even know that we'd consider them family."

"I see," he said, puzzled. Warning bells went off. It was clear from her words, tone and the earlier conversation he'd overheard that Mattie didn't particularly care for her former in-laws. And he couldn't help but wonder why.

Without any family of her own, he'd think she'd want to have the couple as part of her life. And the boys' lives. Especially if they were the only family she or the twins had.

"Joe," Mattie began slowly. "I'm sorry you had to witness our little family discussion this afternoon, but it really couldn't be helped. I don't normally air family business in front of strangers, but at the time, I was more concerned about my sons' feelings than I was about discussing the situation in front of you."

"That was perfectly understandable under the circumstances." His gaze met, and held hers. His heart seemed to do a strange little jig in his chest. "But I wish you could have seen the look on your face when I told you I was there to see your boys."

Mattie laughed. "I can just imagine," she said with a shake of her head. "It's not every day I find an armed man at the door looking for my kids. I have to admit I was a little taken aback. I'm used to the boys telling me everything. We're very close," she added with a smile, more comfortable now that they weren't discussing her behavior or her in-laws. "It's not like them not to confide in me or tell me when there's a problem. And apparently there were quite a few they were keeping from me."

"Sometimes not even mothers can know everything."

"Don't tell me that," she said with a laugh. "I'm a firm believer that mothers, especially *single* mothers are supposed to know everything." At least she prided herself on knowing everything about her boys.

"I think you're too hard on yourself, Mattie. My mom was terrific, but I guarantee you there were things—lots of things—

my brothers and I never told her.'' He laughed suddenly. ''And lots of things we prayed she'd never find out.''

Mattie laughed as well. The man had the most incredible eyes. Deep and dark, and very mysterious. It would be easy to become mesmerized by them, she realized.

''Boys,'' Mattie said with a roll of her eyes. ''I've only got two, so I can't even imagine how your mom handled four. They can definitely be a handful.''

''Twins, especially,'' he added, and she looked at him curiously.

''You sound like you speak from experience.''

He laughed. ''I do.'' He continued to hold her gaze. Something sizzled and sparked between them, but he refused to look away, pleased when she didn't either. ''I'm a twin.''

''You're kidding.'' She couldn't even imagine another gorgeous man who looked exactly like him walking around loose, tormenting poor hapless, unsuspecting women with that tough lean body, or those long, dark smoldering looks.

''Nope. I've got an identical twin brother named Johnny. I'm three minutes older than he is, but other than that, we're absolutely identical.'' At least in looks, Joe thought, thinking of his beloved brother. After his accident, Johnny had been stuck in the mind of an innocent, helpless child. ''And when we were kids, we were as close—and about as mischievous— as your boys.''

She nodded thoughtfully. ''That explains why you didn't even blink when Cody and Conner were finishing each other's sentences.'' She laughed, pushing her hair back. ''It unnerves most people, but you didn't even seem to notice.''

''Nope, it seemed perfectly natural to me. My brother and I used to do it all the time.''

''I thought you were going to tell me you had twin sons.'' Mattie watched his face, saw his eyes cloud, then darken with something she couldn't identify.

''Nope. No kids. I'm not married.''

She leaned her arms on the table and studied him. ''That surprises me, Joe. Someone like you who is so devoted to his family and who seems to love and understand kids so well. I thought for sure you'd have a houseful of your own.''

He shrugged, determined to make light of the situation. This was one area *he* wasn't comfortable. ''I almost got married once, but then I realized that between my sisters and brothers, and all my nieces and nephews, I had more than enough commitments and responsibilities. Thankfully, I realized that before I made a mistake and made two people, and perhaps a few children, very, very unhappy.'' He shrugged, not wanting to dwell on the subject. ''My life is full. I have a job I love, a family I adore and more than enough commitments and responsibilities to keep me busy. I'm very happy with the way things are and I really don't have the time for anything or anyone else.'' He'd been repeating the same refrain for so many years now, he was almost beginning to believe it.

Almost.

As long as he didn't think about the nights he went home alone to an empty house, a house that never rang with love or laughter.

A home that was merely four walls and a space where he rested his head, and not really a home because there was no one there to share it with.

There was only an eerie, empty silence that filled his heart every time he walked through the door.

An image of sweet, helpless Johnny flashed in Joe's mind, and he immediately felt a well of love for his brother. He never thought of looking out for Johnny as a responsibility, but merely as an honor and a privilege. If their situations had been reversed, he knew without a doubt Johnny would have done the same by him, looked after him, taken care of him, protected him. There was never any question about that. *Not ever.* That's how close he and his brother had always been.

So it was only natural that as the oldest, his father had entrusted the care of the family—and especially Johnny's care—to him.

''Sounds like you're a pretty contented man then,'' Mattie said carefully, trying to hide her surprise. She would never have expected him to say he didn't want a family of his own. He just seemed so family oriented.

Regardless of how the man made her feel, it would never amount to anything because he simply wasn't interested in a family of his own. And she came with a ready-made one.

Like her former husband, Joe was a man who clearly didn't want the responsibility of a family, but unlike her former husband, at least Joe was honest enough and mature enough to recognize and admit what he didn't want or need in his life before damaging or destroying other innocent lives because of his own immaturity and inability to accept responsibility.

In spite of her surprise, that knowledge brought on a level of relief. Regardless of his looks or his kindness, Joe was no longer a man she had to worry about, at least not on a romantic level. Obviously he had no interest in or designs on her in that department, so perhaps now she could relax and not worry about the riot of feelings he evoked in her, knowing it wouldn't amount to anything.

"Contented?" He thought about it for a moment, thought about all the things he'd always thought he'd have, the home and family he'd always wanted, the houseful of children he'd always dreamed about.

But he'd always been a pragmatic man and had come to terms with the fact that some things just would never be. He'd made peace with it a long time ago.

"That I am," he said quietly. He glanced up as Gina wound her way around various filled tables toward them with a large pizza in her hands.

Relieved, Joe smiled, anxious to get off this subject. "Ah, finally. I thought I was going to have to start gnawing on the table."

"Nope, not tonight," Gina said as she slid the still-steaming pizza onto the table. "Dig in." She handed each of them extra napkins, and scooped up their soft-drink pitcher to refill it.

"So, what's the verdict, Mattie?" Joe asked, letting the pizza sit and cool for a moment. "Have I passed the test?" he asked with a lift of his eyebrow. "Are you willing to let me teach the boys to play baseball?" He went on before she had a chance to answer. "Make no mistake, it's a big commitment for them and you, as well as a big responsibility. Like I said, it's important that we have full parental involvement and participation. Especially in the T-ball league where we're usually desperate for any help we can get."

"I understand, Joe. I'm working at the at gallery part-time in the afternoons and going to school part-time in the mornings, but I made sure when I set my schedule that I'd have more than enough time for the boys."

"I'm sure you did," he said easily. "So what are you studying?"

"Business administration. Another year and a half and I'll have my degree." She laughed suddenly. "It will be a long haul, but well worth it in the end. I plan to do consulting," she said proudly.

"There's not much call for business consultants in a town this size," Joe said.

"Probably not," she agreed.

"Seems to me that's a big-city job."

"It is," she admitted. "But at least with consulting, I can live anywhere I want and pretty much set my own hours and pace. It will allow me to have a schedule that leaves time and room for the boys, which is my first concern."

"Seems like you've got your long-term future well planned out." So she wasn't planning on staying in Healing Harbor permanently, Joe realized. Just long enough to get her degree.

In some ways, Mattie was exactly like his ex-fiancée. A woman who had a problem with her ex's family as well as a woman not interested in small-town life, anxious to return to the big, bustling city to pursue a career.

Joe sighed softly, wondering why he felt such a well of disappointment. Mattie would never be a threat to his heart. He simply couldn't and wouldn't allow it, not under the circumstances, and especially not knowing all of this about her up-front. So he might as well just sit back and enjoy the feelings she aroused in him. Male feelings that he'd suppressed for far too long.

"So tell me, Joe, exactly what kind of parental involvement

is required for this baseball league?'' Mattie picked up a piece of pizza, blew on it a moment to let it cool before taking a bite.

"In addition to actually helping out the team, you'll need to sign up to work the concession stands at least twice during the season, and volunteer to bring treats for the team probably twice as well.''

Still eating, Mattie nodded, digesting the information. "That's fine.''

"There's a parents' meeting this Thursday night at the town hall. That's in the same building as the sheriff's office. It's mandatory for all parents.'' He shrugged. "I'll introduce all the coaches to the parents, go over the rules and regulations, et cetera.''

"Isn't T-ball pretty much the same as regular baseball?'' she asked with a frown.

Joe smiled. "Yes and no. In T-ball, there's no pitching, so you don't have to worry about kids getting hit with a wild pitch or a wayward fly ball. At this age, kids don't have enough hand–eye coordination or control to actually pitch a ball to a designated place. So the ball is placed on a tee and is hit from there. There's a mandatory participation rule as well. All players must play offense and defense during each game. That way we guarantee that every kid has a chance to play as well as develop his own skills.''

"Joe, are you sure it's safe?'' she asked hesitantly, feeling a little foolish even asking. But she had to, for her own peace of mind.

"As safe as we can make it, Mattie.'' Shaking his head, he laughed at a sudden memory. "I can't and won't guarantee the boys won't get hurt, simply because one year I had a kid walk smack into the concrete water fountain at the park and split his forehead open. A half hour *after* a game.'' He glanced up at her to find her watching him with interest. "His mother was not thrilled,'' he remembered. "The game is as safe as we can make it. The ball we use is only four ounces in weight and is bright orange so it can be seen easily. And even if you're hit by it, it really doesn't do anything but smart for a moment or so. The players are required to wear safety helmets at all times, athletic shoes, preferably with baseball cleats, athletic supporters and gloves. We take every precaution necessary to ensure the safety of all players.''

Mattie nodded, feeling a bit better as she reached for another piece of pizza. ''Okay, so what about practice and stuff?'' This was all totally foreign to her. A new world she'd be traversing with her children for the first time and she wanted to know as much as possible.

''We have practice four times a week for an hour and a half, Tuesdays through Fridays. We have games on Saturday mornings at eleven—except when there's a special game, like for Memorial Day or the big end-of-school parade and game. All players are required to be at all practices unless they're sick or have a major school project. We expect all of the kids to keep up with their studies. It's one of the requirements for being and staying on the team.''

''I understand. And approve,'' she said, pinching off another piece of pizza crust and popping it in her mouth, trying to resist taking another full piece ''But what about Sundays?'' she asked curiously. ''No practice or games?''

Shaking his head, Joe smiled as he helped himself to another piece of pizza. ''Nope. Nothing on Sundays. This is still a small town, Mattie, and Sundays are reserved for family. Church services, visiting family and big Sunday dinners are still a way of life here in Healing Harbor.'' And his Sundays were reserved for visiting Johnny. The whole family—or at least everyone who was in town—went out on Sundays to spend the day with Johnny at the residential home where he lived. They all had dinner together as a family, just as they had done when their folks had been alive. It was the one day the whole family connected regardless of their own busy schedules.

Carefully, Joe set his pizza down and studied Mattie for a moment, trying to ignore the ball of desire simmering low in his gut every time he looked at her. ''I have to tell you, Mattie, personally, I think this would be wonderful for the boys. T-ball isn't just about baseball. It's a way to teach youngsters so many things. Patience. Commitment. Persistence. Dedication. We don't focus on winning or losing, and in fact, that's secondary. What we try to instill in the kids is a sense of feeling good about themselves and having fun.'' He hesitated for a moment. ''Studies have found that playing baseball helps kids in all areas. It especially helps fatherless kids,'' he added softly.

''Why?'' she asked, truly interested. Giving in to temptation, she took another piece of pizza and cursed her waistline.

''Well, for one thing, it will help children learn to interact with one another, as well as with male adults on a regular basis. Something they might not be used to on a daily basis.''

''Yeah, but Joe, what about the kids getting too attached to their coaches?'' She glanced away for a moment. ''You have to remember, my boys have never really had any interaction with adult males, at least not on an everyday basis like this.''

''Believe it or not, boys get more attached to their teammates than they do to the actual coaches. They very quickly develop a sense of camaraderie and commitment to their teammates.'' He shrugged, then smiled. ''Apparently, once the newness of being around adult males has worn off, boys tend to look at coaches more as authority figures than father figures. It's healthy for them, though, to get used to interacting with authority figures, especially children who don't interact daily with their dads. Some dads just don't have the time or inclination to be involved in their kids' lives.'' He leaned closer. ''Just because a boy has a father, Mattie, even if he's living in the same house, doesn't mean he sees or interacts with his kid every day. Lots of boys on our team have full-time dads, but spend more time with the coaches than they do with their own fathers.'' It was a continual source of irritation to Joe. How could a man simply abdicate his parental responsibility? He simply couldn't understand it.

''That's very sad,'' Mattie said, realizing that although her boys might not have ever had a father, they'd always had a full-time, totally involved mother. And perhaps, she realized, that was more than some two-parent kids had.

''Baseball teaches a boy more than just a sport, Mattie. It

teaches young boys how to work as a team, and also gives them a sense of belonging as well as a sense of group support. They learn how to react under stress in a way that's healthy and they also learn good sportsmanship, and that's something that will be an asset to them their whole lives. In addition, they develop a sense of pride in their accomplishments, and a feeling of self-worth with each new skill they master. All of these things will aid the boys' self-esteem now and in the future.''

''Sounds like you're quite an expert on this,'' she said, more impressed than she would have believed.

Thoughtfully, Joe sipped his soft drink. ''I told you, Mattie. I take my responsibilities and commitments seriously.'' He hesitated a moment. ''For the record, I have a degree in criminology with a minor in psychology. *Child* psychology,'' he specified, surprising her once again. ''I knew I was going to make law enforcement a career and that I'd probably be dealing with kids. I wanted as much knowledge as I could get. Working with children has always been a dream of mine, and I wanted to make certain I could understand them as well as help them.'' He seemed a tad embarrassed, and Mattie surprised herself by reaching out and touching his hand.

''I think that's wonderful, Joe. Truly,'' she added with a smile. ''You sound more than qualified, let alone capable of handling young boys.'' And he would have made a wonderful father, she thought, then immediately banished the thought, wondering where it had come from. He'd already made his feelings on that subject clear.

''But what about *your* boys, Mattie?'' he asked quietly, tracing a finger over the top of her hand. She jerked just a fraction, but enough for him to see it. He banked a smile, realizing she was trying not to be so skittish around him, and he had to give her points for that.

There was something very appealing about how nervous she seemed around him. Nervous and, he thought, just a tad too fragile. Someone had really hurt or spooked her, he realized, and he couldn't help it, but it brought out all his protective instincts. The lady needed to know that he wasn't a man who'd hurt her. Or anyone.

And then there were her boys, Joe thought with a wistful little sigh. Adorable pistols—both of them so eager and anxious to please. They reminded him of another set of inseparable twins, he thought with a slight pang.

''Mattie, do you trust me enough to handle your sons?'' He wasn't certain he'd earned enough of her trust yet, but he was confident he would. Eventually.

His question had her heart pumping frantically for a moment, then Mattie silently cautioned herself to relax. He had done nothing to make her doubt him, and in fact, had gone out of his way to make sure she was totally comfortable with him and his qualifications.

So how could she possibly say no?

She couldn't.

Mattie lifted her gaze to his and saw so many things in those mysterious dark eyes, some things frightened her, some comforted her, but she knew that what she couldn't do was make a decision based on her own fears.

Her children deserved more from life than a mother who was afraid of her own shadow, and afraid to let them live or experience life.

Yes, it was a risk. She'd be taking a risk. The boys had never interacted so closely with an adult male before, and they might get too attached; they might also get hurt physically by playing baseball. But she couldn't very well wrap her boys in cotton wool the rest of their lives and keep them in the house just to ensure their safety. That was certainly no way to raise children.

She had to admit there was still a niggling fear knowing that she'd have to spend almost as much time with Joe as the boys would, but she had to get over her discomfort at the feelings the man caused, and realize he wasn't in the least bit interested in her romantically.

Nor was she interested in him in that way.

To even consider such a thing would be ludicrous and foolish on her part. So he made her feel things, things she'd forgotten she could feel. Instead of fearing those feelings, perhaps she should just enjoy them, knowing they would not lead anywhere and, in fact, were harmless.

Perhaps she should just relax around Joe, enjoy the feelings she was experiencing and simply do what was best for her boys.

All in all, if she was going to entrust her sons to a man, who better than Joe? A man who was not only eminently qualified, but more important, a man who had absolutely no interest or designs on her.

He was, she realized, perfect.

Taking a slow, deep breath, Mattie laughed suddenly, feeling better than she had in hours. "Yes, Joe. I think it would be wonderful if you taught the boys to play baseball. And thank you for offering and for caring so much about two little boys' problems." Suddenly a little embarrassed, Mattie glanced down at the last of her pizza. "I really do appreciate everything you've done." She glanced up at him with a sly smile. "Even if I haven't always acted like it tonight."

"Well, I'm relieved that you're no longer looking at me as if I'm dangerous," he said with a laugh, wondering why he felt such a rush of relief by her acceptance.

He allowed himself a moment, just a moment, to savor the feeling of knowing he'd be seeing much more of Mattie Maguire and not wondering why it pleased him so.

He turned his palm over and caught her hand in his. Her hands were so feminine, soft and incredibly delicate. For just a fraction of an instant he wondered what it would be like to feel those incredibly soft, delicate hands on other parts of his body. Clinging to his shoulders as he kissed that luscious mouth senseless. Digging into his arms as he thrust deeply inside her. The thought shocked Joe out of his reverie, causing him to blink guiltily.

He swallowed hard, and felt as if a boulder had mysteriously lodged in his throat. Where the hell had that thought come from? he wondered, looking at Mattie, grateful she couldn't read his thoughts.

Embarrassed, he shifted his gaze back down to her hand,

trying to rein in his thoughts. He couldn't remember the last time he'd thought about a woman in such a carnal way.

Perhaps because he'd never met a woman quite like Mattie. Nor could he ever remember reacting or responding quite so strongly to a woman before. There was just something about Mattie…something that seemed to arouse both his passion, as well as his sense of protectiveness. It was an odd and compelling combination.

Maybe if she dealt with him enough, she'd learn he was trustworthy and stop being quite so frightened—at least of him. And that alone he'd consider worthwhile and a victory.

"So exactly what do I need to get the ball rolling?" she asked, drawing his gaze.

Joe swallowed again, deliberately clearing his mind of all thoughts except the subject at hand. "I've got all the official papers down at the office. If you don't mind, I can drop them off at the gallery sometime tomorrow. You'll need to sign everything, fill out all the insurance forms and include a check for uniforms."

"That's fine." Relaxed now, Mattie let her hand stay in his, knowing that in spite of the increase in her pulse, she had nothing to worry about.

"Practice starts at six-thirty each evening. Ends promptly at eight."

"I don't mind, Joe." Mentally, she began juggling her schedule. She usually studied in the evenings, finishing up any homework she didn't finish during the day at work, but she could probably just bring it with her to practice. Or stay up a bit later and do it after the twins were in bed. It would be worth a little sacrifice to make the boys so happy.

"Good. You'll have to stop by my office maybe Saturday morning and pick up the uniforms. The boys will have to try them on for size, so bring them with you. Oh, and there'll be a list of supplies you'll need to purchase. Make sure you write the boys' names on everything with black, indelible ink." Joe laughed. "If you don't we'll have a couple hundred kids fighting over whose cap is whose."

"Will do." She hesitated. "Joe, is there anything else I

need to do, know or to be aware of, any advice or recommendations for this novice mother?''

Smiling, he gave her hand a gentle squeeze. "Just relax, Mattie. This is going to be wonderful for the boys. The more they learn the more their confidence levels will go up, and the more confidence they have, the easier I think it will be for them to fit in and to do well at school.''

"I hope so,'' Mattie said, chewing her lower lip. "I just hate the thought that they're being teased. It hurts me to know they're being hurt.''

"Kids can be very, very cruel, Mattie,'' he said quietly, feeling a pain from the past settle over him like a billowing fog. He'd learned the hard way just how cruel people—especially children could be—after Johnny's accident. And he'd bloodied more than a few noses and gotten a few himself defending his brother from the taunts and cruelty of kids at school.

He and Johnny had been racing their bikes to the park to play ball the day of Johnny's accident—just as they did every day after school. But on that particular day, a car driven by a driver who was going too fast and who wasn't paying attention, hit Johnny's bike, sending his brother headfirst to the pavement.

Johnny had been severely injured and brain damaged, steeped in the mind of a twelve-year-old child, never to grow or mature beyond that.

"Joe?'' Mattie touched his hand. There were shadows of sadness in his eyes she didn't understand, and for some reason they touched her heart. "Are you okay?'' she asked softly.

Dragging himself out of his memories, Joe smiled, then blew out a breath. "Yeah, I'm fine.'' He reached for his pizza, chewing thoughtfully. "You know, Mattie, I really think it will be good for the boys to have some independence. As you say, you've been a single parent since their birth, so that means they've been totally dependent on you for everything. Baseball will force them to be independent, to do things without depending on you, but instead, depending on themselves and their own skills.'' He grinned as her eyes flashed fire. "A little bit of independence is good for all kids," he chided gently, watching in amusement as she ground her teeth together. "Especially boys."

"I know, but I don't have to like the idea," she muttered crossly. The boys were all she had; all she'd ever wanted. "They're everything to me, Joe."

"I know that, Mattie, and so do they," he said softly, giving her hand another squeeze of assurance. "But they're not going to be young forever, and everything you do now that helps with their self-confidence and self-esteem will help them to become better teens and adults, capable of making good, sound decisions."

"Fine, but I still don't have to like it," she muttered, making him laugh.

"Mattie?" Amusement flickered in Joe's eyes.

"What?" she grumbled, glumly resting her chin on her other hand and staring forlornly at the remaining pizza.

With an amused grin, Joe gave her hand a final squeeze, liking the way her skin warmed against his. "If we hurry, we just might have time to finish this pizza before your boys are ready to move into an apartment of their own."

Chapter Three

"Mattie, lass, has your aunt gone daft?" Clancy Thomas McHugh, a small, spry man with a fringe of white, thinning hair and an impish smile rounded on Mattie the next afternoon, full of Irish indignation. "I'm fearing my eyes are deceiving me. Aye, lass, is it possibly your aunt has really put my latest masterpiece next to a *Calhoun?*"

Standing in the showroom of her aunt Maureen's art gallery, Clancy gave an exaggerated sigh, then shook his head as he placed a hand to his heart and stared woefully at the exhibit wall.

"Aye, lass, if the truth be told, she's broken me heart. Wounded me to the quick she has. Putting me latest master-piece next to this...this..." Whirling, he waved his arm toward the wall where several glorious paintings were show-cased under exquisite lighting. "Abomination." He did a quick two-step that turned into an irritated Irish jig in front of the offending piece. "Aye, I'm shattered beyond repair." He hung his head, peeking at her under the fringe of his white eyebrows. "Me old heart, why, I fear it t'will never recover."

"Now, Clancy," Mattie soothed in a tone of voice she would have used with her children. In the three months since she'd taken over managing her aunt's art gallery, she'd learn that artists were, at times, little more than children. Petulant. Impulsive. Headstrong. And totally, utterly charming. She adored them. "I'm sure that Aunt Maureen didn't mean to offend you—"

"Offend?" Clancy's feet barely touched the ground as he bounced around her, waving his arms madly again. "Offend? Why, simply having this…this…upstart's work in the same…*state* as mine is offensive."

Mattie banked another smile. "Now, Clancy, I think a seventy-five-year-old man with an international reputation in the art world can hardly be called…an upstart—"

"'Tis only because you're a lass that I didn't use anything stronger," he cautioned through narrowed eyes as he rounded on the offensive painting again. "What on earth was the old girl thinking?" he wondered aloud, rolling his eyes toward the heavens as if they could provide the answer.

"I don't know, Clancy," Mattie said, taking his arm to try to steer him away from the wall before he did himself harm. "But you don't have to worry. The piece won't be here long." She grinned with pride. "I sold Calhoun's piece an hour ago. We'll be packing it up and shipping it out later this afternoon."

"Sold? Sold! How much did you steal for this piece of…of…trash?" He waved an arm toward the wall again, making Mattie sigh.

"Now, Clancy," Mattie said, hooking her arm through his and leading him away from the wall and toward the back workroom, hoping to distract him. "You know I'm not allowed to give out those figures. They're confidential." But she'd sold the piece for enough money to make a handsome commission for herself and the gallery. Her portion would go into the bank toward her new car fund.

"Balderdash," he scoffed, waving away her comments like an annoying fly. "Nothing is secret in the art world." He thought for a moment, then brightened suddenly, looking like a mischievous cherub. "Did you perhaps sell it for less than me *Rebellious Gardenias?*"

"Perhaps," she teased, still steering him toward the workroom. She knew once Clancy set eyes on the painting he'd left half-finished in the workroom last weekend, this latest fiasco with Calhoun just might be forgotten. Well, she could always hope.

"Perhaps?" Eyes gleaming, he must have sensed she was softening, and grabbed her hands in his. "Aye, lass, you know I adore you, and have told your aunt what a wonderful find you are." With an elegant gesture, he brought her hand to his lips for a whisper of a kiss. "A treasure to be sure." Still holding her hands, he drew her closer, eyes twinkling. "So tell me, lass, did you sell Calhoun's albatross for less than me *Gardenias?*"

She laughed as she pulled free of him to open the door to the workroom. "Well, Clancy, I can only tell you that you'd not be…shamed by the figure."

"Aye, lass, I knew it!" Delighted, Clancy did another jig around her, clapping his hands in glee. "Sold my *Gardenias* for more. I knew it. Calhoun will never hold so much as a flickering candle to me." He grabbed her cheeks and pressed a loud, smacking kiss to her mouth. "That's me girl, Mattie." He kissed her again, then turned and came to an abrupt halt, his gaze narrowing on his half-finished painting visible through the now-open door.

"Clancy? Are you all right?"

"Aye, lass, now that I've looked at this with a fresh eye, me thinks it needs a tad more yellow for shade and shadowing." Eyes all but glazed in concentration, Clancy moved another step closer to his painting. "Mmm…aye, that's it. That's it!" His feet bounced up and down as his eyes glittered. "I knew the problem would become clear with time." His eyebrows drew together as he muttered to himself. "It's a tad too…green is what it is." His gaze never wavered from his work as he narrowed his gaze. "Off with you now," he said, shooing her away with his hands as he stepped into the workroom. "I've work to be done."

Satisfied she'd averted another artistic crisis, at least for the moment, Mattie sighed, and headed back through the gallery to her desk.

The gallery, which fronted Main Street with plate-glass windows, was divided into three distinct sections. The front was a showcase for artists' work. The middle of the gallery was where her small desk, a file cabinet, her computer and other necessities to run a successful, thriving gallery business were set up, giving her some peace from the foot traffic that wandered in during the day. And in the back was the artists' work room.

The space, small, but incredibly efficient, served as her office. There was a coffeepot—always hot and full—sitting on a small wooden credenza behind her desk. Under it, concealed by a wooden door in the credenza was a mini refrigerator where she kept fruit juice for the boys as well as soft drinks for others.

Since Mattie attended classes in the morning, she spent afternoons at the gallery, relieving her aunt of as much responsibility as possible. She'd fixed her schedule around the twins, and with the grade school just six blocks away, she'd arranged with Charlie, the school-bus driver, to drop the boys off right in front of the gallery every day. It saved her a trip to school to pick them up, and allowed them all to drive home together.

Moving through the gallery now, with the soft, soothing strains of Bach filtering through the quiet air, Mattie glanced out the front glass windows. A patrol car went by and she wondered, as she had several times this morning, if Joe was in the car.

Spending last evening with him had definitely left an impression on her, and considering the fuss she'd made about getting home at eight, the fact that she'd sat and chatted with him over coffee until almost eleven left her feeling slightly off kilter. It had been pleasant, she had to admit, to just sit and relax with a man, talking about her sons, her life.

She'd done little more than think of Joe all day. Mattie laughed at herself. She'd actually caught herself daydreaming about him in class today, an incident that embarrassed her no end.

Smiling at herself for such foolishness, she continued through the gallery, stopping here and there to appreciate a particular painting or to adjust the placement of a sculpture. In the three months since she'd taken over for her aunt, she'd grown to love everything about the gallery.

For as long as she could remember, she'd harbored a secret desire to draw, to paint, but circumstances and the realities of her life had prevented such selfishly frivolous pursuits.

It had been imperative for her to make a living, and she certainly didn't have time to dabble in something that might take years to produce a viable income—if ever.

She'd been forced to be both prudent and practical, living on the little bit of life insurance money Gary had left to her, supplementing that with Social Security payments and part-time work at home so she could always take care of her boys. But it had been a struggle, and now, financially, she and the twins finally had some stability.

Working for her aunt provided not only an adequate income to support them, but she'd also been given her aunt's coach house to live in free of charge. As a bonus, because her aunt was such a well-respected member of the art community, as well as the community of Healing Harbor, and taught classes at the local university, Mattie was allowed to attend the university tuition free. In another year and a half she'd have her business degree, and another year of business experience behind her. Hopefully, those qualifications would allow her to obtain consulting work that would forever secure her and the boys' futures.

Working in the gallery was not all work though, Mattie had to admit. It also allowed her to indulge in the artistic fantasies she'd long held dear, and also to interact with artists, which at times seemed a blessing, and at others, a curse.

As she sat down at her desk now, she reached in the bottom drawer and pulled out the sketch pad she kept hidden there, as well as a small piece of charcoal. She just wasn't up to tackling her homework right now. For some reason, today, she'd been both restless and easily distracted.

Pushing her macroeconomics textbook out of the way, Mattie began to sketch. Quick, short strokes flowed from her fingers, making her smile in pleasure. Knowing she only had a few precious moments each day to take this time for herself, she tried to make the best of them and not feel guilty.

Bright afternoon sunlight flowed in through the plate-glass windows. Cocking her head, she studied her sketch from another angle, drawing from memory. The shape of the jaw needed just a tad more shading to make it a bit more realistic, she decided.

And the eyes, they were much larger, deeper, dominating the planes and angles of that gorgeous face. And then there was that mouth, Mattie thought with a long, heartfelt sigh. Oh, that mouth was incredible, she remembered. Thick and full, it was totally masculine, yet coupled with that slightly off-kilter once-broken nose, it gave the face both character and dignity as well as added interest.

Totally absorbed in her sketching, Mattie didn't hear the tinkle of the bell over the door.

"Good Lord, Mattie, that's wonderful."

Joe's soft, masculine voice right behind her ear startled her, and Mattie let loose a high-pitched screech. The charcoal went sailing one way and she nearly went the other. Gentle, masculine hands on her shoulders prevented her from flying off her chair.

"Easy, Mattie," Joe whispered, his voice warm and soft against her ear. The heat from his hands seemed to melt the material of her cotton sweater, sensitizing her skin, making her feel as if he was caressing her.

"Joe!" Gasping, she pressed a hand to her rampaging heart, more startled and embarrassed than she believed possible. She turned to face him, caught up short by the fact that his face— the face that she'd just so painstakingly drawn from memory— was right there.

He'd gone down on his haunches so that they were eye level, and she blinked at his closeness, then licked her dry lips, realizing if she moved forward just a little their lips would be touching. It took all her willpower not to move a muscle, nor an inch.

"You…you…scared the life out of me." She wished she didn't sound so flustered and breathless. It was hardly the professional image she wanted to project.

"I'm sorry." He flashed her one of those glorious smiles. "I didn't mean to startle you." His eyebrows drew together a bit. "I thought for sure you'd heard the bell. I just stopped by to drop off the papers you need to sign." He laid the sheaf of papers on her desk, trying not to frown. She had that same wonderful perfume on again today, he realized, resisting the urge to bury his nose in the soft crevices of her neck and lose himself in the scent, knowing he'd probably scare a few years off her if he did.

He glanced at the sketch pad still clutched in her hand. Impressed, his eyebrows went up in astonishment. "You didn't tell me you were an artist."

"I'm…not," she stammered, wondering where her charcoal had landed as she tried to close the pad. "Not really."

"No, don't." He covered her hand with his, preventing her from hiding her drawing. "That's not the way I see it," he said, gently prying her hands from the pad and turning it around. "The sketch is really wonderful. And a very good likeness of me."

"Thank you." She resisted the urge to push back away from him, to put some distance between them so she could breathe. He was still too close and it was still too hard to breathe with him so near.

"And I'd say you *were* an artist, Mattie, in spite of your protests to the contrary, and a very good one at that." His gaze met hers and she felt her pulse leap and dance.

Embarrassed beyond belief because she'd been caught drawing him, which meant she'd actually been thinking about him, Mattie licked her dry lips, wondering when her heart was going to stop galloping like a runaway horse.

"It's…it's just something I dabble with," she commented, feeling foolish. Why on earth hadn't she drawn a bowl of fruit or a basket of flowers? Perhaps because neither had been on her mind as much as Joe had been for the past twelve hours.

"Now, why do I get the feeling that you've never shared or showed your work to anyone?" She'd acted as if he'd caught her with her hand in the till. Instead of just...drawing.

"I...I..." His face was so close, she could feel his warm breath flutter across her skin, raising goose bumps and sending her already speeding pulse into overtime.

She glanced at her sketch pad, which he still held in his hand. The temptation to snatch it from him, to hide her private, precious secret was nearly overwhelming.

"I'm...I'm..." She shrugged helplessly, unable to draw her gaze from those mysterious dark eyes. "I guess I'm just not ready to show anyone yet."

"You're just not accustomed to sharing parts of your life with anyone," he said softly, touching her face. Her eyes went wide as saucers, and deliberately he softened his voice, pressing his forehead against hers to calm her. "You've done so much alone, I think that perhaps you forget there are people in the world to share things with, people who will be interested, and who will care about what you care about."

If she could speak, she was certain she would have been able to think of plenty to say. But she couldn't. He was far too close.

"Joe." She swallowed, lifting a hand to his broad chest. She could feel his heart galloping in time to hers. It brought little comfort that apparently he was just as affected by her closeness as she was by his. His mouth was so close, she couldn't seem to think of anything else. The ache of wanting seemed to loom large, nearly smothering her. She just wanted to taste that mouth, taste it just once. Her throat had gone so dry she was certain she'd never swallow again.

"I don't think this is a good idea." Her voice was soft, shaky, and she struggled to find some dignity.

His smile was slow and his gaze never left hers. She looked so wide-eyed terrified, it brought out all his protective instincts, and he tightened his hands on her shoulders.

"Actually, Mattie, I think it's the best idea I've had today."

Without another word, he gently brushed his lips within scant centimeters of hers. She felt the whisper touch of his sweet, warm breath, and could almost feel the warmth of his lips touching hers.

Her breath caught in expectation as she waited for the first touch, the first feel of that warm mouth on hers. Unconsciously, her fingers tightened on his shirt, gripping the material in her fingers, drawing him closer.

"Joe," she whispered, knowing she should stop him, but also knowing she couldn't. She couldn't remember ever wanting anything this badly. Wanting to just feel his touch, his taste.

"Mattie." His breath feathered against her lips, making a rushing ache of yearning twist inside her. Anticipation had her fingers curling tighter on his shirt as his mouth gently, lightly teased hers.

"J-Joe." Her voice was half plea, half prayer. And then his mouth covered hers, firmly, tightly, possessively, and Mattie forgot everything as her head emptied of all thought. Desire hit like a quick-fisted punch, nearly knocking whatever thoughts, and all of the breath, from her as his mouth expertly caressed hers, seducing her lips until she was nearly senseless with shock.

Her fingers curled instinctively, tightening on the material of his shirt, holding on to him, drawing him closer, seeking more of this mindless pleasure that made her forget everything but the man holding her, kissing her.

Her heart seemed to somersault, whirling over and over inside her chest as need blossomed, grew, then exploded in a dizzying blaze of heated desire.

She heard a low-throated moan of pleasure, desire, and was stunned to realize it had come from her. Her body grew warm and weak, needy with a longing she'd never realized existed before, so strong, so powerful, it was all that consumed her, the urge, the need to extinguish the blaze of need and desire that Joe's kiss, his mouth, had ignited.

Frightened by her own feelings, Mattie wanted to stop him, to pull away, but knew she couldn't. Wouldn't. She had never felt any of these wondrous feelings before, had never felt this kind of need, desire for anyone before. The newness was intoxicating and addictive and she wanted to savor the feelings, to bask in them and let them carry her to a conclusion that would hopefully dull this terrible ache of need and yearning burning inside.

Need.

It scared her; she couldn't need anyone, not ever. Especially a man. Especially Joe. It was far too dangerous.

The thought brought her reluctantly to her senses and she forced her shaking fingers to slowly uncurl from his shirt. Pressing the flat of her hands to his chest, she slowly drew back from him, breaking their kiss and contact, embarrassed because her hands—her heart—were far from steady.

"Joe." Her voice was breathless, but the need to say something was urgent. "I'm sorry." She struggled to take a breath, to do something with her shaky hands so she wouldn't reach for him again. Lifting a hand, she touched her lips. They were still warm from his and she felt her pulse kick up again at the mere thought of kissing him.

"I'm not." Stunned by her wildfire response, and his own intense craving to have more of her, to taste more of her, Joe slipped his hands in his pockets, fearing if he didn't, he'd touch her again. And start the wildfire all over again. But she was looking far too fearful and fragile, like a cornered puppy about to get a beating.

The urge to soothe, to protect, was so strong, he wanted to gather her into his arms and simply hold her closely and gently until she calmed down. But he didn't, knowing it would only distress her further.

Instead, he framed her face with his hands and brushed her hair back. It was as soft as silk, as soft as he'd imagined all night long as he lay in bed, thinking of her, dreaming of her, wondering what she'd feel like, taste like. Now he knew, and knew, too, that the knowledge would only make him need and desire her even more.

"In addition to being a fabulous artist, you're a great kisser." He tried to bank the smile at the sharp look she aimed at him. One eyebrow rose in surprise. "Do you always scowl when a man pays you a compliment?"

"Men don't compliment me," she snapped, still shaken to the core.

"Obviously idiots, the lot of them." He flashed her a smile that set her pulse racing once again. "You're far too beautiful and talented not to compliment."

"And you're far too smooth and practiced to take seriously." Deliberately, she made her voice cool, then rubbed her damp, shaky hands over her jean-clad thighs.

"Blame my sisters," he said with a chuckle, running a finger down her nose. Her skin was all dewy soft and creamy ivory. Now that he'd actually touched her, tasted her, he knew he had to have more.

"Your sisters?" she repeated in surprise, glancing up at him.

"Yep, my sisters." Joe blew out a breath, hoping to dispel some of the tension tearing through him. One kiss had knocked him for a loop. "Growing up, my sisters would bring their girlfriends around so they could practice their flirting on me. I was their friendly guinea pig."

"So they weren't flirting with you?" she asked in surprise. Youthful blindness, she decided. Had to be. What woman still breathing wouldn't want to flirt with him?

He laughed, lifting a finger to rub his forehead. "Uh…no, hardly. I was the proverbial…friend." He laughed. "Boy, do teenage guys hate that word. My brother Sal, now, he was the gorgeous heartthrob, the one every girl in town was swooning over. Anyway, all of my sisters' friends practiced their flirting on me, hoping for a chance to really use their skills on Sal. Then they'd feed me the lines they hoped to hear in return. I'm no dummy, I managed to pick up a thing or two, not that it did any of them any good. Sal wasn't interested in any friend of our sisters' since he'd already had his eye on a life mate, and they all knew they couldn't compete with my one true love."

"And she was?"

"Baseball," Joe admitted with a grin. "Stole my heart and never let go."

Mattie couldn't help it; she laughed. He'd done it again, she realized. Diffused her discomfort with humor. "I imagine that left quite a few brokenhearted teenage girls."

"Not really. They still had Sal to work on, and trust me, they made his life miserable. At least for a little while anyway." Joe glanced at his watch and flashed her a smile of regret. "Mattie, I've got to run. I've got to get Angie to the doctor, but I wanted to drop off those papers for you to sign. Don't forget we have a parents' meeting tonight at the town hall." He closed her sketch pad and handed it back to her, then bent and kissed her nose. It was so quick, she didn't have time to object. "I'll see you tonight." He turned and headed toward the door, wondering why the hell his own knees were shaking.

Mattie sat there, stunned and stupefied, too weak and shocked to do little more than watch him walk through the gallery and out the door.

Touching her still-tingling lips, Mattie took a long, slow breath, then carefully let it out. Clamping her teeth together in determination, she took one final glance at the sketch of Joe and slammed the sketchbook cover closed, determined not to even think about the taste or the impact of Joe's lips.

Promptly at three, the school bus chugged to a stop across the street from the gallery. With the Calhoun painting already en route to its new owner, Mattie went to the front door and watched the boys cross the street.

"Mom, Mom, guess what?" Connor yelled, waiting for the light to change before barreling across the street toward her. "Guess what?"

"She'll never guess," Cody said, barreling behind his brother and nearly skidding into her in his excitement.

"Whoa, whoa." Mattie held out her arms to stop their momentum, then led them by the hands inside the gallery. "What's got you two so excited?" she asked with a delighted laugh.

"You'll never guess what Amy Bartlett did today." Cody was bouncing up and down. He'd already dropped his book bag and was looking longingly toward the small refrigerator behind her desk where she kept their after-school snacks.

"Amy again?" Mattie said with a slight frown. "Please don't tell me she threw up today."

"Maaaaaaa!" Cody rolled his eyes in exasperation.

"Nah, she didn't throw up," Connor said, letting his own book bag slide to the floor. "This was even better."

"Much better," Cody said, bouncing up and down again.

"Well, thank heaven for small favors," Mattie said with a grin, ruffling Cody's hair. "So tell me," she said as she ushered the boys through the gallery and toward her desk. "What did Amy do today that was better than throwing up?" She could only hope it wasn't anything too gross. "Cody, don't touch that sculpture, you know the rules," she scolded gently, grabbing his hand before he could touch anything else.

"She gave out party invitations," Cody said, eyes glittering as he grinned up at her.

"Yeah, it's her birthday next week." Connor announced, pushing his glasses up higher on his nose. "She's gonna be six. And she invited us."

"Both of us," Cody said, clearly pleased, excited and still bouncing.

"Can we go, Ma, huh, pul-lease?" Eyes wide, Connor came to a halt to look at his mother expectantly.

"She invited everyone in the whole class." Cody scratched a mosquito bite on his elbow.

"Even Bobby Dawson," Connor added, giving his brother a poke. "Right?"

"Right." Cody stopped scratching long enough to look at his mother imploringly. "So can we go? It's our first birthday party since we moved here, Ma."

Well, well, well, Mattie thought, feeling a surge of pleasure. Perhaps the boys were beginning to fit in at school better than she thought. It was, she realized, something to be grateful for. If the boys were happy here, that's all she needed to be happy.

"Well, I don't see why not. Let me see the invitation."

Both boys scrambled to grab their book bags while Mattie retrieved two bottles of orange juice from the refrigerator, popping off the tops for the boys. She also retrieved a couple of containers of yogurt, knowing it wasn't the boys' favorite snack, but knowing they'd be hungry and would need something to hold them until dinner.

"Here, here." Cody shoved a wadded-up piece of paper at her. "Here's the invitation."

She handed him his juice and the container of yogurt. "There're spoons in my top drawer, honey," she instructed as she took the paper from him. Opening the gaily decorated note card carefully, she read it. Amy's birthday party was next Monday, right after school at the local ice-cream parlor.

"So can we go, Ma?" Eyes shining, Connor guzzled his orange juice, ignoring the little bit that dribbled out of his mouth and down his chin. "All the kids will be there."

"I think so, honey," she said with a smile as he wiped his chin on his school shirt. "You know we'll have to go shopping for a nice present."

"But she's a girl," Cody protested, scowling at his mother. "Do we gotta buy girl presents?"

"Do you get presents on your birthday?" Mattie asked with a lift of her eyebrow.

Cody scratched his head, thinking about it. "Yeah, but we don't know nuthin' about girl presents, Ma."

"Yeah, Ma," Connor piped in. "They don't like bugs, they don't like worms or any other good stuff."

"They don't even play baseball or race cars or do anything else fun."

"Yeah, Ma, they're boring." Connor giggled and gave his brother a poke in the ribs with his elbow. "I'm glad I'm not a girl. They don't got nuthin' fun to play with."

"Girls are not boring, sweetheart," Mattie corrected. "Just…different."

"So what do we gotta get?" Cody asked, rubbing the freckles on his nose.

"Well," Mattie said thoughtfully. "I suppose you could buy Amy some nice stationery."

Both boys looked at her with identical, clueless scowls.

"What's that, Ma?" Cody finally asked for the both of them, making Mattie laugh.

"It's pretty paper to write notes and things on."

"Paper?" The boys broke into fits of giggles, hugging their stomachs. "You want us to buy Amy a piece of paper for her birthday?"

"Ma, that's…stupid," Cody said, frowning. "Everyone will laugh at us."

"It was just a thought," Mattie said, realizing she was probably going to have to be more inventive in order to capture the boys', and of course, the rest of their peers', imagination. The last thing she wanted to do was have her sons laughed at, especially at the very first birthday party they'd been invited to. "Let me think about it," she said with a smile. "The party isn't until next Monday after school. You don't have baseball practice on Monday, so you can go to the party with your friends."

She waited for the explosion of excitement she was certain was coming. The boys had been sleeping when she got home last night, and this morning before school had been as chaotic as usual, so she'd decided to wait until after school to tell them.

Both boys stopped what they were doing. They exchanged looks with each other, then turned their attention to her.

"We can play?" Connor asked in disbelief.

"You're gonna let Officer Friendly teach us to play baseball?" Cody asked with a bit of disbelief of his own.

"Yes, and yes," Mattie said, watching as her boys jumped in the air, whooping and high-fiving each other. Laughing, she tried to quiet them a little. "Boys, boys, quiet down. Mr. Clancy's working in the back room."

"Nay, lass, not anymore." Grinning, Clancy, clad now in a paint-splattered plastic apron over his jeans, stood watching the boys screech and jump around in joy. "So the little lads are excited about something, I see." Eyes twinkling, he wiped his hands on a rag he'd pulled from his back pocket. "So what is it you've done, lass, to make them so happy?"

"Mr. Clancy, Mr. Clancy. Guess what?" Cody rushed up to him, nearly bowling the man over in his excitement as he bounced up and down in front of him. "Me and my brother, we're gonna learn to play baseball!"

"Is that so?" Clancy said, bending down until he could see the lad's freckles, then ruffling the boy's unruly mane of strawberry-blond hair.

"Yep. And Officer Friendly is gonna teach us," Connor added, rushing up to put his two cents in. "Mom said it was okay."

"She did, did she?" Clancy's grin widened as his gaze shifted to Mattie. "Well, then, I'd say you've got a gem of a mum, then, hey, boys?"

"Yeah, and maybe sometime you could come to watch us play."

"When you're not busy painting your hands," Cody said.

"Painting my hands, huh?" Clancy laughed, then wiped his fingers on the rag again. "Aye, son, I can see how it might look that way to you, but occasionally, just occasionally, mind you, I do manage to paint something other than my hands."

"You paint good, Mr. Clancy," Connor, always the diplomat, said. "Our mom showed us one of your pictures once."

"Do you wanna come and watch us play sometime, Mr. Clancy?" Cody asked, tilting his head back. "We're real good learners, right, Connor?" He elbowed his brother for confirmation. Connor bobbed his head up and down, nearly dislodging his glasses.

"Well, my little lads, that's very kind of you to ask. Very kind, indeed, and I just might take you up on your offer," Clancy said as he frowned at the substance the boys were eating. "What on earth have you got there?" he asked, picking up Cody's container of yogurt and giving it an inelegant sniff, then wrinkling his nose.

"Yogurt," Cody said with a scowl and a shudder. "Banana yogurt."

Clancy was still studying the container, his face almost a mirror of young Cody's. "Banana yogurt you say? Hmm." He lifted his gaze to Mattie. "Do you mind, lass, if I borrow the little lad's…yogurt? It's just the right color of yellow I've been searching for." Before she could respond, Clancy slipped two chocolate bars from his back pocket. "Here, my little lads, I'll make you a trade." Cody and Connor quickly gave up their yogurt for the candy. "Now, it's back to work for me." Yogurt containers in his hands, Clancy winked at the boys. "Congratulations, lads." He tipped an imaginary hat to them. "I'll be seeing you at the ballpark. Enjoy your chocolate."

"Mr. Clancy's neat, Ma," Connor said, ripping the wrapper off his candy bar, preparing to take a big bite.

"Yeah, even if he does talk funny," Cody added with a grin.

"He talks that way because he was born in Ireland, honey," Mattie explained, reaching out and snatching the candy bars from both boys before they could take a bite.

"Dinner is in less than two hours." She broke one candy bar in half and slipped the other in the top drawer of her desk. "You can share one."

"Aw, Ma," Cody complained, rubbing his stomach. "I'm starving."

"Good." She smiled and handed him his half of the candy bar. "That means you'll eat your dinner then." She handed Connor his half as well. "Now, I've got a few things to do before Aunt Maureen gets here, so you know the rules. You can sit at my desk and draw or read until it's time to go home." She lifted the boys' book bags from the floor. "Do either of you have homework?"

"I got vocabulary words," Cody said around a mouthful of chocolate.

"Okay, go to the bathroom, Cody, and then Connor can help you with your vocabulary."

"But I don't have to go to the—"

"By the time you get there you will," Mattie said knowingly, pointing toward the rest room. With a sigh, Cody slunk off, head down as Mattie watched him, her heart full of love.

"Ma, why you smiling?" Connor asked, clambering up on her chair. She turned to him, her heart overflowing.

"Because I love you guys." Ruffling his hair, she bent and planted a kiss on his cheek, then wrapped her arms around him tightly, burying her face in his neck, savoring his little-boy smell. "Just because I love you."

Chapter Four

"Mattie, I've been trying to get Joe Marino naked since the moment I laid eyes on him."

"Aunt Maureen!" Mattie flushed to the roots of her hair, still surprised by her aunt's outrageous way of always speaking her mind.

At seventy-three, Maureen McBride was artistic by birth, outrageous by choice, and eccentric simply because it delighted her to be. And Mattie adored her.

"I wasn't trying to get Joe *naked*—"

"Pity." Maureen smiled at her beloved niece over the rim of her coffee cup. They had just finished dinner and were sitting at the kitchen table, chatting over a last cup of coffee.

"W-we just shared a pizza last night," Mattie stammered. "*With* our clothes on," she specified nervously.

"I can think of a lot more exciting things a woman might share with Joe Marino than a pizza," Maureen said, patting her head of platinum hair, which was scraped back tightly against her head and coiled into a sophisticated chignon. "A lot more indeed." Propping her chin on her hand, Maureen sighed dreamily. "Joe has that wonderfully incredible body with all those planes and angles. Not to mention those muscles." Maureen batted her false eyelashes theatrically. "Now, if I were twenty, dear, no, perhaps thirty years younger, I just might give you a run for your money."

"I'm not interested in Joe that way," Mattie protested, not wanting her aunt to get the wrong idea. She wasn't about to mention the fact that she'd kissed Joe at the gallery this afternoon. Or rather, Joe had kissed her. Well, maybe they'd kissed each other.

Even though she hadn't been able to stop thinking about that kiss, Mattie was certain it wasn't going to happen again, so why bother talking about it.

"Don't tell me you didn't even *notice* the man's body?" Shock filtered across her aunt's face, then her eyebrows drew together. "Maybe I'd better check you for a pulse," she said with exaggerated concern, laughing at Mattie. "Don't look at me like that, dear. I'm an artist. The human body is supposed to fascinate me. Besides, I may be old, but I'm certainly not dead." Her blue eyes twinkled as she patted Mattie's hand with her own. "And I'd say Joe's body is more than fascinating for any woman at any age." Maureen paused to sip her coffee, smoothing down her flowing blue silk caftan. "It's a pity *you* didn't take more notice."

"Oh, I noticed all right," Mattie finally admitted, trying not to grin.

"You did?" Maureen beamed at her. "Well, good for you, dear." She patted Mattie's hand in approval. "Perhaps there's hope for you after all."

"Hope?" Mattie repeated suspiciously, making Maureen sigh.

"You know, there are a lot of women who have had bad first marriages."

"Aunt Maureen—"

"No, let me finish." Maureen held up one scarlet-tipped hand. "Even though you've never discussed it, I know that things weren't…easy with Gary, even before he died. And I know, too, that you and the boys had a very hard time of it afterward.'' Maureen sighed, then fiddled with the gold cross around her neck. "I will always regret not being there for you, dear. It was unforgivable.'' Tears swam behind Maureen's false eyelashes and she sniffed elegantly, extracting a silk monogrammed hankie from the pocket of her caftan to delicately dab at her eyes.

"Aunt Maureen, don't,'' Mattie said softly. "Don't blame yourself. You had no idea what I was going through, because I chose not to tell anyone.'' Especially her aunt, because she knew how her aunt would worry.

"Pride, my dear, can lead to ruin,'' Maureen cautioned, waving her hankie in the air. "Anyway, as I was saying, one bad experience shouldn't put you off men forever. I mean, really, dear, if you get a bad hamburger do you swear off beef for the rest of your life? No, of course not. You simply chalk it up to experience and go on, learning from your mistake.''

"Aunt Maureen, a husband isn't exactly like a hamburger,'' Mattie said, trying not to grin.

"You're quite right, dear. At least a bad hamburger can be tossed out and replaced with something of quality rather quickly.''

Now Mattie did laugh. "Well, there is that. However, if you get a dog from the pound and he turns out to be rabid, why on earth would you willingly go back and get another?'' Mattie grinned simply because her aunt looked so troubled. "Besides, I've already got two wonderful males in my life.'' Mattie glanced behind her, toward the kitchen window where the boys were out playing in the backyard. "They fill my life completely.''

"Yes, dear,'' Maureen said quietly, leaning forward to study her niece intently. "But what about when they're grown and you suddenly find yourself all alone?''

"You're alone,'' Mattie pointed out, not wanting to think about that time when her boys would be grown and on their own. And she would indeed be all alone. "And you love your life.''

Maureen looked away for a moment. "Yes, that's true,'' she admitted carefully. "But don't think there aren't times I

wish I would have married and had a companion of my own."
She glanced at Mattie. "It does tend to get lonely, dear, especially now that I'm finally old enough and successful enough to have the time and money to do whatever I want. It would be nice to have someone to do it with and then of course there is the advantage of having a nice warm body to cuddle up with during a long, cold winter night."

"You could always get a dog," Mattie suggested, making her aunt laugh.

"I'd prefer something that's perhaps trained enough *not* to have to be walked or fed during the night. And I do think there might be a man or two around who actually fits the bill." Maureen thought of Clancy and almost blushed. For twenty-five years he'd been hinting at his feelings for her. She almost sighed in frustration. Now if the dang man would only stop hinting and *do* something, maybe they'd get somewhere!

"Are you unhappy, Aunt Maureen?" Concern etched Mattie's forehead as she studied her aunt carefully.

"Unhappy?" Maureen thought about it for a moment, then her face brightened into a beautiful smile. "No, not at all, dear. I'm quite content, really. I have my work, my friends, and now you and the boys…" Her voice trailed off. "It's just that at times, I'd like to have someone to share my life with, that's all," she added with a shrug.

"Well, you know, it's not too late. You're still a beautiful, vibrant woman, and I know for a fact you have a lot of admirers."

"True, all of it," Maureen said with a laugh, taking a sip of her coffee. "And something I promise to give serious consideration to as soon as I have a moment of time." And as soon as Clancy worked up enough nerve to actually tell her how he felt about her. How a man could express himself so brilliantly in his work, but then be a complete and utter mute about his feelings never failed to frustrate her. She smiled brightly at Mattie. "Now, tell me what happened at the gallery today. Anything I should know about?"

"I sold the Calhoun." Pride lit Mattie's eyes. "And the buyer didn't even bother to haggle over the price."

"He paid full price?" Astonished, Maureen's eye's widened.

"Full price," Mattie confirmed. "In cash yet. I shipped it out myself this afternoon"

"Man must have been drunk," Maureen decided, then laughed and picked up her coffee cup. "Here's to another sale." She toasted Mattie's cup with her own. "And another bountiful commission. For both of us." Maureen sipped her coffee. "Did you notify Calhoun? I'm sure he'll be pleased."

"I called and left a message with his maid." Mattie hesitated a moment. "But Clancy was in the gallery at the time. Working." She laughed suddenly. "He was quite put out that you'd hung a Calhoun right next to his latest masterpiece as he called it."

"I'm sure he was. And he must have given you an earful," Maureen said knowingly, eyes twinkling in amusement. Her heart warmed just at the mention of Clancy's name, but she, too, had been hiding her feelings for the man for so long it had become second nature. "It's a good thing I love…those two mischievous men—and make a fortune on their work." She added with a knowing look, "Or I swear I'd be tempted to toss their quarreling butts out of my gallery and my life."

"Yeah, but think how boring life would be then," Mattie said, draining her cup and pushing back from the table. "Aunt Maureen, I hate to run, but if I don't I'll be late for the parents' meeting."

"I know, dear." Maureen hesitated. "But there's something I've been meaning to tell you since you got home today."

"What?"

"Last night, while I was staying with the boys, Evelyn Maguire called for you."

Mattie froze and a chill raced over her. "My former mother-in-law called last night?"

"Such an unpleasant woman," Maureen said with a barely concealed shudder. "She was almost downright rude when I told her you weren't available. She insisted on knowing where you and the boys were."

"And did you tell her?"

Maureen's chin lifted regally. "I most certainly did not. I informed her that I was not the hired help, nor did I take orders from anyone, let alone *her*." Maureen's eyes chilled. "I told her I'd be happy to relay any message to you, but her interrogation of me was over." Feeling guilty, Maureen glanced up at Mattie. "Then I hung up on her, dear. I'm sorry, Mattie, perhaps it was rude, but that woman does try my patience. She doesn't have a civil word for—"

"No, no, it's perfectly all right, Aunt Maureen." Temper was simmering low in Mattie's gut. She'd been far too busy today to even think about phoning her in-laws to have a talk with them about their comments to the boys.

Now that she knew that Evelyn Maguire had phoned last night—and been less than pleasant to her aunt—whom they unfairly blamed for her and the twins leaving Chicago and them—Mattie knew she couldn't put that call off much longer. It was time to have a serious discussion with her former in-laws, something Mattie was not in the least looking forward to.

"I'm sorry Evelyn was rude to you, Aunt Maureen. I promise you it won't happen again."

"Oh, Mattie, please." Maureen waved her hand in the air to dismiss Mattie's concerns. "Don't even bother wasting a moment worrying yourself about her or me. Besides, others much more experienced than her have tried to insult me and failed." Maureen smiled and held out a bejeweled hand to Mattie. "I'm made of stronger stuff than that. Just remember, dear, she can only upset you if you let her." She gave Mattie's hand a squeeze. "Now, run along before you're late. I'll get the boys bathed and put to bed right on time, so please don't worry."

Maureen stood up, then picked up her coffee cup and saucer to put in the sink. She paused at the window to watch the boys playing for a moment. She did love them so. All of them. She turned back to Mattie with a smile. "We'll be just fine. I promised they could watch a movie if they got into the tub and their jammies without a fuss. And a bowl of buttered popcorn for each afterward if they helped me clean the kitchen.''

''You don't have to clean up, Aunt Maureen, I can do it when I get home.''

''Nonsense, dear. I don't mind. Besides, it's good for the boys to know their way around a kitchen.'' Maureen winked at her. ''A helping hand now and again is not a bad thing, Mattie.'' Mattie's fierce streak of independence, of insisting on doing everything on her own was a constant sense of worry.

''Okay, but just make sure they're in bed by eight.'' Mattie bent and kissed her aunt's softly lined cheek. ''I love you.''

Maureen enfolded Mattie in a hug. ''And I love you, too, dear.'' She drew back amidst a cloud of French perfume. ''Now, run along before you miss your parents' meeting.''

''There can be several hundred fans in the stands all shouting and cheering, and six assistant coaches on the field, all shouting directives, but I guarantee you the only voice your child will here is…'' With a smile, Joe waited a beat, glancing around the crowded town hall. ''His mother's or father's.''

Standing in front of the room, with his assistant coaches seated behind him, Joe waited for the laughter to subside. He gave the same speech every year and knew no matter what, half of what he said tonight would be forgotten with the first crack of the bat.

''So it's imperative, parents, that if you're at the games, or in the stands, you don't give any direction to your child during the game. So, let's make it easy on the kids, and let the coaches coach the game. Fair enough?''

Sitting in the back of the room, Mattie applauded with the rest of the crowd as she watched Joe, amazed at how comfortable he seemed standing in front of a crowd speaking.

Although she'd been incredibly nervous about seeing him after this afternoon, and the kiss they'd shared, when she walked in, he'd been busy talking to one of the other parents and had merely given her a nod and a wave, much to her relief.

He was dressed casually tonight, and she realized it was the first time she'd seen him out of uniform. She had to stifle a laugh when she thought of her aunt Maureen's comment about getting him out of his clothes.

Tonight, his jeans were well worn and threadbare in spots, hugging his long, muscled legs like a second skin. His black, short-sleeved T-shirt outlined the muscles of his chest and shoulders in a way that almost had her—and every other woman in the audience, mother or not—gaping. He wore battered tennis shoes on his feet, well worn, and obviously well loved, judging from the condition of them.

"Remember, parents, you are an integral part of our team. Positive reinforcement, regardless of errors or mistakes, is the name of the game. Winning or losing is not the most important objective. We're striving to give kids a sense of pride and self-esteem, and the ability to know that they can learn and do well." Forcing a smile, Joe tried hard to remember his prescribed speech, and tried just as hard not to stare at Mattie. Looking at her did something to his insides, made them shift, and soften.

Since that wildly incredible kiss they'd shared this afternoon, he'd been unable to think of anything but her.

Until today, he was certain he knew his speech by heart, after all, he'd given the same blasted speech every year for the past dozen years.

But by the time he got back to his office this afternoon, after Angie's doctor's appointment, the impact of Mattie's kiss had knocked every tangible, sensible thought, every word of his speech right out of his head.

All that filled his mind was her.

He'd sat at his desk, kicked back in his chair and merely stared into space, daydreaming away most of the afternoon. On more than one occasion Clarence had come in, scratching his head, asking him if he was ill.

No, insane was what he was. Why on earth had he kissed her? He'd been asking himself that all afternoon. But then again, maybe he wouldn't have if he'd have known the kind of wallop one kiss of hers would pack.

He hadn't had a clue. He'd been knocked for a loop and

left dangling somewhere in no-man's-land. A place he had to admit, he'd never, ever been before.

But he also had to admit he'd never kissed anyone like Mattie. Kissed a woman and then found himself as desperate as a dying man for more.

When she'd walked in tonight, his heart had done a belly flop in his chest, and his throat had gone so dry, he couldn't even find his voice, so he'd merely waved to her, fearing he'd sound like a frog if he tried to speak.

His gaze had followed her as she walked down the aisle to her seat, hips swaying seductively in those slim-fitting jeans she favored. He was afraid he wouldn't be able to concentrate if he looked at her.

So, deliberately, he'd focused his attention on the big black-and-white clock at the back of the room. But his gaze kept idly shifting to Mattie.

She was seated in the aisle, near the back of the room, but as far as he was concerned there was no one else *in* the room.

Just Mattie.

His gaze had been hovering on her or near her from the moment she'd walked in tonight. The town hall held almost two hundred and was filled to near capacity tonight, and it was a good thing, too, he thought, or he'd be tempted to simply march right down the aisle, haul Mattie to her feet and kiss her senseless. Again.

Instead, he forced himself to concentrate on his speech.

"Any questions?" Joe waited, but no one raised a hand. "Okay, one final matter to take care of, then I'll let you go home. You all know my sister Annie. She's here somewhere. She'll be coordinating the volunteers for each game." Joe craned his neck to look for his sister. "Annie, raise your hand so everyone can see where you're sitting. Especially me," he added, making everyone laugh.

When the woman next to Mattie raised her hand, Mattie's eyes widened. Another of Joe's sisters, she thought, looking at the woman. Like Gina, she was petite and dark-haired, but rather than a flowing, wild gypsy mane of curls, Annie had a sleek, sophisticated cap of hair the color of midnight with a fringe of spiky bangs covering her forehead. Rail thin, she wore up-to-the minute designer clothes and was absolutely stunning. Mattie put her age at no more than perhaps twenty-two or twenty-three.

Obviously, good looks ran in the family, Mattie thought.

"Okay, everyone knows where Annie is. She has a sign-up sheet for volunteers for each game. Please make sure before you leave you sign up to volunteer your time for at least two games. That's mandatory. Now, any other questions?" Joe waited a moment, then smiled as the crowd shifted restlessly. "Then I guess that's it. Thank you all for coming tonight."

Joe waited for the applause to stop, then mingled with a few of the parents, shaking hands, or speaking to someone here or there, occasionally letting his gaze search the crowd for Mattie. He hoped to see her for a few moments before she left.

"Hi, I'm Annie. Joe's sister. You must be Mattie Maguire." The young woman seated next to Mattie extended her hand with a smile.

Mattie laughed as she took the woman's hand. "With all these people here, how on earth did you know who I was?"

"Easy," Annie said with a laugh of her own, glancing around. "I know everyone else in town. Besides, I've seen you around school."

"So you're attending the university?" Mattie said with a smile, picking her purse up and slinging it over her shoulder. "What are you studying?"

"Culinary arts," Annie said with a grin.

"Ah, so you want to be a chef like your sister Gina?"

Annie wrinkled her pert nose. "Yes, and no. What I'd really like to do is open a bona fide catering firm with full, commercial kitchens and an experienced staff that can handle everything from school banquets to full-scale weddings."

"Sounds very ambitious. And tiring," Mattie added with a chuckle, wondering why she hadn't spotted Annie at school, then realized she could have, but wouldn't have known she was Joe's sister.

Sensing the crowd moving toward them, Mattie decided she'd better get the ball rolling before Annie was surrounded by a mob of people. "Well, as long as you're sitting right here, Annie, I guess I'd better sign up before you get mobbed."

"Good idea." Annie reached beneath her seat and pulled out a clipboard. "You can volunteer to either work the concession stands for a game, bring after-game refreshments for the team or just sign up and let the coaches decide what they need most that day."

"I think that's what I'd like to do, since I have absolutely no experience at this."

"Just relax," Annie said, filling out the sheet for Mattie with a pleasant smile. "My brother makes it all sound very official and complicated, but it's not really. It's just a great time and something fun to do with your kids." Annie grinned. "As long as you don't take it too seriously."

"Thanks," Mattie said.

"Hey, what are you two whispering about?" Joe asked with a grin. He enfolded his sister in a bear hug as she stood to greet him and accepted the kiss on the cheek she gave him, all the while letting his gaze drink in Mattie. He was afraid she'd leave before he had a chance to talk to her.

"The town's most eligible bachelor," Annie teased, glancing at a now standing Mattie.

He laughed. "Warning Mattie already?"

"You bet," Annie said saucily. "We single women have to stick together." Another parent came up to sign up for the volunteer sheet, so Annie grabbed her clipboard off the chair. "Duty calls, Joe," she said, giving him another kiss on the cheek. "I'll see you later." She waved at Mattie. "It was nice meeting you, Mattie."

"You too, Annie," Mattie said, turning to Joe. He was standing close enough to her that she could smell his scent. It was familiar now, an earthy, woodsy scent that was distinctively, disturbingly male. "Are all your sisters so sweet?" Mattie asked, figuring it was a safe subject. Now that she was face-to-face with him again, she felt a bit nervous, wondering what—if anything—to say about this afternoon.

"Usually," he confirmed, rubbing a spot of tension that had settled in the back of his neck. "Except for Angie." He grinned at her, and she realized how exhausted he looked. "She's a tad…cranky right now."

"And with good reason," Mattie said, grateful that conversation with him still seemed easy and comfortable. "How far along is she?"

Joe was thoughtful for a moment. "Well, the baby's due the first week in July. This is the first week in April, so—"

"So, she's in her last trimester, and probably as big as a house and uncomfortable to boot. No wonder she's cranky. She has every right to be," Mattie said in sympathy. "She probably feels like someone's playing the bongos on her kidneys, and sticking pongee stakes in her back."

Shuddering at the thought, Joe cocked his head and looked at her. "That's just about the same sentiments she expressed this afternoon at the doctor's office," he admitted with a grin, cocking his head to look at her. "How did you know?"

She laughed. "I've been through it, remember?"

"Yeah," he said quietly, touching her elbow. "I remember." He had to touch her, he realized. He couldn't simply stand here, with her so close, and not touch her. It was as if her touch would fuel his soul. "I'm glad you came tonight," he said softly, not wanting to add that after this afternoon he'd worried that he might have scared her off.

"Seems to me someone told me this meeting was mandatory, remember? If I want the boys to play and I do, then I had to come to the meeting."

"Mattie, have you eaten?" he asked abruptly, steering her by the elbow out of the aisle and toward the door. He wanted to escape while most of the parents were busy talking to each other, or waiting to sign up with Annie. "Because I haven't. Not a morsel all day, and I'm starved. If you haven't eaten, I'll buy you a cheeseburger. The diner should still be open and if it's not, I'm sure I can sweet-talk Freddy into opening for me."

"I've already eaten, Joe," she admitted, allowing him to hustle her down the quiet hallway toward the town hall back door. "And I—I really should be getting home," she stammered as he took her hand and all but tugged her along with him.

"Nonsense. Your aunt's with the boys, right?" He held on to her tight, fearing she'd bolt.

"Well, yes."

"Then there's nothing to worry about. They're in good hands." He stopped just as they stepped out into the night, letting the town hall door close softly behind them. She almost bumped right into him, but caught herself just in time, placing a hand on the broad width of his chest for balance.

He was standing under a fading streetlight with the moon's silhouette shadowing him from behind. With most of the town still inside, the streets were quiet, dark and nearly deserted at this hour.

"It's been a long time since I stood in the moonlight with a woman," he said softly, reaching out to run a finger down her cheek. "I'd forgotten how nice it is."

Nervous, Mattie's gaze darted around. She looked everywhere but at him, fearing if she did, she'd be lost in the depths of those dark, mysterious eyes again.

"Although I'd prefer it if the woman didn't look like she was going to make a run for it at any moment." He brought her hand to his lips for a whisper of a kiss and Mattie's heart began to slam erratically in her chest. "You're safe with me, Mattie."

"Safe." She had to swallow. The touch of his lips on her hand had sent her pulse skittering one way and her brains scampering another.

"Yes, you're safe with me, Mattie." He wiggled his eyebrows at her. "I'm the sheriff, remember?"

"But you're also a man," she said without even thinking.

"Ah, so there's the rub," he said, unable to drag his gaze from her panicked one. He sure did wish she'd stop looking at him as if he was the kind of person who'd enjoy ripping fins off a fish. "It's the man part that makes you nervous. I wasn't quite sure you'd noticed."

She laughed, pushing her hair off her face, wishing she didn't feel as if the two of them were all alone in the world. It was just so dark and quiet out now. "Oh, I've noticed, Joe." A woman would have to be blind not to notice he was a man.

"Well, I'm glad to hear that." He kissed her hand again and she resisted the temptation to yank it free. He was making her unbearably nervous. "I'd hate to think that you weren't aware of exactly who was kissing you this afternoon."

Her gaze flew to his and she tried to swallow but found she couldn't. "Yes, well, that kiss." How on earth was she supposed to forget, when her whole body tingled with the memory?

"So you do remember it?" There was a smile on his face, so she knew he was teasing her. She wasn't quite certain that she wanted to be teased about something that had unnerved her so. It made her feel particularly self-conscious.

"Ah…yes, Joe, I remember it," she stammered, trying to tug her hand free. He held on.

"Good, but just in case." He moved so quickly, she didn't have time to protest. His mouth was there, hovering over hers, making her mind empty and her pulse race. "I thought I'd better refresh your memory," he whispered.

"Joe." She had enough time to think to put her hand to his chest, certain she was going to stop him, to protest, then his mouth was on hers, warm, soft and demanding, and she forgot everything, curling her fingers into his shirt to hold on as the whirlwind grabbed her, and scooped her up, tossing her world upside down.

Embers of desire flared to life, scorching her reason, devouring her resistance. Mattie was certain she was going to pull back, to put him in his place, but she didn't.

Hating herself for her own weakness, her own need, she gave herself to the kiss, to Joe's patiently tender lips, sliding her hands up his broad shoulders, then diving into his hair to cling as the world spun, spinning her with it.

Joe pulled her closer, trying to settle the unbearable knot of need that had settled somewhere inside the moment he'd laid eyes on her. That knot had only tightened, grown since the kiss they'd shared this afternoon, leaving him desperate for more.

"Joe." Shaken, Mattie used all the willpower within her to break away, to pull away from his kiss. His embrace. Deliberately, knees shaking, she stepped back and hopefully out of his reach.

Her vision was glazed, her heart pounding, and the world still felt as if it were spinning. "I'm sorry, Joe—"

Grinning, he tenderly brushed a strand of hair off her cheek. "I do believe you said that this afternoon."

"Yes. Well." Mattie licked her dry lips, tried to swallow, then ran her damp hands down her jeans. "I really don't think this is a good idea." She wished her body wouldn't react quite so traitorously whenever he was near. It was annoying.

"Actually, I think it's a fine idea." He cocked his head to look at her. Her face was partially lit by the streetlight and he could see the fear, the uncertainty in her eyes. Once again, it set off all his protective instincts and he wanted to gather her in his arms and hold her close until she was no longer afraid. Of anything. Especially him. "I think I told you that this afternoon."

"Yes, but—"

"But it was simply a kiss, Mattie," he said quietly. "Nothing more. Nothing less. Surely you've been kissed before?" he asked with a lift of his eyebrow.

Now she felt ridiculous. "Of course I've been kissed, Joe," she snapped. But not like this, never like this. Never had a kiss simply made her blind and deaf to rhyme or reason. Her chin lifted. "Plenty of times."

"Good. Then you should know as the song says, 'A kiss is just a kiss.'" He reached for her hand again and started walking down the street, away from the town hall. "Since you've already eaten dinner, would you mind keeping me company?" Still holding her hand, he flashed her a grin, grateful he'd have her to himself at least for a little while longer. "I hate eating alone."

''Fine,'' she said, not knowing what else to do. He was talking about eating and she was still reeling from the touch of his mouth on hers. How on earth did the man change gears so quickly? She snuck a glance at him. He looked perfectly cool, calm and collected, unlike the firestorm raging inside her. Blast the man!

Perhaps she was the only one affected by his kiss. Perhaps she was the only one who felt as if an explosion rocked the world every time their lips met.

And if she was, she was darned if she was going to let him know it and embarrass herself further.

So, it was *only* a kiss, she thought, lifting her chin. Fine. Then as long as it was *only* a kiss, there was no point in thinking about it again, or letting it happen again.

''Making an old woman like me open up this late at night. Ought to be a law, Joseph. At my age, a body should be able to relax and enjoy life. Not be cooking and cleaning in a diner at all hours of the day and night for some spoiled specimen of a male.'' Freddy gave an inelegant snort. ''And I ought to charge you double for making me dirty up my grill again after I just spent an hour cleaning it.'' Frederica Devereaux, known simply as Freddy to everyone in town, scowled at him as she poured him another cup of coffee, sloshing it dangerously close to the rim.

The bangle bracelets that littered her wrists in a rainbow of glow-in-the dark shades clanged and glittered every time she moved her arms in her white, off-the-shoulder peasant blouse.

She pointed one nail-bitten-to-the-quick finger—which was as bony as her shoulders—at the plate in front of Joe laden with food. ''Now, you make sure you eat everything on your plate, you hear me, Joseph? I didn't cook all this grub just to have it wasted.''

''Yes, ma'am,'' he said, glancing up at her and trying to smother a grin. ''I promise to clean my plate, Freddy.''

''Yeah, promises, promises. You know what you can do with your promises.'' Her razor-sharp, heavily made-up eyes cut to Mattie. ''And what's wrong with you?'' she demanded, pointing her bony, arthritic finger at Mattie's full plate. "Don't like my cooking?" Freddy cocked her head and scowled at Mattie so the pencil-thin lines of her eyebrows looked like a black beetle lying across her forehead. "Now, don't tell me a pretty little thing like you is one of those bark-and-berry buggers?" With a sigh, Freddy shook her Brillo-pad head of hair, which this week was somewhere between apricot and auburn and a bit of every color in between.

Mattie swallowed, and tried not to cower against the back of the cracked red vinyl booth, more than a little intimidated. The woman was probably two inches shy of five feet tall and she couldn't weigh more than eighty pounds dripping wet. But, apparently someone forgot to tell Freddy that, because she had the forceful personality of a mile-wide linebacker.

"A…bark-and-berry bugger?" Confused, Mattie glanced from Freddy to Joe, looking for some help, or at least an explanation.

"She means a vegetarian," Joe offered helpfully, leaning across the table. "Freddy's not real fond of vegetarians."

"Bark eaters, the lot of them," Freddy announced, nodding. "All those leafy greens and sprouts tossed with fermented fungus. It's a wonder they all don't start sprouting branches and glowing in the dark. Don't know how a body's supposed to survive on food fit for rodents." Freddy slapped a hand to the table, making Mattie jump in alarm. "Man needs to have a good slab of beef, strong protein." She nodded her head vigorously. "And a few carbs don't hurt none, either." She pushed Mattie's plate closer, setting her bracelets to clanging and jangling again. "Now, dig in," she ordered with another scowl as she let her heavily made-up eyes slowly go over Mattie. "You could use a few pounds." Freddy elbowed Joe. "She's a bit scrawny, Joseph, don't you think?"

"Uh…yes, ma'am." Helplessly, he shrugged at Mattie, who in turn glared at him. Scrawny, indeed.

"Thought so," Freddy announced smugly, giving Mattie a satisfied look as she pushed her plate another inch closer before turning back to Joe. "You and the family having dinner with Johnny this Sunday?"

Chewing a bite of his cheeseburger, Joe nodded, then wiped his mouth. "Yes, ma'am."

"Good. See that you stop here on your way to dinner. I'm making Johnny one of those coconut custard pies he so favors. I want you to take it out to him." She laid a hand on Joe's shoulder and her face and eyes softened. "You tell Johnny that Freddy said hi. Will you do that for me, Joseph?"

Touched by her unending kindness toward his entire family, but especially Johnny, whom she'd never forgotten, Joe's heart warmed. He nodded once more, then reached for Freddy's bony hand and brought it to his mouth for a kiss of gratitude. "I'll do that, Freddy. And thank you."

"No point in you thanking me." She snatched her hand back, but Mattie noticed the pleased flush that climbed her rouged cheeks. "Pie's not for you," she pointed out. "It's for Johnny. You can't even handle what you've got in front of you." She wagged a finger at him. "Now get to work on that plate."

"Yes, ma'am." With a nod, she started to walk away. "Don't forget to leave my check, Freddy," Joe called, his voice echoing across the empty diner.

Freddy turned on him, one beetle brow raised. "You wake me up, make me cook, now you want me to be doing arithmetic at this late hour as well?" With a snort, she shook her head. "Men. Always wanting something from us. Lord knows what we're supposed to be doing with them. It's too late for me to be adding figures tonight just 'cuz you got a hankering for some dinner. Now finish your food so I can go home and get these old bones in a hot tub. And don't you be forgetting to stop by here Sunday, either. I'll call Clarence and have him put it in that fancy planning book of yours."

"Thanks, Freddy." Joe took another bite of his cheeseburger, his gaze on Mattie's.

"I am not scrawny," she said defensively, leaning across the table to speak softly so Freddy didn't hear her and rear back around toward her. The woman scared the daylights out of her!

Joe laughed, then held up his hands in a self-protective gesture. "I know, Mattie, I know. But I figure I'm not old enough or big enough yet to argue with Freddy." He grinned, then popped a French fry in his mouth. "Neither are most people in town."

"She is a…character," Mattie said, taking a sip of her soft drink and glancing across the spotlessly clean but empty diner, which ran toward red vinyl seats and fading Formica. "This is the first time I've been in here," she admitted.

"You're kidding." Joe drew back, surprised. "I couldn't live without Freddy's cooking. Every day, promptly at noon, she delivers the diner's daily lunch special to the sheriff's office. Been doing it for as long as I can remember. First for my father, and now for me."

"Your father was the sheriff, too?" Mattie asked, and Joe nodded.

"Yep. And his father before him. A Marino has been sheriff of this town for almost two hundred years."

"That is amazing," Mattie said, picking up a fry of her own to nibble on. "So your family really has deep roots in this town."

Chewing thoughtfully, he nodded. "Absolutely. My family came here in the early 1800s." He shrugged. "We settled in and have been here ever since with no plans to leave," he added firmly. "I can't even imagine living anywhere else."

"I'm amazed that your dad never moved to the city."

"Why?" Joe asked. "What does the city offer that Healing Harbor doesn't?" He popped the fry in his mouth and waited.

Mattie shrugged, picking at her plate. "I don't know, Joe. Better-paying jobs, maybe. With a family of eight, I'm sure your dad could have found a better-paying law enforcement job in the city."

Joe shook his head. "Maybe, but some things are more important than money, Mattie. At least they were to my dad. And to me," he added softly.

"Well, that's true," she agreed, thinking of her in-laws and their continual offer to basically "buy" her sons from her by giving her a lump sum of money to do whatever she wanted with her life as long as she turned over care and custody of her children to them. "I never thought money was the be-all and end-all everyone else thought. For me, it was merely a means to make life easier for me and the boys."

"I can understand that. Money is only important when you don't have it and need it. But once you do have it, and the need for it is gone, you realize how many more important things in life there are. Things money can't buy," Joe added quietly, thinking of his brother. The settlement from Johnny's accident was secured in a trust fund for his brother's lifetime care, yet all the money in the world couldn't make his brother whole again. So what good was it?

"Yeah, I know," Mattie said, resting her chin on her hand and realizing she was tired. It had been a very long, exhausting day. Mattie sighed, glancing around the quiet diner. "You know, Joe, I have to tell you, I was very skeptical about moving to a small town after living in a big city. I thought for sure I'd miss the hustle and bustle, not to mention the convenience of everything. You know, rapid transit, taxis, buses, fast-food restaurants open twenty-four hours, but it's funny, I don't miss any of it." She sighed again, feeling tired and content. "I've really come to love this sleepy little town."

"Yeah?" he said, pleased.

"Yeah," she agreed, stifling a yawn and then flashing him a smile. "I think it's been very good for the boys."

"What made you move, Mattie?" he asked curiously, polishing off his burger and pushing his plate away to reach for his coffee.

Mattie shrugged, not wanting to explain about the continual harassment from her in-laws. "Lots of things. First, the boys were starting kindergarten in January, and I knew that if we were going to make the move I wanted to do it before they actually started school. I think it's very hard for kids to be moved around during a school year, so I wanted to do it so they could start in one school and remain there without having to worry about uprooting them midterm."

"Yeah, I imagine that would be hard in the adjustment department."

"Then, when my aunt Maureen announced she wanted to

semiretire, close her gallery in Paris and return here to Wisconsin to open a smaller gallery, she made me a fabulous offer that I simply couldn't refuse. It came at the perfect time for the boys and me.''

"Use of her coach house and a position at the gallery?"

"Manager of the gallery," Mattie correctly proudly. "I was both thrilled and excited. I've always had an interest in the arts, and my aunt was my very favorite person growing up. I used to spend two weeks a year with her here in Healing Harbor every summer. She'd take a beach house on the water somewhere, and she and I would spend the time swimming, sunbathing, walking the beach and just talking."

"Did you ever tell her about your artistic talent?" Joe asked quietly, remembering how embarrassed she'd been this afternoon when he'd walked in and caught her sketching.

"No." Mattie said softly, shaking her head and feeling self-conscious again, knowing Joe had discovered her secret.

"And you've never shown her or anyone else your work, have you, Mattie?"

She shook her head. "No, of course not. I told you. It's just something I dabble in."

"That's a shame, Mattie, like I told you this afternoon. You have talent, real talent. As much as anyone in that gallery."

Although pleased by his appraisal, she laughed off his comments. "Joe, the gallery is a professional gallery, designed for professional artists. I'm a rank amateur with no credentials and even less talent. I'd hardly go around showing my work to anyone, let alone putting it on display for the entire world to see." The mere thought sent a shiver through her. Her art was so private, the one thing that was hers alone. She couldn't bear to have it critiqued simply because she wasn't good enough.

"Well, I think you're wrong, Mattie," he said quietly, letting his gaze meet hers. "I saw your sketch of me. And I think it's every bit as good as anything on display in the gallery, and I think you've underestimated yourself. In fact, I believe your sketch is good enough to sell." He leaned across the booth and reached for her hands before she could snatch them away. "Will you sell me that sketch, Mattie?"

"Sell it to you?" she repeated in shock. "Don't be ridiculous, Joe, after all you're doing for the boys, I'll give it to you. If you really want it," she added, making him smile.

"I do, Mattie. I do. But I'd feel better if you let me pay you for it. After all, professionals get paid for their work."

"Yes, but I'm not a professional, Joe, and I wouldn't feel right taking money from you." Yet, she felt ridiculously pleased that he'd even offered, and thought her work good enough to pay actual money for. "You're welcome to the sketch, but I do need to add a few finishing touches before I give it to you."

"Fine." He gave her hands a squeeze. "Thanks, Mattie. This means a lot to me."

"You two about done over there?" Freddy called from behind the counter. "I'm gonna be able to pack groceries in these bags under my eyes if I don't get me some shut-eye pretty soon."

"Finished?" Joe asked, and Mattie nodded, pushing her half-eaten plate of food away. "Let's go, then, so Freddy can get some sleep."

Mattie slid out of the booth, grabbed her purse and slung it over her shoulder as Joe dropped an enormously large bill on the table as a tip.

"Night, Freddy." He waved at her. "Thanks again."

"Welcome, Joseph, and don't forget about that pie."

"I won't." Joe pushed open the diner door and he and Mattie stepped into the dark night. If possible it was even quieter and more deserted now than before. "Come on, I'll walk you to your car." Taking her hand, they walked in silence for a few moments before Joe began to talk.

"Don't forget we have an all-team meeting tomorrow night."

"I won't. Do I have to stay?"

"No," Joe said, leading her through the little gangway that separated the town hall from the building next door. "It's just for the team. Then sometime on Saturday, can you stop by the office and pick up the boys' uniforms?"

Mattie frowned a bit. "Yes, but I don't know what time. I have to work on Saturday."

"No problem. If you can't make it, Mattie, I can always drop them off." Joe smiled as they reached her car and he turned her to face him. "Besides, if it's all right with you, I'd like to drop by on Saturday and help the boys with a little practice. Since this is their first year, I'm sure they'll need a little extra help, even with the basics."

"Joe, that's very nice of you." She glanced down, unable to continue staring into his eyes. It did something to her heart, her pulse and her common sense. "I really do appreciate it."

"No problem." He trailed his knuckles down her cheeks in a tender gesture. "Drive safely. I'll see you tomorrow."

She swallowed, a little disappointed that he didn't appear to have any interest in kissing her again. "I will." She dug her car keys out of her purse. "Thanks for the snack. And for the introduction to Freddy," she added with a grin as he took her car keys from her to open her door.

"You're welcome." He held the door while she climbed in. "Drive safely."

"I will." She hesitated, not really wanting to leave.

"Good night, Mattie." He really didn't want to say goodnight yet. Deliberately, he slipped his hands in his pocket and stepped back from the car, realizing that he'd been playing with fire all day. And perhaps it was best to call it a day before he got singed. Something about Mattie seemed to scramble his senses and affect his judgment in a way no other woman had in a long, long time. And right now what he needed, he realized, like it or not, was some distance. "See you tomorrow."

"Good night." Mattie shut the door, then started the car, aware that he was simply standing there, watching her. As she pulled away, Mattie couldn't help thinking about the evening and Joe. He was an incredibly kind man, the kind who could steal a woman's heart. Fortunately, her heart was protected.

Chapter Five

"Connor, remember what I told you," Joe said as he stood in the imaginary infield of Mattie's backyard early Saturday afternoon and tried to get the boys acclimated to the basics of T-ball. "Point your belly button where you want the ball to go."

"But my belly button doesn't got a pointer," he announced, making Joe laugh.

"Remember what I said about the bat. It's not toothpaste. Don't squeeze it. Just close your fingers around it and let them rest comfortable around the knob of the bat. See those red buckets we set up? That's your outfield. Those are the other team's players and they're going to do their best to catch your ball and stop your rotation around the bases. So where do you want to hit the ball, Connor?"

"In between the red buckets?" he asked hopefully, glancing at Joe, then shoving his glasses up his sweaty nose.

Kids were smart as whips, Joe thought, glancing at Cody who was fidgeting over on second base. "That's right, son,"

Joe confirmed, then frowned a bit. "Keep your eyes on the ball as you bring your swing around, Connor. Are you ready?"

Squinting in concentration, Connor stopped abruptly and shook his head. "No. I gotta go to the bathroom, Coach." The bat slid out of his hands and he made a mad dash toward the back door of the house, leaving Joe and Cody laughing.

"Okay, sport, your turn." Joe turned toward Cody and motioned him toward home plate. "Let's see what you can do."

Grinning, Cody loped toward home plate, anxious to have a turn. He picked up the bat and did everything as Joe had instructed them to do.

"Think you're ready to try to hit the ball?"

"Yep."

Joe grinned. "Well, then, son, go to it." Joe backed up a bit, not even certain Cody would be able to connect with the ball, but if he did, Joe needed to be prepared to show the boys not just offense—hitting—but defense—stopping the ball in the infield—as well. And he wanted them to learn the right way from the beginning. It made things easier in the long run. If they could learn to anticipate the ball's path and angle toward it rather than chase it, they'd be much better ball players.

Cody squinted for a moment, staring hard at the ball, then took one practice hit, before going through the age-old batter's ritual of squinting to put the outfield in perspective, kicking dirt, then settling the bat comfortably over his shoulder while he set his feet.

Amused, Joe watched the ritual, knowing the young boy was only imitating what he'd no doubt seen on television.

Cody's first swing met air, whistled through it and nearly knocked the boy off balance with its velocity. The ball stayed on the tee as if mocking him. Cody muttered something under his breath Joe couldn't hear, but he decided it was time for some positive encouragement.

He didn't want the boys to get discouraged early on. That had a tendency to make young players feel embarrassed and resentful, and soon, lose their desire to play and, more importantly, to learn and have fun.

"It's okay, Cody. Even the best miss sometime. Remember,

just follow through with your swing and keep your eye on that ball.''

Cody's eyes narrowed, focused, and before Joe could utter another encouraging word, he heard the crack of the bat as it hit the four-ounce orange ball and sent it airborne.

Joe's mouth dropped open. He stood in the middle of the outfield, his hand shading his eyes from the sun, and followed the trajectory of the soaring ball with his eyes.

''Ho-ly cow,'' he muttered in disbelief, shaking his head as he watched the little orange T-ball finally bounce to the ground, then roll to a stop far behind the small red buckets that indicated first and second base. He turned his attention back to the young boy, and studied him for a moment, nearly dumbfounded. ''Uh…Cody?'' he called hesitantly.

''Yeah?'' Cody was grinning like a loon.

''Uh…do you have something you want to tell me?'' Joe asked.

''Like what?'' Cody asked in confusion, wrinkling his nose.

''Uh…have you done this before?''

''Done what?'' Cody asked, scrubbing at his freckled nose.

''Played baseball? Batted? Hit a ball?'' He didn't care what they called it, this kid was apparently a natural.

''Nah,'' Cody admitted. He slipped his safety helmet off to give his head a good scratch, leaving his strawberry-blond mop standing on end. ''Me and Connor, sometimes we fool around throwing a ball, but we never had bats to hit before.''

One eyebrow rose. ''Throwing the ball,'' Joe said in amusement, walking toward home plate and Cody. He cocked his head, studied the boy. ''And are you telling me you can throw a baseball as good as you can hit one?''

Cody had to think about it for a moment. ''Nah,'' he decided with a shake of his head. ''I can't throw so good, but Connor can.''

Joe's gaze traveled to the house where Connor was still using the rest room. ''Connor can throw good,'' he repeated before shifting his gaze back to Cody. ''As good as you can hit?''

Cody shrugged. ''Nah, better. But he can't run real fast.''

Joe swallowed, draping an affectionate arm around the boy's skinny shoulder. "Better?" he repeated hopefully. "Your brother can *throw* better than you can *hit?*"

"Yep." Cody's head bobbed up and down.

"What did I miss?" Connor called, racing back into the yard while tugging up his pants and swiping his still-damp hands down them.

"I hit the ball." Cody giggled. "Far. Real, *real* far."

Connor's eyes widened, then gleamed. "Awesome." He looked up at Joe. "Can I try now?"

"You sure can, son," Joe said, draping an arm around Connor and drawing him close as well. "And then I think I'm going to see how you two handle the infield. And throwing," Joe added, a gleam in his eye.

"I told ya, I don't throw so good," Cody admitted, shuffling his toe in the dirt. "Connor's better." He lifted his head, feeling embarrassed. "Lots better," he added glumly.

Joe gave him a reassuring squeeze around the shoulders. "That's okay, Cody. Remember what I said. Not everyone can be good at everything. If you have one thing you are good at, then you practice it, work on it until you're the best you can be. Does that sound fair?"

Cody shrugged. "Guess so."

"Well, Cody, from what I've seen, you have the makings of a first-class batter—"

"I do?" Eyes glittering in excitement and pleasure, Cody beamed, then began to bounce up and down. "I really do?"

"You sure do." Joe glanced behind him to where the orange ball had come to a rest. The hit still amazed him and he shook his head. "I don't reckon I can recall seeing many boys your age hit a ball that far."

"Really?" Cody bounced harder.

Joe laughed. He was having a ball with these kids. "Really."

"Can I have a turn now?" Connor asked, glancing up at Joe and squinting behind his glasses.

"Yep, I think it's your turn," Joe confirmed, giving each

boy an affectionate squeeze. He glanced at Cody, who was still bouncing. "Uh, Cody? Do you have to go to the—"

"Yeah," he said glumly, making Joe laugh. "I'm going. I'm going." He turned and trudged mournfully toward the house. And the bathroom. "Be right back," he called over his shoulder as he bounded up the back stairs and yanked open the door.

Working at the kitchen counter, Mattie squeezed the last lemon into the pitcher of fresh lemonade she was making and glanced out the window just in time to see Joe, with his arm around each of her sons, bend his head and say something to them, something that had both her boys grinning in delight.

Watching them, something inside Mattie's heart shifted, softened and yearned, a yearning so sharp it was almost painful.

Joe was so good with them, she thought wistfully, feeling the pull of yearning grow stronger. Growing up, he was the kind of man she'd always dreamed of having as a father to her children. Kind. Patient. Understanding. Caring. And more than anything else, willing to give of himself and his time, openly and without reservations to his children.

Joe had been at the house since very early this morning, keeping his promise to spend as much time as possible with Cody and Connor today, and arriving before the boys had even had their breakfasts.

She couldn't remember a time when her sons had been so excited. Or so happy. For a moment, she leaned on the counter and just watched the three males together, her heart filling unbelievably full. It was clear the lads adored Joe. Simply adored him.

And his affection for them was just as genuine.

The yearning, so much like an ache in her heart, surprised her. She hadn't thought or yearned for things she didn't and wouldn't ever have in a very long time. But right now, watching Joe with her boys, she realized that because of him, that yearning that she'd buried so many years ago, when all of her hopes and dreams for a wonderful husband and family of her own had been so cruelly dashed by Gary's immature, childish actions and rejection were suddenly flickering to light again.

For a moment, she wondered what it would be like to have a husband like Joe. A man like him as father to her beloved boys. Not having any real experience with the scenario, she wasn't even sure she could imagine it. Perhaps because between the time of her youthful dreams of happily-ever-after and the cruel bite of reality, she'd realized how futile and useless dreams could be.

They prevented you from seeing things as they truly were. Although reality could be harsh and cold at times, there was nothing about it that led to broken dreams or empty promises. She'd merely been seeing things—and her life and the boys—the way it was for so long, that seeing what other possibilities there could be simply never entered the equation.

Perhaps because she knew that seeing other equations, other possibilities meant she'd have to open herself and her heart to someone again. A man. And Mattie was no longer sure she was even capable of doing that.

And even if she could see it as a possibility, it could never be a possibility with Joe. He'd already made it very clear he was *not* interested in a family or children of his own. And getting emotionally tangled up with another man who'd felt the same way had left her in the position she was in now. She never intended to make the same mistake twice. Not ever.

With a sigh, Mattie shifted her gaze from the window to the fresh pitcher of lemonade. As much as the boys wanted to spend the entire day with Joe, it just wasn't possible. She had to go to work, and for today, they'd have to go with her.

"Look, boys," Joe called with a smile when he saw her walk down the back steps carrying a pitcher of fresh lemonade and three glasses. "Reinforcements with refreshments."

"Hi, Mom!" the boys caroled, dropping their gloves and the bat and barreling toward her. "It's hot, and we're thirsty," Connor said with a grin, racing up to her.

"Well, I've got a whole pitcher of fresh lemonade for you."

Joe took the pitcher and filled the glasses, then handed one each to the boys, carefully helping Cody until he had a solid hold on his, before draining his own glass in one long swallow.

It was ridiculous, Mattie thought, but as she watched Joe tip his head back, and watched the muscles of his throat move as he drank, she felt a punch of pure lust that nearly staggered her.

Must be the heat, she decided, swiping her hand down her jeans. Watching a man drink a glass of lemonade was hardly the stuff to get all hot and bothered about, but she had to admit, everything Joe did seemed sexy. It was beginning to annoy her simply because she'd become so vividly aware of it. And him.

"I have to tell you, Mattie, I'm very impressed." Joe glanced down at the boys with an affectionate smile. "Your sons are naturals."

Mattie glanced from one sweaty, freckled face to another. Both boys were beaming and their eyes were alight with excitement.

"They are, are they?" she asked, more pleased than she would have believed.

"I hit the ball real far, Ma," Cody said, taking another gulp of his lemonade. "Real, *real* far," he repeated, rolling his eyes for emphasis. "Joe says I got a good arm."

"You do, do you?" Mattie ruffled his hair, noted it was damp and tangled. Extra-long baths with shampoos tonight, she mused. "Well, I'm very proud of you."

"And I can throw good," Connor added with a grin of his own. "Joe said so."

"I never doubted it for a minute," Mattie said with a grin of her own, taking Cody's empty glass from him before he dropped it.

She had to admit, Joe had been right about one thing. She could fairly see the confidence brimming over in the boys from the praise they'd received from Joe this morning. It warmed her heart to know that her kids were feeling good about themselves and their abilities. And she knew it was Joe and his influence that had given them that extra bout of confidence.

"Something wrong, Mattie?" Joe asked quietly. He'd been watching her since she walked out in the yard, and if he wasn't mistaken, there was something shadowing her eyes, looked like something sad to him. He wondered what had caused it.

She managed a smile. "Yes and no, Joe." She shifted her gaze to her sons, knowing they were probably going to be upset and disappointed by her news, but it couldn't be helped. Such was the life of a single, working mom.

"I hate to break this up, boys. But Aunt Maureen called from Milwaukee. You know she had to go interview a new potential artist for the gallery and review his work?" She waited for the nods. "Well, Aunt Maureen is tied up in Milwaukee and won't be able to sit with you while I go to work today." She smiled to try to soften the blow. "So I'm afraid you're both going to have to go with me to the gallery today."

"Awww, Maaa." Cody's wail was first, followed quickly by Connor's.

"Can't we just stay here with Coach Joe and keep practicing?"

"I'm sorry," Mattie said with a sympathetic smile. "But Joe is not a baby-sitter. And I'm sure he has plenty to do today. In addition to coaching, don't forget he's also the sheriff of this town."

"Yeah, but Ma—"

"I'm sorry," she said more firmly. "But there's not much I can do about this."

"Can't we stay alone?" Cody asked, earning a look and a raised eyebrow from her.

"Not in this lifetime, sport," she said with a laugh. In spite of their obvious disappointment and displeasure with her, they could still make her laugh.

"It's not fair," Cody complained, looking beseechingly at his mother. "It's just not fair."

"I know," Mattie said with a sigh, feeling the weight of guilt land heavily on her shoulders. "There's nothing I'd like better than to let you boys stay out in the warm sunshine playing baseball all afternoon, believe me, but it's just not possible. At least not today," she added, hoping to soften the blow. She went down on her haunches and lifted two despondent little chins in her hands. "But I'll tell you what. How about if we get a pizza and rent a movie tonight? Would you like that?"

The boys exchanged looks, as if weighing their choices. It wasn't playing baseball all afternoon, but it was better than nothing.

"Yeah, we guess so," Connor said, scuffing the toe of his cleats into the dirt.

"Uh, Mattie?"

She stood and looked at Joe. "Yes?"

He rubbed a hand over his stubbled chin. "If it's okay with you, I mean, if you don't have a problem with it. I can stay here with the boys—"

"But—"

"Wait, let me finish." He held up his hand to stop her protests. "Clarence has things covered down at the office. Annie and Sophie are at the office handling uniform pickups. They do it every year, so they really don't need me this afternoon." Flashing her that killer smile, he shrugged his massive shoulders, then dropped his arms around the boys' shoulders so they formed a formidable front. "So, it really wouldn't be a problem." He glanced down at the boys. "And I'd love to do it. We can really use the practice time, to boot."

"Can we, Ma, pul-lease?"

"We'll be good. Honest, Ma, can we?"

"We won't be any trouble. Really."

Mattie's gaze went from one hopeful face to another, torn between doing what she felt was best, and doing what would make her sons happy.

"I can even run the kids down to the office and get them fitted for their uniforms," Joe added as she wavered, weighing everything. "That way I can also check in with Clarence and make sure everything is under control."

"But Joe, what about—"

"Come on, Ma, pul-lease?" Cody stepped closer and would have grabbed her hand to tug on it if she hadn't been holding the tray with the lemonade pitcher and glasses on it. "We'll be good, honest, Ma. Pul-lease?'' Hope shimmered brightly in his eyes, and Mattie's heart softened. She glanced at Connor and saw the same hopeful expression and sighed.

"Joe, are you sure about this?'' she asked. "Because it's not necessary. Really. The boys have gone to the gallery with me plenty of times. It's really not a problem.''

"I'm absolutely sure,'' he confirmed. "And if I can have more lemonade, I might even be persuaded to cook dinner,'' he added with a wiggle of his eyebrows, surprising her.

"You can cook, too?'' she asked, trying not to gape at him as she poured him more lemonade. What? Was he a super-hero? Was there anything he couldn't do?

He laughed. "Well, let's just say that Gina and Annie are the culinary geniuses in the family.'' He grinned sheepishly, winking at the boys. "I'm what you might call the culinary idiot.'' His words sent the boys into fits of laughter. "But I know how to warm and how to microwave,'' he added proudly, making her laugh. "Hey, stop laughing, they're useful skills.''

"I see. But cooking dinner isn't necessary or required. As long as you're going to spend the afternoon with the boys, the least I can do is cook dinner for you.'' She leaned close and spoke directly into his face. "And I'm not a culinary idiot.'' She grinned. "Honest.''

"I believe you,'' he said softly, leaning forward to brush his lips against hers.

Stunned and startled, Mattie jumped back as if he'd lit a torch to her, glancing guiltily at the boys. She'd never, ever kissed a man in front of them and had no idea how they'd respond.

She'd been playfully lost in the moment, unaware of just how close she'd been. Or he'd been.

"You kissed a girl,'' Cody complained, swiping a hand across his own mouth as if he could wipe away the offending action.

"Yep, I did,'' Joe agreed, smiling at her. "Do you mind?'' he asked Cody, who looked up at him, eyes wide.

''Why would you want to kiss a girl?'' Cody asked, eyebrows wrinkled in total disgust. ''Girls are yucky.''

''Yeah, well, come back and tell me that in ten years,'' Joe responded with a laugh. ''And your mom's not yucky. I like kissing her.''

''You do?'' Connor asked, wide-eyed. He glanced at his mom as if some reason for wanting to kiss her would magically appear, then he glanced back at Joe. ''Why?''

Slightly panicked by the question, Joe looked at Mattie.

''Hey, don't look at me for any help. You got yourself into this mess,'' she added, trying not to grin. ''You're on your own here. I've got enough problems answering other…life questions.''

''Thanks,'' Joe muttered, glancing down at Connor, who was waiting patiently for an answer. ''Well, I like kissing your mom because…because…I like her,'' he finished lamely. ''You like your mom, don't you?''

''Yeah,'' Connor and Cody both said, sliding a glance toward her.

''And you kiss her, don't you?'' Joe was on a roll here, and figured if he handled this right, he wouldn't get derailed by two five-year-olds. Again.

''When no one's around,'' Cody admitted in a near whisper.

''Okay, then. So I kissed your mom because I like her even though you and your brother were around. Sometimes I kiss your mom when you two are not around,'' Joe added with a shrug and a laugh when Mattie groaned and covered her face with her hand. ''Is that okay with you boys?''

Cody and Connor exchanged glances, then both shrugged their shoulders. ''Guess it's okay.''

''Yeah, we don't care if you wanna kiss girls or our mom, but it's weird,'' Cody decided, scratching his head. The kiss forgotten, Cody was anxious to get back to practice. ''So Ma, can we stay with Joe?''

Mattie sighed. Her insides were still rioting after the brief kiss Joe had just given her. If she'd been concerned about the boys' reaction, she had to admit Joe had handled it admirably.

The boys apparently didn't think or care one way or the other. As long as they weren't the ones required to kiss a girl.

"Yes, honey, you can spend the afternoon here with Joe." They started hooting and hollering, jumping up and down and giving each other high fives. "But," she added in her best parental voice, causing them to stop jumping and turn to her, waiting. "I want your absolute word that you'll listen to Joe. Do everything he says, and no fighting or arguing, agreed?" She couldn't look at Joe right now, knowing she'd blush. She was going to have to say something to him about kissing her in front of the boys. It just wasn't something she was totally comfortable with, but then again, she wasn't comfortable with him kissing her. Period. Not that she didn't enjoy his kisses. She did, perhaps too much, and that's what worried her.

"We promise, Ma."

"Scout's honor," Cody added.

"Do you promise to behave, and to listen to whatever Joe tells you?"

"Mattie, don't worry," Joe said, affectionately pulling the boys closer. "They'll be fine. We'll all be fine. So go on to work and don't worry about a thing."

"Yes, but…" Mattie's voice trailed off and she shrugged, feeling ridiculous. "Joe, the boys have never stayed with anyone other than their grandparents and Aunt Maureen."

"Mattie, with seven brothers and sisters, not to mention more nieces and nephews than I can even remember, I've spent more time with kids than probably you have. I'm also a certified lifeguard, not that there are any pools or water nearby except for the lakeshore, which is a good mile away, but just in case some tidal wave or monsoon should drop from the sky and hit Wisconsin this very afternoon, I'm prepared for it. Totally. And I'm also trained in emergency medical care, so as long as I don't try to cook anything, and a tidal wave doesn't descend, I think we're all pretty safe." With his gaze on hers, he lifted a hand and laid it to her cheek. "Don't worry, please. We'll be fine." His eyes seemed to be pleading with her: *Trust me.*

And Mattie found herself wavering, lost in the depths of those mysterious dark eyes.

"Mattie?" His voice, soft as a whisper, gentle as a caress, washed over her, and Mattie wanted to shiver.

Joe watched her, waiting. He knew that this was a test for him. A test to see if she could trust him enough to leave her precious sons with him, knowing that he'd guard their lives with his own.

Considering in all her years of parenting, Mattie had never had anyone she could trust, share parental responsibility with or lean on, he understood that she might have a hard time letting go.

But at some point, she had to know and acknowledge what he'd been telling her all along. He was totally and completely harmless. He'd never do anything to hurt her or her boys. Or anyone else for that matter.

And for the life of him he couldn't understand why it had become so important to have Mattie's trust. Perhaps because he knew she didn't give it freely or often. That made it all the more special and precious to him.

"Yeah, Ma, we'll be fine."

"Yeah, so it's okay, you can go to work." Cody all but gave her a push to get her going before she could change her mind.

Mattie blew out a breath, then dragged a hand through her hair. "Okay, but remember what I said," she cautioned, her gaze still on Joe's. He could read the uncertainty, the fear in her eyes, and met it with a smile of reassurance. "I'll be home about five."

"We'll be right here," Joe told her as she forced herself to turn and walk toward the house. At least if she was alone at the gallery, she'd be able to call her former mother-in-law, something she not only dreaded, but had put off for a day already. Like it or not, she had to call Gary's mom and have a talk with her.

Just the thought was enough to ruin Mattie's day.

Foot traffic in the gallery was always heavier on weekends than during the week. Today had been no different. By four-thirty Mattie had a blistering tension headache, partially because she'd been far too busy since she'd walked in the door to even have a morsel to eat, and partially because she'd been talking almost nonstop to customers from the moment she'd come in and relieved Colleen, the part-time college student she'd hired to handle the morning shift.

But, on the bright side, she'd sold two paintings and a sculpture, and had put an additional sculpture on hold for another customer. The commissions she'd earned today would go a long way toward helping her purchase a desperately needed new car. Well, a different car, Mattie amended as she filed away the last invoice of the day. She wasn't certain she could afford "new" yet, but a newer, different car, one that was a bit more dependable than the one she now drove would suit her purposes fine.

With a sigh, Mattie used her knee to close the file cabinet, and reached for the soft drink on her desk. Her sketch pad was lying facedown under a pile of papers she'd yet to file. The day had started out slow, at least for the first fifteen minutes, fifteen minutes she'd used to work on Joe's sketch.

Picking it up now, she couldn't help but smile at his image. He'd asked her if she'd sell the sketch to him. And no, she wouldn't. Not after all he'd done for her and the boys. She would give it to him—as a gift. But not until she was totally satisfied it was the best it could be.

Although Clancy was in the back workroom finishing up the painting he'd started last weekend, she was alone otherwise. And it was blessedly quiet finally.

With a sigh, Mattie sank down in her chair, pressed a hand to her aching back and reached in the drawer for her charcoal. She had to make that call to her former mother-in-law before she left for the day, but it could wait just a few more minutes. She really needed a few minutes of peace and calm, do something that would give her pleasure and hopefully help stem the pounding headache that had taken up residence inside her head.

Cocking her head to get a better view of what she'd already

drawn, Mattie narrowed her gaze and began to sketch, fleshing out the area around Joe's cheeks and jawline. She'd made them too small initially. Not at all proportionate to the rest of his face. He had a broad, masculine face with beautiful planes and angles, planes and angles she wanted to capture in the sketch.

Biting her lip in concentration, she made light, feathery strokes along his hairline and around the sides of his scalp, expertly drawing the texture and shape of that gloriously thick, black hair. She always focused on the hair as one of the crucial parts of a sketch. It helped to give the entire face depth and definition, and allowed her to see what areas needed more work, more shading, or less. Deeper lines, or more perspective.

With a smile, she began to work on the mouth and found her own mouth curving into a smile when she remembered the way that mouth felt, tasted. A quick thrill rolled over her, causing her skin to prickle and her heart to pound.

Lord, the man could kiss, she thought with a grin. Or maybe it had just been so long since she'd kissed a man, she'd forgotten how pleasurable it could be.

No, she decided. Joe was one expert kisser. She couldn't remember ever being kissed the way he'd kissed her. Nor could she ever remember responding to a simple kiss so wildly.

As she finished the lines of that full, sensuous mouth, Mattie sighed, then glanced at her watch and almost jolted out of her chair. Good Lord! She'd been sketching for almost half an hour! Time flew when she was engrossed in drawing, more so than at any other time. And as much as she would like to just close the world off for several hours and finish her sketch, she couldn't. She had responsibilities to the boys and obligations to her aunt that she simply couldn't ignore, especially if she wanted to get home on time.

She'd phone her former mother-in-law, then call it a night.

With a sigh, Mattie dropped her charcoal back into the drawer, laid her sketch pad on the desk and reached for a tissue to wipe the remnants of charcoal dust off her fingers.

She stared to pick up the phone to dial, then decided that

with the way her head was pounding, she'd better take a couple of aspirin *before* she called. Talking to her former in-laws always gave her a headache anyway, simply because it was so frustrating and futile, so why add to it now? She reached in her desk and pulled free the bottle of aspirin she kept there, shaking two free and downing them quickly with her soft drink.

Trying not to grimace at the chalky taste, she quickly picked up the phone and dialed her former mother-in-law before she could change her mind. This had to be done, so she might as well get it over with.

It took three rings before the phone was picked up.

"Evelyn, it's Mattie. I'm returning your phone call."

"That was several days ago," she accused. "I expected you to return my call sooner."

"I'm sorry, but with work and school, things have been a bit hectic. This is the first opportunity I've had." Mattie hesitated. "Evelyn, there's something I need to discuss with you."

"What?"

Mattie took a quick, silent breath then plunged in. "The last time the boys were at your house for the weekend, they overheard you and Bob talking, and apparently the things they overheard upset and scared them very much."

"That's ridiculous. I would never do or say anything to scare or upset my grandsons."

"Nevertheless, Evelyn, they did overhear you and they were scared." Mattie knew she had to persist or she'd be run over and bulldozed by this woman once again. "And I'm afraid that this isn't something I can allow to continue."

"What on earth do you mean?" Evelyn demanded. "Are you saying I can't see my own grandchildren? That's ridiculous. They're my blood."

"No, I'm not saying you can't see them." Mattie took a deep breath and tried to hang on to her temper. "But what I am saying is if you're going to continue to see the boys, then I'm going to have to ask you and Bob not to discuss them while they are there. They're not babies any longer, Evelyn, and understand far more than you think they do.''

''What exactly was it that I supposedly said that scared and upset them?''

Mattie pressed a finger to her temple and began to massage it as she closed her eyes. ''They overheard you telling Bob that if they came to live with you, Bob could be their daddy and teach them to play baseball.''

''Well, it's the truth. I see nothing wrong with stating the truth.'' Evelyn huffed out a breath. ''The boys would be much better off living here with us. Why, you yourself said that with work and school you're very busy. How much time can you truly devote to the boys? Bob and I are both retired. They could have our full attention if they lived with us.''

Mattie blew out a breath and counted to ten. ''Evelyn, we've been through this several times. Cody and Connor belong with me. I'm their mother. I would never, ever agree to give up custody of my children. Not to anyone,'' she added firmly, and especially not to her. ''My sons are my life and I'm totally devoted to them.''

''So you say,'' Evelyn snapped. ''But every time I call, you're off somewhere and the boys are with that Maureen woman.''

Mattie's temper was threatening to go straight past simmer to boil. '''That Maureen woman' happens to be my aunt, and she adores the boys and would never do anything to hurt them.'' Frustration and anger had her voice and tone sharper than she intended. Mattie took another deep breath before continuing. ''I have to work and earn a living to support us, Evelyn, and I'm sorry if you don't approve of the method or the manner in which I do it, but that can't be helped. That certainly does not mean that my children are neglected or not given enough attention. Lots of single parents work, Evelyn, and still raise happy, well-adjusted children.''

''Nevertheless, Mattie, there's no reason for the children not to come and live with Bob and I. What I said when they were here was the truth. They'd be better off living with us. I don't understand why you insist on being so stubborn about this,

Mattie. If you sent the boys to live with us, you'd be able to have more free time for yourself.''

Mattie shook her head, grasping the receiver so hard her knuckles turned white. "Evelyn, I don't want or need free time for myself. All of my time is devoted to Cody and Connor and I like it that way. We're a family, and I think it's time for you to recognize that."

"What kind of family do you think you are?" she demanded with a derisive snort. "The boys are always with a sitter, you're always working, and they don't have a father. Boys need a father, Mattie, and Bob is more than willing to take over that responsibility. Besides," the woman added, "we can give them so much more than you can."

"Things," Mattie snapped. "You're talking about giving my sons *things?*" Mattie wondered if her head could implode from fury. It wasn't things the boys needed, but love. Unequivocal, unconditional love. Something she was certain the Maguires had never understood. "Material stuff isn't what my children need, Evelyn. And the boys had a father, remember? A father who didn't want them," she snapped, barely able to contain her tears or her anger.

"Be that as it may, Mattie, we can't change the past, but we can correct the situation in the future. Bob and I think you're being terribly selfish."

Mattie's eyes slid closed and she pressed her hand against her forehead, hoping to stave off the pain. "Evelyn, I'm sorry you think I'm being…selfish." She could barely get the word out. "You're entitled to your opinion. I just don't happen to agree that wanting to raise my own children is being selfish. I consider it responsible, Evelyn, something I don't expect you to understand."

"Yes, but—"

"Listen to me very carefully, Evelyn." The pounding in her head grew stronger, radiating behind her eyes and into her temples. "The boys are *my* sons, and we're a family. We always have been, we always will be. And I think it's about time you and Bob acknowledge and accept that." Mattie inhaled deeply. "Now, I'd appreciate it if you'd stop saying things that both scare the boys and undermine their security and stability. Am I clear, Evelyn?'' Pulling the silent receiver from her ear, Mattie glared at it, before pressing it to her ear again. ''Evelyn?'' With tears blurring her vision, Mattie realized the woman had hung up on her.

Frustrated, she slammed the receiver down and swore softly, sinking back down in her chair as the tears came faster.

It was like talking to a brick wall. She'd been doing this tap dance for the past five years and right now she was so very tired of it. Tired and angry. Why couldn't they just leave her alone? Why did they have to undermine the boys' security and constantly judge her unfairly?

Reaching for a tissue, Mattie swiped at her eyes, then her nose, sniffling deeply. Then she gave in to the frustration, buried her aching head in her hands and let the tears come. Something she rarely allowed herself to do, but today, it just had been too much. Far too much.

''Aye, Mattie girl, you're still here, good. I was wondering—'' Clancy came to an abrupt halt, his eyes rounding when he caught sight of her. ''Are you *crying,* lass?'' The mere thought almost had him dancing away.

Lifting her head, Mattie sniffled, then wiped her nose, raising tear-stained eyes to his. ''No, no, no, I'm not crying, Clancy,'' she lied, mortified that he'd caught her. She managed a watery smile. ''Really, I'm not.''

''Aye, lass, I can see you're…*not* crying,'' he said with a lift of his eyebrow. Clancy peered at her the way a man might peer at a lit stick of dynamite someone had just dropped down his pants.

There was nothing that could drop a man to his knees and make him feel like a drunken Druid faster than a woman's tears. Aye, he'd rather face a firing squad.

With a sigh, Clancy knew he couldn't just walk away now. Nay, not and be comfortable. It was clear the lass was hurting. Deeply. And it pained his heart to know that something or someone had hurt her.

''Ah, lass,'' he said with a large sigh and a shake of his bald head. He peered into her face, almost nose to nose, then his gaze softened and he drew her close to him in a gentle hug, still shaking his head in confusion. "Now, tell me, lass, tell old Clancy who 'tis who's hurt you and made you *not* cry."

Drawing back, he raised a fist and made a face, making a valiant attempt to look fierce. All he did was succeed in looking comical. He thrust his fist into the air, as if hitting an imaginary opponent and Mattie found herself laughing.

"Aye, it'll be a good poke for them, right smack in the kisser if I learn their name."

Clancy was an artist whose hands were one of his most valuable gifts. He would no more punch anyone and risk damaging his hands than he'd jump out the window.

Touched, Mattie kissed his cheek. "Thank you, dear Clancy. That's the nicest thing anyone has ever said to me." She kissed him again.

"Hummph, then it seems to me you haven't had nearly enough nice things said to you." He drew back to look at her, then dug a rumpled handkerchief from his pocket that had a bit of paint dabbed on it and pressed it into her hands. "Mop up your face now. Aye, that's a girl," he said with a grin as she did as she was told. "Can't have the little lads seeing their mum *not* crying, now, can we?" He watched as she did what she was told, then took her hand in his, giving it a comforting pat.

"Mattie girl, I'm sorry that you're hurting." He kept patting her hand as if it would make everything all right. "Is there anything I can do, lass?"

Sniffling, Mattie shook her head. It hit her then how much she'd come to care for Clancy since she'd moved to Healing Harbor. In some ways, he was like the father she no longer had.

"No, Clancy, but thank you for asking. And for caring," she added, drying the last of her tears and flashing him a smile. "I'm sorry, I didn't mean to upset you." She managed another smile. "And I'm sorry, but I didn't hear you before. Did you need something?"

"Aye, I was going to ask—" His voice broke off abruptly

as he reached around her to pick up her sketch pad. "What's this, Mattie girl?" He studied the sketch with an artist's eye, appraising, assessing, judging, and Mattie felt her face flame. "Are you bringing in more competition for me?"

"It's...nothing, Clancy. Just...just a rough sketch," she stammered.

"Rough sketch," he repeated with a laugh. "Nay, there's nothing rough about this, Mattie girl. It's a very good likeness. Sheriff Joe, if my eyes aren't deceiving me." Narrowing his gaze, he studied the pad.

"Y-yes, it is," she confirmed nervously.

"Hmm, a very good likeness, indeed." He continued to study the sketch thoroughly, thoughtfully, and Mattie was torn between pride over his compliment and embarrassment that he'd found out her secret.

"Who did this, Mattie?" Clancy's gaze narrowed suspiciously on the sketch pad. "'Tis that new pipsqueak artist from Milwaukee your aunt has been sniffing about for weeks?" He gave a noisy, inelegant snort. "Aye, so she's taken this new fellow on, has she? He's to be her new pet then?" He all but sneered, shaking the sketch pad at her.

Confused, Mattie shook her head. "Clancy, this isn't a new artist. It's not an artist at all—"

His eyes rounded again. "You would be lying to me now, lass, to cover for your aunt?" He looked aghast, and Mattie flushed.

"Good Lord, Clancy, I would never lie to you." She touched his hand. "Not for anyone." Self-consciously, she glanced at her sketch pad, sorry she'd ever taken it out today. "I'm telling you it was no artist who did that." Mattie swallowed hard, mortified if she had to admit she'd been the one who drew the sketch.

He cocked his head and looked at her. "I've been an artist for most of my life, lassie, and I know another artist's work when I see it." He leaned close, eyes twinkling with charm now. "So if this is a secret, I'd like to know why." He grinned into her face. "What is the old girl up to this time?" He straightened and sobered suddenly as a shadow crossed his features. "Aye, lassie, tell me, is…he someone special to your aunt, is that it?" He looked so wounded, Mattie wanted to put her arms around him and give him comfort.

"No, Clancy. No." She shook her head, trying to figure out what was going on. If she didn't know better, she'd think Clancy was jealous of another man because of her aunt. If she didn't tell him the truth, it could cause serious problems for Maureen. On the other hand, if she did tell him, she risked looking the fool. Taking a deep breath, Mattie knew she had no choice.

"Clancy, it wasn't an artist who drew this. It was…me." Too embarrassed to look at him, she lowered her gaze and wanted to wince when he merely stared at her as if she'd just announced she was about to give birth to a banjo.

"Yours you say?" he repeated in disbelief, glancing up at her.

"Yes," she admitted numbly with a nod of her head. "It's mine."

"Aye, so that's the way the wind blows, lass." He was quiet for a moment, tapping his finger against his lip in concentration. "Do you have any more?" he asked, glancing at her.

"Any more…what?"

He laughed and shook his head. "Work, lass. Do you have any more of your work?"

"I…I…" Before she could answer, he began flipping the pages in her sketchbook.

"Aye, so here's one of the little lads." He grinned broadly. "It's a good likeness, lass. Very good." He winked. "You've captured the mischief in their eyes very well. Adorable imps they are. True mischief-makers. Aye, they should make you proud."

She laughed. "They do." She hesitated, then added. "Most of the time."

He continued flipping pages, pausing when he came to the sketch she'd done of her aunt one afternoon when Maureen had been sitting out in the garden. "'Tis beautiful," he said quietly. His eyes grew dreamy and a smile curved his mouth.

"Aye, she's always been such a beauty, Mattie, hasn't she? You've captured the grand old dame's essence perfectly as well."

"Clancy—"

"Why haven't you shown these to anyone?" he demanded, making her even more nervous than she already was.

"Show them?" Shocked, Mattie shook her head. "Good Lord, Clancy, this is just something I dabble in. They certainly aren't good enough to show anyone."

"Aye, so now you're an art critic as well, lass?" He rocked back on his heels, relieved and delighted. "I remember what it was like when I first started out. Aye, lassie, it was embarrassing and humiliating to know I wanted something so desperately, something I wasn't sure I could ever attain, mind you." He draped his free arm around her shoulder and cocked his head toward hers as if confiding a great secret. "'Twas like a great big secret buried very deep in my heart, so deep I feared sharing it with anyone." He glanced at her, then smiled in understanding. "Aye, Mattie, you see, lass, I was scared to death to show my work to anyone as well. I couldn't bear the thought of someone telling me I wasn't good enough or talented enough. And that's what we fear most in our heart of hearts, isn't it, lass?" His smile and his gaze were gentle. "Or worse, we fear they'll laugh, or worse yet, not feel anything when they look at your work. That's it, isn't it?"

She merely stared at him, wondering how he could know what was in her heart. How could he know what she'd never expressed to another living soul? Knowing Clancy understood exactly what she'd harbored deep inside for so long almost made her want to weep again.

"Y-yes," Mattie stammered.

"Let me tell you a story, Mattie girl. A very, very long time ago, when I was still very young—and quite handsome if I do say so myself," he added with a wink, making her laugh, "I was in Paris, attending art school."

"That's when you met Calhoun, right?"

"Aye, a dismal memory, that one," Clancy said with a smile before continuing. "Anyway, one day after art class, I was in a small café across the street from school, sketching my heart out, when this incredibly beautiful woman approached me. I couldn't speak at first, I could only stare because she was so beautiful." He sighed in remembrance. "It was love at first sight," he admitted softly, then brightened. "At the time, I thought for certain she was an angel sent by the fairies to tempt me into misbehaving, and for her, aye, I would have done it, too." He laughed suddenly, shaking his head. "Aye, we were all so young then, Mattie girl, foolish as well. This beautiful angel told me she owned an art gallery right around the corner and wanted to see my work. Apparently she'd been watching me in the little café for days, and wanted to see what I'd been working on." Nostalgia made his eyes warm and his lips curve. "When I stammered and stuttered over showing anyone my work, let alone this beautiful creature, she scoffed at me and told me that an artist's work was meant to be seen and appreciated. Not hidden and hovered over." Laughing, he shook his head. "'Twas the first time in my life anyone had ever called me an artist."

"It was Aunt Maureen?" Mattie asked in surprise, wondering why she'd never put it together before. Clancy was in love with her aunt!

"Aye, lass, 'twas the beautiful Maureen." His eyes twinkled with unabashed love. "We made our first deal there and then. She viewed my work and had a very critical eye, even then, mind you. No pushover was she. Anyway, we made an agreement with only a handshake, and have stuck to it to this day. I'd do the paintings, she'd handle the showing and selling of them." He glanced around the gallery. "That was more than twenty-five years ago, lassie, and I never regretted my decision. Not ever."

"You make a good pair," Mattie said with a smile. "But Clancy," she prodded softly, "if you were in love with Aunt Maureen, why didn't you ever tell her?"

For a moment he looked aghast again, then shook his head. "Aye, lass, at first, I had nothing to offer her, nothing but myself," he added with a small smile. "And then…well…" He shrugged helplessly. "I guess I never told her for the same reason you don't want anyone to see your work." His smile was sheepish. "Fear, pure and simple. She was always so achingly beautiful, like one of Botticelli's angels, I couldn't even fathom that she'd care a fig for someone like me." His shoulders lifted and fell. "I was a poor artist, not without some romance in him, but it just never seemed the right time." He sighed with regret. "However, I'm not about to let you make the same mistake. You've got talent, Mattie. As much as anyone in this gallery. I want you to promise me you're going to show your work to your aunt."

Her heart was pounding in triple time. "Clancy, I don't think I can do that."

"Balderdash, lassie," he said with a dismissive wave of his hand. "You owe it to yourself and to your aunt." He laid a gentle hand to her cheek. "If you don't, Mattie girl, imagine how it would hurt her, to know that she's got one so talented in her midst, in her very own family yet, and you didn't trust her enough to let her see your work."

Mattie sighed, then pushed her hair off her face, frowning. "I never thought about it that way."

"Aye, I know, lass, but you know as well as I that's the way she'd take it if she knew." His gaze softened on hers. "You don't want to hurt the old girl, now, do you?"

Mattie shook her head, feeling a sinking feeling in her stomach. "No, of course not, Clancy. I'd never do anything to hurt Aunt Maureen." The mere thought was too distressing to even contemplate.

"Then tell her, dear, or rather, *show* her." Eyes twinkling mischievously, Clancy leaned close. "Of course, if you'd like, I'd be happy to show her." His grin bloomed. "Seeing's how it might help me score some points with the old girl."

Mattie laughed at his logic. "And how will you manage that, Clancy?" she asked, finding the idea intriguing.

"Well…" Thoughtfully, he stroked his chin. "I could tell her I've found a marvelous new artist. Then show her your sketches. Imagine her delight when she learns they're yours."

"Delight, huh?" Mattie repeated dubiously. "She might hate them, Clancy, then what?"

"Then what?" He chuckled. "Mattie dear, if she hates your sketches will you still continue to sketch?"

"Of course," she answered automatically, not even bothering to think about it. "I sketch for my own pleasure, Clancy—"

"Aye, then, lassie, I rest my case." He patted her cheek. "And therein lies the proof that you indeed are an artist. We may fear what others say, lass, aye, it's only natural, but no matter what, we still trudge on, doing what we must because we can do nothing else." With a brisk nod, he grinned. "As it should be."

"Clancy?"

"Yes, dear?"

"I adore you," Mattie said with a laugh, throwing her arms around him.

"Aye, and I you, lass." He held her close for a moment. If he'd ever been blessed with a fine lass of a daughter, he'd want her to be just exactly like Mattie.

"And I'll let you show my sketches to my aunt if you promise to tell her how you feel about her."

Clancy's face clouded for a moment. "Tell the beautiful Maureen how I feel?" He almost shook his head, then realized perhaps now, finally, it was time. He looked at Mattie, saw the hope in her eyes and decided the time was right. Aye, after more than twenty-five years, and following her halfway around the world to be near her, perhaps it was time to confess what he'd harbored for so long in his heart. "Aye, lass, you drive a hard bargain."

"Then you'll do it?" Mattie asked hopefully.

"Well, I certainly can't just burst out with the news," he said with a quick grin. "But, methinks it might be time to start courting her." He laughed. "Of course, she could simply turn a deaf ear, but…" He glanced down at Mattie's sketches. "If you've got the courage to face your fears, then how could I do less?"

"Thanks, Clancy." She hugged him tighter, then kissed his cheek again. "She might surprise you."

"Aye, lass, she might indeed." His heart began to thump

at the mere thought of finally having his beloved Maureen after all these years.

He couldn't wait to share the news about Mattie with Maureen, as well. She needed to know what a treasure she had right under her nose. And it would please her so, he realized, knowing how much she cared for the lass.

He drew back and looked at Mattie. "Now, lass, are you done...*not* crying for the day?" he asked with a grin, and she nodded, then laughed.

"Yes, Clancy, I am."

"Good, then. It's time for you to go home to the little lads," he said as he rubbed a hand over his own tired eyes.

"I think that's the best idea I've heard all day." Mattie glanced at him, then leaned forward and kissed his cheek, realizing how much better she felt now. "Thanks, Clancy."

"Aye, lassie, you're welcome. You're very, very welcome." With a sigh, he tucked his handkerchief back in his pocket. "You run along now, lass. I've still got some work to do, so I'll lock up when I leave."

"You're sure you don't mind?" Mattie asked as he took her arm with one hand and picked up her purse with the other, pressing it into her hand. "Nay, not at all." He grinned as he hustled her to the door, holding on to her sketch pad tightly. "Run along now," he urged, opening the door for her and all but pushing her through. "I've got work to do."

With a sigh, Mattie nodded, glancing back through the plate-glass windows of the gallery, wondering what on earth Clancy was up to.

Chapter Six

"Boys, I'm home," Mattie called as she wearily let herself in the front door. The heavenly scent of something cooking assaulted her and she nearly swooned. She still hadn't eaten a morsel all day and her empty stomach was protesting loudly. "Boys?"

"This boy's in the kitchen," Joe called from the kitchen.

After peeling off her suit jacket and dropping it on a dining-room chair, Mattie went into the kitchen, drawn by Joe's voice and the heavenly aroma.

"Hi," she said with a grin. He turned from the stove to grin back.

"Hi yourself." His gaze studied her for a moment, then one eyebrow lifted in question. "Rough day?"

"Boy, that would be an understatement." Nervous, she slipped her hands into the pockets of her jeans, then glanced around. "Where are the boys?"

"Upstairs in their room. They've been so quiet, I think they're plotting to overthrow the government."

''Which one?'' she asked with a laugh, stepping closer to him and the stove.

''I don't think they're particular.''

''What smells so wonderful?'' she asked suspiciously, trying to see what he was stirring. At the moment, she was standing so close to him, the only thing she could smell was his magnificent male scent. It almost made her weary legs weaker.

''Dinner,'' he replied, blocking her view with his body.

''Dinner?'' One eyebrow lifted and she gave him an arch look, trying to see past him. ''Should I call the paramedics now? Or wait until after we've eaten?''

''Hey, hey, no fair. I didn't cook it.'' Turning to her with a wooden spoon in his hand, he grinned. ''I just warmed it up.''

''Warmed it up?'' She stepped around him, lifted the cover on the pot and inhaled deeply. ''Spaghetti sauce?'' She glanced up at him, aware that he was mere inches from her. Close enough for her to feel his body heat.

''Yep. Gina's specialty. There's chicken Parmesan warming in the oven, along with garlic bread. The boys and I tossed a salad—and I do mean tossed in the literal sense, so be careful where you step,'' he added with a laugh, making her glance down at the floor. ''I've got a bottle of Chianti open and waiting, and as soon as the water boils and the pasta cooks we can eat.''

''Joe.'' Moved, she shook her head, not certain what to say. ''You didn't have to do this,'' she said softly, forcing herself to meet his gaze in spite of what it did to her pulse. ''I could have made dinner when I got home. I told you that.''

''Yeah, I know.'' Lifting a finger, he brushed a stray strand of hair from her cheek. ''But it was no big deal. When I took the boys to get their uniforms, Gina offered to send dinner over. I may be a culinary idiot, but I'm not a fool. I'm not about to look a gift horse in the mouth.''

Impulsively, she leaned forward and gently touched her lips to his. ''Thank you. I really appreciate it, especially tonight.''

He slid his arm around her waist to hold her in place. ''What happened today that put those shadows under your eyes?''

Cocking his head, he looked at her more closely. "If I didn't know better, I'd swear you'd been crying." When she didn't answer, but merely glanced away, he sighed. "Okay, if that's the way it's going to be. Turn around," he ordered, and she blinked in confusion at him.

"Excuse me?"

"Turn around," he instructed, taking her by the shoulders and turning her so her back was facing him. He set down the spoon, then lifted both hands to her shoulders and gently began to knead.

"Oh God," Mattie groaned. "That feels wonderful."

"It should," he commented, moving his fingers in a circular motion across her shoulders. "You're tight as a strung wire back here. Lower your chin," he instructed, and Mattie did, feeling his fingers dip into the back of her hairline, caressing her neck and lower scalp.

Her eyes slid closed and she swayed back against him, the last of her energy draining. The pounding in her head was finally, slowly easing with the expert touch of his fingers.

"My word, Joe, where on earth did you learn to do this?" Her voice was soft, dreamy, as her entire body relaxed and responded to his touch.

He shrugged. "When you play baseball, you end up with a lot of screaming muscles. It helps to have them massaged."

"Does this mean I have to take up baseball?" she asked, wincing as his fingertips touched a particularly tight, painful spot.

"Not with those fancy nails you're not."

"Sexist," she teased.

"Realist," he corrected, gently turning her toward him so she was facing him. "How long have you had this headache?" he asked, surprising her.

She tried to open her eyes, but as his fingers slowly pressed and caressed her temples, she simply didn't have the will-power or the energy. "A couple of hours," she admitted, taking a slow, deep breath.

He was standing right in front of her, close to her, and she could feel his heat, feel his touch, and it was wreaking havoc with her pulse.

"You know, Mattie, they have this new wonder drug…it's called aspirin. It works wonders on headaches."

"I know." She sighed, lost in the feel of his fingers and the resulting lethargy that was stealing through her. "I took some, but they didn't help."

"Have you eaten?"

"You mean today?" she asked, and he laughed.

"Well, that answers my question, I guess." His fingers moved just above and below her collarbone and began to gently massage. "You know, you take wonderful care of the boys, but you're falling down on the job when it comes to taking care of yourself."

She hadn't really heard what he said; she was too busy concentrating on what he was making her feel. The warmth of his hands, the gentleness of his fingers was making her whole body tingle. If he moved his fingers down just a few inches, he'd be caressing her breasts.

The mere thought had her nipples tightening, puckering, and Mattie took another long, deep breath, trying to ignore the feelings storming through her.

Slowly, she blinked her eyes open. He was watching her with a curious expression on his face.

"I feel much, much better, Joe," she said softly. "Thank you."

He slid his hand to her cheek. "You're welcome." His gaze stayed on hers a moment longer than necessary, then he slowly lowered his head until his mouth covered hers.

Too tired and drained to fight what she was feeling, Mattie gave in to the sensations storming her body and leaned into him, wrapping her arms around his neck, threading her fingers through his dark, silky hair and hanging on as he took the kiss deeper.

She felt the soft slide of his tongue, accepted it, relished it, wanting, yearning for more.

When his hands slid to her hips to draw her even closer, so

her softness was pressed against his hardness, she didn't protest, she merely savored the feelings.

His hands slid up her buttocks, to her waist, then up her back, drawing her ever closer until they were pressed tightly together, shoulder to hip, with no room for more than a breath between them.

Her fingers tangled, tightened in his hair and she moaned softly, arching in to him, wanting something she couldn't or wouldn't name.

With her heart thudding and her pulse scrambling, Mattie knew she was on dangerous ground. Boggy ground. And if she wasn't careful, she would slip and fall.

And this time, she wasn't certain she'd be able to pick herself back up again.

Reluctantly, she drew away from him, eyes glazed with passion, lips full and flushed from his.

"I...I...." She had to swallow in order to speak. "I'd... better go check on the boys," she stammered. After everything that had happened today, she was totally depleted emotionally, which left her feeling terribly vulnerable. She wasn't used to it and it threw her off balance.

Where Joe was concerned, she knew she had to keep her defenses up. Way up, and at the moment, with the day she'd had, and the way she was feeling, she knew it was an impossibility.

"Fine, Mattie. I'll pour the wine. You go check on the boys." His eyes gleamed in amusement as he flashed her that killer smile. "But I'll still be here when you come down." He picked up the wooden spoon and began to stir the pot on the stove.

Why, she wondered wearily, did that sound like a promise? A promise that left her smiling.

The boys weren't exactly planning a covert military act, but instead, were plotting and planning something a bit more personal.

Sitting on the carpeted floor of the bedroom they shared, they tried to figure out how to accomplish their objective.

"You heard what Grandma said," Cody reminded his brother with a frown as he curled his legs under him and picked at a scab on his knee. "Grandma said little boys *need* a father. We need one."

"How come?" Connor asked, digging through the numerous toys in their overflowing wooden toy box for several metal cars and a couple of action figures.

"Dunno," Cody admitted with a shrug. "Maybe it's a rule or something."

"Like having to wear our seat belts?" Connor wondered, and Cody shrugged his skinny shoulders again.

"Guess so."

"So how we gonna find one?" Connor wondered, racing two metal cars against one another until they went crashing and careening into the wooden toy box.

"Beats me." Frustrated, Cody sent two of his favorite action figures careening across the floor of blue carpeting as they engaged in an imaginary battle. "I don't know how we find one."

"Me neither," Connor agreed, shrugging his shoulders helplessly and leaning back against his bed.

"Maybe we could ask someone," Cody suggested, scrubbing a fist over his freckled nose.

"Who?"

Cody crawled on his skinned, scabby knees across the carpeted floor to retrieve his men. "Well, we can't ask Grandma," he said with a scowl.

"Definitely not Grandma," Connor agreed with a scowl of his own. "Not Grandpa, either. 'Cuz then he'll think we don't want him to be our dad."

"Well, we don't," Cody said, turning to his brother, hands defiantly on his narrow hips.

"Cody," Connor wailed, flinging his hands in the air. "We can't tell Grandpa we don't want him to be our dad."

"How come?"

"'Cuz." Connor frowned a bit, his eyebrows drawing together over his blue eyes as he tried to figure this out. "I think it might hurt his feelings or something."

"Yeah, maybe," Cody agreed, glancing at his brother. "But then who we gonna ask?"

"Dunno." Connor heaved a heavy, world-weary sigh, then curled his legs under him as he lowered his chin to rest in his hand. He did his best thinking this way. "But someone else has gotta know how we could find us a dad."

"Yeah, but not just any dad," Cody specified. "He's gotta like little boys. Like us."

"Yeah," Connor agreed. "And he's got to like baseball."

"A lot," Cody confirmed with a nod of his own head. He picked up his favorite plastic action figure, shoving the other one—the one missing an arm, and more than slightly wounded from a previous battle—into the already bulging pocket of his pajamas. "And he's gotta not be too old," Cody added, straightening the helmet on his action figure.

"Or have 'rthritis." Connor brightened. "And he's got to be nice."

"*Real* nice," Cody confirmed.

"And maybe he could like to do 'rithmetic." Connor dug in his brother's pocket for the wounded action figure to run around in a circle, up and over his bare foot, then back down again, making he-man growling noises deep in his throat. "Bobby Dawson said 'rithmetic is real hard." Connor glanced up at his brother. "And you get lots of problems you have to bring home to do."

"We have to bring work home from school?" Cody asked, rolling his eyes in disgust and making Connor shrug. "That can't be right. Why would they make us bring work home to do?"

"Dunno." Connor shrugged again. "That's what Bobby Dawson said."

"Boys?" Mattie knocked gently at the door. The boys exchanged frantic glances as the door gently opened. "Here you two are," she said with a grin.

"Uh…hi, Mom," Cody said, looking guilty and hoping she hadn't heard them talking.

"Hi yourself." Mattie sat on Cody's bed. "So what are you guys doing?"

They exchanged glances and Mattie wanted to sigh. They were at it again. Up to something, no doubt.

"Nuthin', Ma, honest," Connor said, eyes wide and sincere. "We was just talking and playing with our guys." He held up the wounded action figure to show her.

"I see." She looked from one to the other. "Did you have a nice day?"

"Awesome," Cody said, bouncing up and down on his knees. "Coach Joe and us, we stayed outside practicing almost all day. We got real dirty and sweaty," he crowed proudly. "And Coach Joe, he told us lots and lots of stuff about baseball."

"He did, did he?" Mattie reached out and ruffled her son's hair, pleased to see him so excited and happy.

"Yep," Connor confirmed. "And he said that if we keep practicing we'll be real good baseball players."

"Well, sweetheart, I think Joe's right. If you want to be good at anything, you need to practice. That's how you get good." She glanced around their room, absently smoothing down the blue-and-white *Star Wars* bedspread covering Cody's bed. "I see you picked up your room, too. Thank you. That was very nice of you to do without being told." If she hadn't seen it with her own eyes, she wouldn't have believed it. Getting the boys to pick up after themselves was like trying to tap-dance down a ladder blindfolded in backless high heels.

"Coach Joe helped," Cody said. "He told us that if we're going to be baseball players we have to be re...re..." Cody scowled as he struggled with the word.

"Responsible?" Mattie supplied helpfully and Cody bobbed his head.

"Yeah, that's it."

"And we already had our baths and washed our hair," Connor added. "Coach Joe let us wash our hair all by ourselves." Connor giggled. "But he helped us rinse it with a bowl."

"A bowl?" Mattie repeated with a lift of her eyebrow, wondering how bad the bathroom was after three males with a bowl had used it. "Well, that's a new one."

"He said when he and his brothers were little, his mom always rinsed their hair with a bowl."

"Yeah, and we cleaned up the bathroom, too," Cody added with a grin. "Coach Joe's nice."

"Yes, he is," Mattie agreed, wondering how long the boys would remember the things Joe had tried to teach them this afternoon. It was nice, she realized, to have another adult, a male adult interacting with her sons, giving them a male perspective on things. It was something they had never had, and she realized now, listening to them, that perhaps it was something they truly needed.

She realized how grateful she was to Joe for staying with them today, and for all the kind and wonderful things he'd done for them in the past week. It was amazing what the impact of one person on two little boys could be, even in just a week.

"Yeah, Ma, Coach Joe's *real* nice," Cody added, glancing at his brother. Identical-twin faces broke out in identical, mischievous grins, making Mattie very nervous, not to mention slightly suspicious. Lord, she hoped they weren't up to something. Again.

"Yeah, Ma, and Coach Joe, he likes baseball." Connor was grinning from ear to ear.

"A lot," Cody confirmed.

"I know," Mattie said, amused.

"Yeah. And Ma, he likes us, too."

"Yes, Connor, I know that, too."

"And we like him," Cody added, giving his brother another look and a grin.

"I'm glad," Mattie said slowly, trying to figure out what was going on.

"Ma?"

"Yes, Cody?"

"Could you ask Coach Joe something for us?"

"Sure, honey, what?"

"Could you ask him if he likes 'rithmetic?" both boys said nearly in unison.

Mattie frowned, totally confused. Where on earth did this

question come from? "You want me to ask Coach Joe if he likes…arithmetic?"

Twin strawberry-blond heads bobbed up and down furiously. "Yep," both boys said, grinning widely.

"Okay, fine," Mattie said with a shrug. "I'll ask him." She stood up. "In the meantime, dinner will be ready in a few minutes."

"Can we play until then?" Cody asked, glancing at Connor.

"Sure." Mattie bent and gave each of them a kiss on the top of their clean, shiny heads. "I'll call you when dinner is on the table." Mattie walked to the door, then hesitated a moment. "Oh, I almost forgot." She smiled, slipping her hands in her jean pockets. "I got Amy's birthday present."

"What? What? What did you get?"

She smiled. "You know the ice-cream parlor across the street from the gallery? The one you two always want to go into?"

"Yeah?" both boys said in unison.

"Well, I bought Amy a gift certificate for the ice-cream parlor. It's like money," she explained when both boys looked confused. "Each month for the next year, Amy can go into the ice-cream parlor and get a free sundae, soda or malt. Anything she wants."

"You're kidding," Cody said, scratching his head. "For free?"

"Yep. She just has to give them her gift certificate, and anything she wants—up to a certain dollar amount—is free."

"Cool," Cody said with a grin. "Can we have one of those things for our birthday?"

Mattie laughed, grateful she'd found something the boys approved of. "We'll see, honey. Your birthdays are not for a long time yet." She looked at her sons again. "Are you guys by any chance up to something?" she asked curiously, looking from one to the other.

"No, Ma, honest," Cody said solemnly.

"And we're not in any trouble, either," Connor volunteered before she had a chance to ask.

"All right," she said slowly. "But you know if you ever want to talk to me about anything, anything at all, I'm here."

"We know, Ma."

"And you don't want to talk to me about anything, at least not right now, right?" she asked with the knowledge that only a mother would have.

"Right," both boys said, grinning at each other again.

Mattie sighed. "Okay, then. I'll call you when dinner is ready."

Cody waited until he was sure his mom had gone downstairs before getting up to close the door. He turned to his brother.

"You thinking what I'm thinking?" Cody asked.

"Yeah, he likes us, he likes baseball and he even likes Ma. He kissed her this morning, remember?"

"Yeah, yeah," Cody said, bouncing up and down and beaming brightly. "I almost forgot."

"And I don't think he's got 'rthritis or nuthin', or else he couldn't run or play baseball, right?"

"Right!" Cody's eyes were shining with excitement.

"Now, if he likes to do 'rithmetic, our problem will be solved!"

"They're both out like lights," Joe whispered to Mattie as he glanced at the boys, who were sprawled on her living-room floor, sound asleep.

She chuckled softly. "I know. Wait until morning when they realize they fell asleep during the middle of an *Invaders* movie. They are going to be so upset." Her face filled with love as she glanced down at her boys, her life.

"Well, the movies don't have to be returned for a couple of days yet. I'll leave them here so the boys can finish watching them tomorrow."

"Oh, Joe, you don't have to do that," she protested. He'd not only had dinner waiting for her, but he and the twins had gone to the video store and rented several movies for them to watch this evening. At first, the thought of spending an entire evening with Joe, even with her sons present, had made her nervous, but everything had gone very well.

The dinner was fabulous, the one glass of wine she'd allowed herself, along with Joe's excellent massage, helped her to relax and shed some of the tension of the day, and the movies had successfully lulled her mind so that most of the day's irritations were forgotten. Almost.

"Let me help you take them up to bed," Joe said, keeping his voice low so he wouldn't wake them.

"Take Cody," she suggested, getting up to scoop Connor off the floor. Fortunately, she'd made him take his glasses off the moment his eyes started drooping. Getting his glasses off while he was sleeping was always an experience. "He's a bit heavier."

Carefully, with Joe following her, Mattie carried Connor up and laid him in his bed, pulling the blankets up and kissing him good-night on the cheek.

"Coach Joe?" Cody murmured sleepily.

"Yes, Cody?"

"I like you." Cody wrapped his arms around Joe's neck to give him a good-night hug, and everything inside Joe melted into a warm pool of love.

How on earth was it possible to lose his heart to a thirty-pound bundle of mischief? he wondered as he tucked Cody into bed.

"I like you, too, sport," Joe whispered, giving the boy a kiss on the forehead.

Mattie turned as Joe was settling Cody into his bed. Her heart softened when she saw Joe kiss her son good-night.

With a sleepy groan, Cody rolled over, burrowing deeper into the bed, making her smile.

"They look so peaceful," Joe said quietly, glancing at her.

"Yeah, well, many an adult has been lulled by that look," she said, bending to kiss Cody's cheek. "Don't let it fool you."

Joe grinned, reached for her hand and led her out of the bedroom. "They're wonderful kids, Mattie," he said as he led her down the stairs. "You've done an incredible job with them."

She sighed, more than a bit tired herself. "Thanks, Joe,

believe it or not that means a lot to me.'' Pushing her hair off her face, she bent to pick up the throw cover that she'd tossed over the boys when they fell asleep. ''Single moms rarely know if what they're doing is right or wrong.'' Slowly, she began folding the throw, aware that he was just standing there, watching her.

With the boys upstairs asleep, they were alone in the house for the first time. ''It's usually not until our kids are grown that we have any inkling of whether or not we did a good job.'' She laid the comforter on the back of one of the Queen Anne chairs in the living room.

''Well, I don't think you have anything to worry about, Mattie. You're doing just fine.'' He reached for her hand again. ''Come sit with me for a minute.'' He tugged her down beside him on the couch. ''Now, we didn't get much of a chance to talk tonight.''

Feeling slightly nervous with him so very close, she laughed. ''Joe, we've been talking all night.''

''Well, I guess you're right. But we've been talking about the team, baseball, the first game, and hey, by the way, what was all that stuff the boys were asking me about arithmetic?'' he asked with a confused shake of his head.

Mattie shrugged. ''Beats me.'' She laughed suddenly. ''But I have a feeling we might not want to know.'' She hesitated for a moment. ''I think they're up to something,'' she admitted with a slow smile. ''Again.''

''Up to something? The boys?''

She laughed because he looked so surprised. ''Yes, the boys. They were incredibly interested in whether or not you liked arithmetic—''

''Yeah, I know, but why?''

She shrugged again. ''I honestly don't know. It makes no sense to me, but somewhere in their five-year-old minds it does, and until they're ready to come clean, we can only…imagine what they're up to.'' Trying not to shudder, she rushed on at the look on his face. ''Don't worry, it's generally not anything dangerous, just…mischievous,'' she added, unable to contain her amusement. From the look on his face, she had a feeling he hadn't quite dealt with any kids quite like hers.

"I see," he said, clearly not seeing anything of the kind. "Now, Mattie, why don't you tell me something else." Taking her hand again, he traced his fingers over the skin, wondering why she felt so incredibly soft all the time. And she smelled wonderful. She had on that sneaky feminine scent again, the one designed to drive a man crazy. So far it had been doing a pretty good job.

Even though he was sitting right next to her, warming her with his body heat, and holding her hand in his, she leaned back against the couch, determined to relax.

"Okay, what would you like me to tell you?" she asked with a smile. "Anything in particular, like the population of the planet? Or just general things like grass is green and radishes are red, that sort of thing?"

"No, actually, I'd like you to tell me why you were crying earlier today."

"Oh." He had her there. She was not an experienced or skillful liar, it just wasn't in her nature. She felt the truth, no matter how embarrassing or awkward, was always the best way. She had to set a good example for the boys, which was why she was so adamant that they always tell her the truth. She couldn't very well demand less of herself.

He lifted his hand from hers and ran it the length of her hair, playing with the ends for a moment. "You were really tense and upset when you came home, Mattie. I don't think I've ever seen you that upset."

"No," she admitted with a sigh. "It's been a long time since I was that disturbed."

"Who upset you?" His gaze went over her face, tracing every beautiful feature, coming to rest on that tantalizing mouth.

"Joe, it's a really long, boring story." She managed a smile. "Not a pretty one, either. Nor one that I think you'd be interested in."

"Try me," he persisted, unwilling to allow her to shut him out. He realized he wanted to know everything about her.

She glanced at him for a moment, thinking about how just earlier today she'd wished and longed for someone to share her troubles with, to get another's perspective. Joe was offering that to her now.

Mattie took a deep breath. "I had an argument of sorts with my former mother-in-law."

"The boys' grandmother, right?" he asked carefully, and she nodded. "I take it from what you've already told me that you two aren't close."

Mattie laughed, but the sound was harsh. "*Close* is hardly the word I'd use. She hates me," she admitted sadly, trying not to feel sorry for herself or embarrassed by her admission.

Surprised, Joe drew back. "Mattie, maybe you misunderstood her. I can't possibly imagine anyone hating you, let alone the boys' grandmother. Surely she has to admire what a wonderful job you've done with her grandsons?"

"No, Joe," Mattie began carefully. "She doesn't think I've done a wonderful job with them. In fact, she wants me to let her and her husband raise them because she thinks she and Bob can do a better job." Lifting her head, she met his gaze and managed another weak smile. "She thinks I'm being selfish for wanting to raise my own children." The absurdity of the situation just struck her and she wanted to weep again.

"Mattie, is this woman a drunk?"

She couldn't help it, she laughed, then remembered how wonderful it was to talk to Joe. No matter what the situation or the circumstance, he always managed to find a way to make her smile about it, to make it seem as if it was going to be all right.

"No, Joe, she's not a drunk," she finally managed to say when she'd stopped laughing.

"Then I don't understand." He shook his head. "You are one of the most wonderful, loving, natural mothers I've ever seen. Totally devoted and in tune with your boys. It's clear your life revolves around them and you adore them."

"Yeah," she admitted, worrying her lower lip and hoping she wasn't about to cry again. "I know."

"And they adore you, so how on earth can this woman

accuse you of being selfish for wanting to raise your own children? And worse, think *she* could somehow do a better job?''

''I wish I could give you a logical answer, Joe, but I can't.'' Mattie took a deep breath. ''Their son, Gary, the boys' father—''

''And your late husband, right?'' This was clearly dangerous ground, he realized immediately. Her shoulders stiffened and he saw the emotional gates slam down again, trying to keep him out.

Not this time, he thought firmly.

Joe had a feeling whatever had made her so wary and mistrustful of men stemmed from her past relationship with her husband. If he was ever going to get her to trust *him,* he had to understand why she didn't trust men in the first place, and he had a feeling the conversation they were having was a good place to start.

''Y-yes,'' she admitted with a nod, embarrassed that she had to confess that she'd had such poor judgment in marrying a man like Gary. ''He was Bob and Evelyn Maguire's only child. He was born late to them, long after they'd given up hope of conceiving, and as a result, they spoiled and indulged him his whole life.''

''Charming. Well, then, that certainly qualifies her to raise your boys,'' Joe muttered sarcastically, making her smile again.

''I got pregnant shortly after Gary and I were married, but he wasn't interested in having a child.'' Her voice had dropped to a hushed, hurt whisper and Joe felt something soften and ache deep inside him. ''He just wasn't ready, nor did he want the responsibility.''

''It was a little late for that, don't you think?'' Joe muttered. ''Go on, I'm sorry.''

''Anyway, Gary went to his parents, told them he didn't want the baby.''

''You've got to be kidding me. He actually went to his parents and told him he didn't want his own baby?''

''Afraid so,'' she admitted.

He looked at her for a long moment, almost afraid to ask his next question. "And what did they say?"

Mattie glanced down, trying to gather her emotional strength before she went on, knowing that it was going to be hard. She'd never told anyone this before. Not anyone, and she realized now why.

It was both embarrassing and humiliating to know that she'd been so naively foolish to choose a man who was so reckless and irresponsible, and even more embarrassing to admit that she'd been too young to do much more than accept his treatment and make the best of a very bad situation.

But Joe had asked, and she wasn't about to sugarcoat the truth or lie to him.

"Gary's parents asked me to…take care of the pregnancy," Mattie said slowly, feeling a lump form in her throat at the mere memory. "They said it was unfair to burden Gary with the responsibility of parenthood when he clearly didn't want a child, and wasn't ready for it." Her vision blurred from unshed tears and she had to swallow hard past the lump in her throat.

"Exactly how did they want you to 'take care' of the pregnancy?" Joe asked, turning to face her and unconsciously clenching his fists at the sheer, raw pain he read in her face, her eyes.

Fury and frustration that he hadn't been there to protect her, to prevent this, swarmed him like angry bees, and he had to clamp down hard on the emotions that streaked through him.

What she was telling him simply didn't compute. Not in his mind, his heart or his world. He simply couldn't comprehend what she was telling him. This was her husband and her in-laws? My God, what kind of people were they?

"They wanted me to terminate it." Her response came out soft and shaky, and she lifted eyes blurred by tears to his, hating that she had to tell him all this, but knowing it might do her some good to finally get it out, to talk about it. She'd held all these emotions inside for so very long, now she feared they'd come spewing out like a volcano that had been capped far too long.

"Terminate?" he repeated dully, as if he'd never heard the word before, and if he did, hadn't understood its meaning. "They wanted you to terminate your pregnancy?" Shock had his eyes narrowing and his fists clenching. "Are you sure?"

"Yes, Joe," she admitted quietly. "I'm very sure. But I refused. I adamantly refused." With a sniffle, she shrugged. "I didn't care whether Gary or his parents wanted my child. Or children, as it turned out to be. I did, and that was all that mattered to me."

"You were right, Mattie," Joe said. "These people aren't drunks. They're merely insane." He blew out a breath and dragged his hands through his hair, trying to make some sense out of this. "Obviously insanity must run in their family, since your former husband clearly inherited it from his parents."

She laughed, unable to believe that she could. "Well, yeah, that's what I thought, but hey, I was in the minority at that point."

He turned to her and the look on her face made every protective instinct he'd ever had rise to the surface. He wanted to grab her in his arms and hold her close, and never let anyone hurt her again.

"What happened, Mattie?" he asked gently.

Shadows flickered over her face, but he could still see the pain, the tension, the remnants of a betrayal that cut far and deep into her soul. He wanted to hit something. Hard.

"When I refused to terminate the pregnancy, Gary left me. He moved back in with his parents and resumed his bachelor lifestyle."

"Wait a minute." Joe held up his hand, wanting to make sure he was getting this right. "Are you telling me your husband *abandoned* you while you were pregnant, and his parents approved of it?" His voice was so shocked, Mattie wanted to smile.

Now, why did she know instinctively that Joe was the kind of man who would never be able to understand a family behaving in this manner? Would never understand such selfishness and cruelty.

He was so deeply rooted in his family, brothers, sisters,

nieces, nephews, not to mention how involved he was in the lives of the people in town, the players on his team and even her own sons, that she knew Joe was not a man who could even comprehend the actions of Gary or his parents.

Knowing Joe was so totally outraged, appalled and, yes, even shocked by what Gary and his parents had done to her, not only validated her own feelings toward them, but also made her realize just how wonderful a man—no, a *person*—Joe was. A rare and unusual person who truly understood the real meaning of the word *family*.

And for some reason, the knowledge made the yearning deep inside her grow.

"Joe, they didn't simply approve of it, they *encouraged* it," she admitted quietly. "They were certain if Gary left me alone to fend for myself, I'd be forced to 'come to my senses,' as they put it, and do what they asked."

"That's nothing short of emotional blackmail," Joe snapped. Not to mention cowardice on her husband's part.

"Yeah, I know." Mattie shrugged. "But it didn't work." Her chin lifted defiantly. "I adamantly refused to even consider their request." She shrugged. "I've been blessed with an incorrigible stubborn streak, Joe, and when I make up my mind about something, especially something I felt this strongly about, there's no way anyone can change my mind. I *was* going to have my baby, or babies, as it turned out, whether they liked it or not, and I didn't care what they did to me, or what they put me through. I was not going to buckle under and give in to their ridiculous demands."

"Good for you, Mattie." He dropped an arm around her shoulders and pulled her close. "Good for you." He resisted the urge to wrap both arms around her tightly, to stand between her and anything that would try to harm her or the boys. "Okay, now tell me the rest. What happened after Gary abandoned you and the babies and moved back in with his parents?"

Lacing her fingers together even tighter, Mattie glanced down at her hands and carefully prepared to tell him the rest.

"Two months before the twins were born, I was struggling

to take proper care of myself, and the babies, and still hang on to my job even though I was sick as a dog and big as a house. The doctor warned me about twins coming prematurely and wanted me to stay in bed the last three months, but it just wasn't possible.''

''Wait a minute, Mattie. What about your aunt Maureen? Couldn't you have gone to her for help?''

''I could have,'' Mattie began slowly. ''But my aunt had moved to Paris years ago and had a very successful gallery there, not to mention a life and friends. I knew if I told her what was happening to me, she'd abandon everything in her life to help me with mine.'' She glanced up at Joe. ''And I couldn't do that, Joe. I simply couldn't. Aunt Maureen worked a lifetime to garner the reputation she now enjoys both in Europe and here in the States. I couldn't ask her to give all of that up simply because I'd made silly, foolish choices.''

''I understand, Mattie.'' And he found he did. It was just like Mattie to consider someone else's life, wants and needs ahead of her own. Which also explained why she wasn't used to sharing any part of her life. How on earth could she expect anyone to be there for her when her own husband hadn't been?

Swiping at her nose, Mattie flashed him a brave, wan smile, then continued. ''Anyway, Evelyn Maguire—Gary's mother— called me at work one afternoon, hysterical. Gary had been killed in a car accident.''

She heard how flat and emotionless her voice sounded, as if it were echoing in a long, dark empty room. She wished she could dredge up some emotion for the loss of the man she'd once been married to, the man who had fathered her children, but she couldn't.

Gary had killed every ounce of love and affection she had for him long before his fatal car accident.

She lifted her face so she could see Joe's beautiful features. She needed to see him right now, needed to know he was right here by her, and that she wasn't alone.

Perhaps it was silly. But she'd been alone through this long, awful ordeal, and had never had anyone to unburden herself to. Now that she did, she realized that it had built an invisible bond between them, a bond that seemed to draw her closer to him.

She had to swallow before continuing. "Gary's parents had bought him some fancy sports car for his birthday. He loved to race it, and he loved to drink." She shrugged, realizing she felt nothing inside for the man she'd been married to. Nothing. "He just happened to do the two together one too many times. He was killed instantly."

"Mattie, I wish I could say I was sorry, but it's hard to dredge up any sympathy for someone who was so downright cruel to his own wife and children."

"Once Gary died, his parents had a change of heart." She glanced up at him, and gave in to the temptation and allowed herself to lean against him and accept his comfort. She'd never realized how much she'd missed, or how wonderful it was to be able to share something like this with another.

"What do you mean a change of heart?" Joe searched her face, not certain what on earth was coming next. Although after what she'd just told him, nothing else would surprise him.

"After Gary's death, they encouraged me to go through with the pregnancy."

"Because they wanted custody?" he guessed, and she nodded.

"Gary was their only child. With him gone, my children were all they had left of him. From the moment Gary died, up until today, his parents have never stopped trying to get me to give custody of the boys to them."

"Are you telling me these crazy people first wanted you to terminate your pregnancy because their irresponsible son wasn't man enough to be a father, then after his death, they wanted you to go through with the pregnancy and then give the child, or rather, the children, to them to raise?"

Mattie sighed. "Yep, that's about it," she admitted, watching as a myriad emotions crossed Joe's face.

"I think I've heard just about everything now." Joe shook his head. "And how on earth could they even think that you'd turn your own boys over to them?" Joe shook his head again.

"Talk about reckless, irresponsible parenting. Your former in-laws could be the poster children."

"I know, Joe. They've done just about anything you can think of to get me to change my mind. When the boys were first born, they offered me money—"

"You mean they tried to *buy* your sons?" he asked, appalled once again.

"Well, I'm sure they wouldn't put it that way, but that's what it amounted to."

"Good God."

"I, of course, refused. I desperately needed money to support the three of us, of course, but not that bad. I used the small amount of life insurance Gary had left me, and of course the monthly Social Security I received from Gary's death, because the boys were still minors. I made up the difference working at night from home." She sighed. "I did the best I could, but Evelyn and Bob Maguire have never stopped pressuring me to turn the twins over to them to raise." She hesitated a moment. "Just today, Evelyn accused me of being selfish for wanting to raise the boys myself."

"Today?" he asked with a lift of his eyebrow. "Is that why you were crying this afternoon?"

She nodded, then sighed. "Evelyn called a few days ago and I returned her call today from the gallery, and was sorry I did. Once again, she chastised me for leaving the kids with my aunt while I worked, and for being selfish for not turning the boys over to them, since she believes they can do a better job raising them, and give them more than I ever can."

Stunned, Joe merely stared at her in the flickering candlelight for a moment. "This woman had the audacity to call you *selfish?*" Temper laced his tone, making his words clipped and sharp.

"Yeah," Mattie said with a weary sigh, rubbing her temple. Just thinking about her phone call this afternoon was enough to bring back her stress headache. "She reminded me again that she and Bob can give the boys so much more than I can."

It hurt Mattie to have to admit it was probably true. The Maguires were very well off financially and could probably provide the boys with material things she'd never even thought of or considered. But she knew that material things didn't compare to unconditional love, a *mother's* unconditional love.

"So, they can give the boys things, so what?" Joe's gaze caught and held hers. Something deep and dark flickered within the depths of his eyes. "Based on their history and the way they raised their own son, they can't give the boys the important things, like morals, values and character." Joe shook his head, his anger building.

His temper was a fearsome thing when unleashed and ran toward cold, unbendable steel. He rarely allowed it free rein simply because he knew how ferocious it could be, but now he didn't even bother to try to rein it in. His feelings toward the twins' grandparents were strong, very strong, and he knew it would do no good to try to control his temper, not on this issue, or with his feelings for these people.

"How can you even speak to them after the way they've treated you?"

Mattie smiled. "Because, Joe, in spite of my feelings, they're still the boys' grandparents." She glanced down at their hands. "And family is very important to me. I really don't have anyone else but Aunt Maureen, and I thought it was best for the kids to at least know their grandparents, although lately I'm not so sure about that."

"Well, Mattie, you're a better person than I am. I'm not so sure I'd be so generous if I'd been the victim of these people's terror tactics." He was thoughtful for a moment, watching her. "Is that why you moved from Chicago?" he asked. "To get away from them?"

"Partially," she admitted. "I wanted to get away from the Maguires' constant pressure, but I also wanted to move somewhere the boys and I could have a real future. I needed to finish my degree but I also needed to work while I was doing it. My aunt gave me an opportunity to do both. When I told the Maguires I was moving, they were absolutely beside themselves. It really was awful," she remembered, chewing her lower lip. "But I knew it was best for the twins and I. But I did promise that the boys could spend at least one weekend a month with their grandparents. That seemed to appease them somewhat.''

''But they still haven't given up on pressuring you to give them custody?''

''No,'' she admitted with a sigh. ''They haven't. I really don't think they ever will, Joe.''

He sighed, then shook his head. ''Mattie, I've got to tell you. I don't have a clue how on earth you've endured this kind of treatment.'' But it certainly explained why she was so mistrustful of people, especially men, and why she was so very, very cautious about letting anyone interact with her children.

''I have to admit, if it had been me, I would have put as much distance between my in-laws and myself as I could possibly get. They really don't deserve to be part of your life or the boys', not after what they've done and continue to do to you and your sons.''

''Perhaps,'' she admitted hesitantly. ''But, Joe, I do feel some sorrow for them.'' She glanced at him. ''They lost their only child and they have to live with that for the rest of their lives, knowing their only son is gone. As a mother, I cannot even begin to fathom or comprehend how they deal with that. It has to make you just a little…crazy, don't you think, to lose a child?''

''Well, I'm not a parent yet, but I see what you mean. Still, that doesn't excuse their behavior.''

''No, Joe, it doesn't.'' She smiled and reached for his hand, closing her own over it. ''But it helps me to remember that, when they upset me so much I just want to…scream.''

He shook his head. ''Mattie, I thought I was too old to be surprised by anything, especially a woman, but you've totally surprised me.''

''Me?'' She drew back. ''Why on earth have I surprised you?'' She smiled. ''I haven't done anything any other mother wouldn't have done.''

''Ah, now, there's where you're mistaken, Mattie. A lot of women would have simply caved in, given the Maguires custody and taken the money and run. Think how easy your life would be.''

''Easy?'' She considered the idea, then laughed. ''Maybe, but not richer, not fuller. The twins have given me things no amount of money could ever buy.''

''I know that. But that's you. Some other woman might have taken out their anger on the boys and not let them see their grandparents.''

''I suppose so,'' she agreed. ''But what good would that have done, except hurt my own children?'' She shook her head. ''My job, as their mother, is to make sure I always put their needs ahead of my own and to make sure I take care of them as best as I can until they can take care of themselves.'' She shrugged. ''When they're older, they can make the choice whether they want their grandparents in their lives or not. But that's not a decision I'd ever make for them.''

''Yep, like I said, you're pretty incredible.'' He was quiet for a moment. ''Mattie, thank you for sharing all this with me. For trusting me enough to tell me.'' He glanced down at their joined hands. ''I know it couldn't have been easy for you, and now I understand why you're so wary and suspicious of men—''

''I'm not—''

''Mattie.'' His grin stopped her words. ''Whether you realize it or not, you are, and I fully understand that. But as I told you the very first night, I'm not someone you have to fear. Not on any level. I'll never do anything to hurt you or your boys.'' With his hand still in hers, he drew her close, brushing his lips gently against hers. When he heard her soft sigh, felt the pressure of her trembling hand on his chest, he deepened the kiss, drawing her closer.

Mattie felt the sigh of longing whisper through her, tugging her heart, tangling her emotions.

She was certain Joe meant it when he said she didn't have to fear him on any level, but Mattie knew better.

She couldn't help but fear what he was doing to her scarred, fragile heart.

Chapter Seven

By the first of May, spring had abdicated its hold to summerlike temperatures, causing a heavy dose of spring fever for most of the residents of Healing Harbor, especially for Mattie, who was counting down the hours until her first semester of school and last final were over.

With her life, and almost every spare minute of her time totally dominated by baseball, she almost couldn't remember a time when the boys *hadn't* been involved in baseball. Or when Joe hadn't been a daily part of their lives.

He spent several hours with the boys almost every evening after the official team practice ended. He'd have dinner with them, and then after dinner, he'd turn Mattie's backyard into an imaginary ball field again, where the boys could practice and hone their baseball skills.

Joe had quite easily and effortlessly became a daily part of their lives, and Mattie had to admit, it was wonderful to be able to share part of her life with another adult.

If there was any fear about the boys getting too attached to

Joe, it was offset by the positive impact Joe was having on their lives and their confidence.

Watching them play, and play so well under Joe's tutelage, filled Mattie with such a sense of pride, she realized that introducing Joe into her sons' lives had only had positive consequences.

If she worried about her own growing feelings for Joe, Mattie comforted herself with the knowledge that nothing could ever come of it simply because Joe was not interested in having a family of his own. He'd made that perfectly clear, and she wasn't a woman who disregarded something a man seemed so sure of. So she felt confident that in spite of her growing feelings she was definitely on safe ground.

This morning, as she gratefully finished her macroeconomics final—the last exam of the year—Mattie slung her heavy book bag over her shoulder, bid farewell to a few classmates, then hurried down the steps. The university was not air-conditioned, and even though it wasn't yet noon, the heat inside the classroom had been stifling.

With a sigh, she pushed through the heavy metal doors, then glanced back at the building with a grin, feeling foolishly proud of herself.

She'd completed her first semester of school here, and now, only had two more to go to receive her degree. Yes, it had been difficult, she mused as she cut across the crowded campus and headed toward the student parking lot, but it had been well worth it.

She was now that much closer to her goal of securing the future for her and the boys.

Lost in thought, Mattie laughed at herself when she realized she must have gone down the wrong aisle in the parking lot. Her car wasn't there. With a sigh, she shifted her book bag higher on her shoulder, then double backed the way she'd come, darting through rows of cars.

After going up and down several aisles, Mattie began to frown. Yes, she'd been terribly distracted this morning, worried about her final and a few minutes late, but surely she couldn't have forgotten where she'd parked her car.

After twenty more minutes of searching, Mattie found the aisle where she'd parked. She'd parked next to a car-repair shop's van, one with a dented front bumper. She remembered it only because she'd thought it was funny that a car-repair shop wouldn't bother to fix its own vehicle.

But the spot next to it, where she'd parked her battered little car, was empty.

"I don't believe this," she muttered, turning in a full circle and shading her eyes to check out the entire line of cars. Her car was nowhere to be found. "Who on earth would want to steal that piece of junk?" she wondered aloud, trying not to get upset.

Her car might indeed be a piece of junk, but it was *her* piece of junk, and the only transportation she had. With so much going on in her life right now, she couldn't afford to be without a vehicle, nor could she afford to buy a new one just yet. Her new-car fund wasn't quite full enough to handle a purchase yet. Another two months and several more commissions and she'd have enough money, but for right now, she didn't.

And the thought infuriated her.

"Damn!" With a shake of her head, Mattie turned and headed back toward one of the buildings to report the theft of her car, wondering how on earth she was going to get everything done today she needed to without wheels.

Joe loved patrolling during this peaceful, quiet time of the morning, especially on warm, sunny days like today. Kids were in school, most parents were working and the town was still except for the occasional yip of a dog or the blare of a horn.

Traffic was generally at a minimum, allowing him to get through and around town in a fraction of the time it generally took during what was considered rush hour.

Sipping the coffee he'd picked up at Freddy's diner on his way out on patrol, Joe leaned his elbow out the window, anxious to feel the warm sun on his skin.

Each year winter seemed to get longer and longer, he

mused, so that those first warm days of summer were greeted with great anticipation.

The weather had turned a couple of weeks back, promising a very hot May. The mere idea delighted him because it meant that the end-of-the-semester baseball game, picnic and celebration would be well attended.

With a sigh of deep contentment, Joe glanced at his watch and decided he had plenty of time to stop by to see his sister Angie. She had less than nine weeks to go until her delivery, and he had to admit he was getting more nervous and tense as the days wore on.

His radio squawked to life just as he turned the corner off of Main Street, heading toward Angie's house.

Joe reached for his radio. "Yeah, Clarence, what's up?"

"We got us some trouble over at the college, Joe."

"Trouble?" he repeated with a frown. "What kind of trouble?"

"Ms. Maguire just called. Seems her car's been stolen."

"Who on earth is stupid enough to steal that old piece of junk?" Joe wondered aloud with a shake of his head.

Clarence laughed. "Don't reckon I know, Sheriff, but I told her someone would be right over to take her statement and a report."

"Okay, Clarence. I'll get right over there. Anything else comes up, just give me a holler."

"Will do."

Joe replaced his radio receiver, then did something he rarely did: turned on his siren. He didn't want to keep Mattie waiting.

When Joe pulled his squad car in to the university parking lot, he spotted Mattie sipping a soft drink and sitting on the back end of a battered white pickup truck, talking to a grizzled old man wearing greasy coveralls and a battered blue baseball cap sporting the faded words Ziggy's Car Repair.

Joe pulled to a stop in the empty spot beside them as Mattie jumped down from the truck. She was dressed for comfort today in a pair of ivory shorts and a matching short-sleeve cotton sweater that emphasized every feminine curve, nearly making his mouth water.

Her tangle of hair was pulled back into a ponytail, but a few strands had escaped and now framed her face, making her look very young and very beautiful.

He felt that familiar clenching in his gut. Happened every time he looked at her, touched her. And as the days went by, he never seemed to get enough of looking at her or touching her, he realized.

"Can you believe this?" she asked him with a smile as he climbed out of his squad car and glanced around the lot. "That heap of junk is on its last legs…who on earth would steal the blasted thing?"

"Actually, I can believe it," he admitted, leaning forward to brush his lips against hers in greeting. Her hand immediately went to his chest, and she glanced back at Ernie, the trucker, who was suddenly watching them with a great deal of amused interest.

"Joe," she murmured, pulling back and fighting the urge to blush as she glanced at Ernie again.

"Yes, Mattie?" Joe replied innocently, his eyes twinkling devilishly. He knew she still wasn't totally comfortable with the ease in which he touched or kissed her, but she was getting better.

At least she didn't jump or jolt now, nor did she continually try to back away from him. And he was pleased that he seemed to be making progress in getting Mattie to trust him. He was, after all, a very patient man.

"What happened?" he asked, glancing up and down the aisle again.

"I wish I knew," she admitted, still flustered that he'd kissed her in public. Again. "I was running late this morning." She smiled. "Cody couldn't find his book bag. He couldn't remember where he'd left it, so by the time we did a search and seizure and found the blasted thing, it was too late for the boys to take the bus, so I drove them to school. Then, I drove straight here. Joe, I park in almost the same place every day, so I don't lose my car simply because I always have so many things on my mind. But when I came out of my last final this morning, my car was gone.''

''And you're sure it's not in another aisle?''

''Yeah, I am.'' She turned toward the pickup truck. ''I remember this truck. I parked right next to it.'' She leaned close to Joe so Ernie wouldn't hear her. ''I remember it only because it's all smashed up in the front end.''

''What's so unusual about that?''

She laughed, shading her eyes from the sun as she glanced at the truck. ''Joe, it's a truck for a car-repair shop.''

One eyebrow rose and he returned her smile. ''I see your point.'' He looked around again. ''Okay, Mattie, why don't you get in the squad car? We can drive up and down all the aisles and check for your car, but if we don't find it, we'll have to file a theft report.''

''Okay.'' She turned to the truck driver. ''Thanks for the soda, Ernie, and for a place to rest until the sheriff got here.''

''Welcome,'' he called with a wave of his greasy hand. ''Anytime. Hey, Sheriff?''

Joe glanced over at him. ''Yeah?''

''If I get my truck stolen, do I get a kiss when you come to take the report, too?'' Cackling loudly at his own joke, Ernie waved them away. ''See you later, Mattie. Good luck finding your car.''

''Thanks, Ernie.'' She waited until Joe climbed in beside her. ''Sorry about that, Joe, but you asked for it.''

''True.'' He reached over and gave her hand a squeeze, then kissed her again. This time she didn't back away, but merely slid into the kiss with that soft sigh he'd come to love hearing.

The urge to take the kiss deeper, to do more than kiss her, to ease the ache that had continued to grow inside from the moment he'd laid eyes on her was strong. But vividly aware that they were in the middle of the university parking lot, Joe reluctantly ended the kiss, then started his car and began slowly driving up and down the aisles, scouring the lot for her car.

''Do you have car insurance, Mattie?''

''I do, Joe, but only liability. My car is too old to have theft coverage on it. The insurance company doesn't even offer it on a car that old.'' She glanced out the window, hoping against hope to see her car. ''It's not worth anything to them, but it's sure worth a lot to me.''

He could hear the distress in her voice. ''Listen, Mattie, if your car is really gone, and I suspect it is, you're going to need transportation.''

''No kidding,'' she said with a sigh, trying not to get upset. She'd been wrangling every angle in her mind on how she could afford a new, or rather a different, car right now, and every way she figured it, she came up short.

She knew that she could ask her aunt for an advance on her salary or commissions, but she really wasn't thrilled with the idea. She preferred to spend only the money she had in hand and not borrow against the future.

Having to watch her pennies so very carefully over the past six years had taught her to be very cautious with money. Thinking and rethinking every single purchase and planning it like a major assault. Not having money only made you appreciate it when you did have it, but that didn't mean she was about to become reckless now.

But she also couldn't afford to be without transportation. She had to go to work, and although if push came to shove she could walk to the gallery from the house, still, there were other considerations.

Like the boys' baseball practice, doctor visits, grocery shopping. As a busy working mother she could not afford to be without a car. But she couldn't afford to buy another just yet.

''Mattie, you're looking real worried here.'' Her eyebrows were furrowed and she was biting her lip in a way that always meant she was worried.

''Of course I'm worried, Joe. It appears I've just lost my only means of transportation, and at the moment I really can't swing another car.''

Joe was thoughtful for a second as he turned down the last aisle of the parking lot. ''Mattie, why don't you use my car for the interim? My personal car,'' he specified. ''I've got the squad car, so I don't really need it.''

"Joe, I appreciate that, truly I do, but I don't think that's a very good idea."

"Why?" he asked with a frown.

"I'm not sure it's entirely ethical for you to be using your squad car for personal business, and then of course, if I'm seen driving around in your personal car I imagine tongues are going to wag, don't you think?"

"Not any more than if I let you drive the squad car," he replied with a smile. "I thought my own car would be a bit less conspicuous."

"Joe, I appreciate the offer, but I'd never want to put you in a spot that might be an embarrassment to you, your family or your position."

It was the first time in memory, Mattie realized, that she'd had any backup or someone to lend a hand or offer support during a crisis, and she realized it was a wonderful feeling, knowing she wasn't totally alone and out on a limb. It was also a luxury, she realized, one she not only couldn't take advantage of but knew she couldn't come to depend on. She knew it was best to depend only on herself.

"I never really thought about it that way." Joe considered several other options as he pulled out of the university parking lot and headed down Main Street. "I'll tell you what. How about if I let you borrow my car and I borrow Angie's?"

"Your sister's? Don't you think she might need her car? You did tell me her husband's overseas, didn't you?"

"Yep, he is."

"Well, then, I'd think she'd want to have use of her car, then. Especially while she's pregnant."

"Actually, she can't drive even if she wanted to." He glanced at her, then explained. "Doc Mayfield told her yesterday that until the babies are born, she's not allowed to drive. She's too far along right now. Not to mention the fact that, according to her, she can't fit comfortably behind the wheel anyway. So giving up the car wouldn't be a hardship or a problem for her at all."

"Babies?" Mattie grinned. "Did you say babies, as in more than one?"

It was his turn to grin as he turned to her. "Man, you're good. I don't know that anyone else would have picked up on that." He grinned. "The doc called Angie this morning. She had another ultrasound yesterday and apparently she's carrying twins. Girls," he added as his grin widened.

"Joe, that's wonderful. She must be thrilled."

He laughed, turning her hand over in his and lifting it to his mouth for a kiss. He couldn't be near her without wanting to touch her, kiss her. "She is, but right now she's also very, very uncomfortable. And a tad cranky."

"I know the feeling," Mattie said with a laugh. "Been there, done that."

"Did you ever want more children, Mattie?" he asked, glancing at her. He had no idea where the hell that question had come from. All he knew was that he'd been thinking about it, wondering about it for weeks now. She was so good with children, not just her own, but all children.

He'd been watching her on the practice field nearly every day for the past month, and was continually amazed at the calm and patience she displayed with all the players from the youngest and clumsiest, to the eldest and experienced, Mattie was a marvel.

"More children?" She hesitated for a moment, trying to hide the rush of yearning that surfaced at the mere thought of being able to have another child. "I always wanted a houseful," she admitted softly, feeling an ache in her heart where she'd long ago buried her maternal desire. She rubbed the spot, hoping to rub the ache away. "But when I realized what a mistake I'd made marrying Gary, I realized that my twins were probably the only children I'd ever have. I certainly didn't intend to have any more children as a single mother. I had a hard time supporting the two I had, and getting married again was out of the question." She forced a smile she didn't feel. "So I'm eternally grateful I had the twins, knowing that they are the only children I'll probably ever have." She shrugged. "I try not to wish for things I can't or don't have, or that never can be."

"I see," he said quietly, trying to digest everything she'd

told him. Now he understood so much better why she never wanted to get married again. Who would after what she'd been through? That wasn't what he'd call a marriage, no, it was more like being a prisoner of war, with her husband and in-laws as her captors.

"Can I buy you lunch before I drop you off at the gallery? We can run by the diner, and fill out the paperwork on your car while we're at it."

"Sounds good, I'm starving." She hesitated, knowing the matter of using his car wasn't quite settled yet. "Joe, about your car—"

"Mattie, don't worry about Angie, please? I do enough worrying about her for both of us. Trust me on this one. Someone in the family takes her to the doctor, grocery shopping, and everywhere else she needs to go. So borrowing her car won't be a hardship on anyone. Truly."

"Your family really does stick together and support one another, don't they?"

He met her gaze, and knew she was thinking about the Maguires and how they could have made her life so much easier but deliberately chose not to.

"That's what family does, Mattie," he said quietly. "At least my family. We depend on one another, help one another, and always support one another. It's the only way we know how to do things."

Mattie turned and glanced out the window, watching the pretty, tree-lined streets of town roll by, wondering why Joe's words made her feel so sad. Perhaps because she knew she'd never have that kind of wonderfully supportive family. Not for herself. Or her children.

"That's wonderful," she finally said, banking her own emotions and turning to him. "Truly. You have one incredible family."

"So does that mean you'll use my car?" He shook his head. "Mattie, you need to be practical here. As you've said, you've got to get to work, you've got errands to run, the boys' schedule to maintain, and don't forget about their practices. I could always pick them up and bring them home—"

"Good Lord, Joe, I could never impose on you like that."

"Fine," he said, totally ignoring her protests. "Then it's settled. If you use my car, you won't have to impose on me, right?"

"This is some kind of male logic to confuse me, right?"

He grinned. "You got it." He didn't let her utter another word of protest. "Now, I'll drop the car off at the gallery this afternoon before you close."

"Joe—"

"Mattie." He pulled in to an empty parking spot in front of the diner and turned to her. "I think it's only fair to warn you that it might be better if you didn't argue with me in front of Freddy." He grinned boyishly as he traced a finger down her cheek. "She's a mite possessive about me."

"She is, huh?" Mattie said with a grin. "Guess you've got women all over town panting after you."

He sighed. "Well, since my brother Sal—the real Marino family heartthrob—is no longer available, I'm a poor substitute." He feigned a heavy sigh. "It's a rotten job, but someone has to do it."

Mattie knew when to give up a fight. "Okay, I'll use your car on one condition."

"I let you have your way with my body?" he asked hopefully, wiggling his eyebrows at her and making her laugh. "Repeatedly?"

"Close, but not quite. You have to let me pay you for the use of the car."

"Pay me?" he said, insulted. "Mattie, you can't pay me, but I'll tell you what you can do."

Suspicious now, she looked at him warily. "What?"

"I'd like you and the boys to have dinner with me and my family on Sunday." It was time for Mattie to meet the rest of his family, especially Johnny. He wanted her to see exactly why he'd made the choices he had in life. Why there could never be anything more than friendship between them, and he wanted her to see that he took his responsibility to his family seriously—unlike the Maguires who clearly had no understanding of the word *family*.

He wanted the boys to meet Johnny as well, simply because he was certain not only would the boys enjoy it, but Johnny would too. And if the truth be told, he was also hoping Johnny would be able to offer some additional pointers to Cody and Connor on their batting technique.

"Dinner?" Surprised and confused, she shook her head. "You want me and the boys to have dinner with your whole family?" She knew how important Joe's family was to him, knew, too, how sacred their Sunday dinners together were. She felt honored that he'd invited her and the twins to join them.

"Yeah, Mattie. I'd really like it if you would." He reached out and tucked a stray strand of hair behind her ear.

"And how does our having dinner with you and your family fit into the category of me repaying you?"

He wiggled his eyebrows again. "You have to bring dessert. A couple dozen of those fabulous brownies you baked for the boys to take to class last week would work out just fine for Sunday. Fair enough?"

She laughed. He was offering her the use of a car for a couple dozen brownies? "Fair enough."

He leaned over and kissed her again. And then once more until her eyes slid closed and she was clutching at his shirt, her heart thudding along with his. Reluctantly, he drew back, remembering he was parked smack-dab in the middle of town. In his squad car. Hardly what he'd call a professional move.

"Great." Lingering over the kiss, his gaze lovingly went over her face. "But if you ever change your mind, Mattie, the offer still stands." Grinning, he wiggled his eyebrows yet again, leaning his forehead against hers. "You can have your way with my body anytime, anywhere."

Mattie resisted the urge to sigh dreamily, wondering how he'd react if he knew his body had been on her mind. A lot. He looked fabulous in his baseball uniform, but lately, she'd been fantasizing about getting him *out* of his baseball uniform.

"Thanks," she responded, swiping her suddenly damp palms down her shorts. "I'll keep that in mind." *Locked* in her mind and in her heart, she thought, where her fantasies and feelings about him would forever remain, and thus, keep her...safe.

"Lassie, did you bring them?" Clancy all but danced around her the moment she pushed through the glass door of the gallery that afternoon. "Do you have them, lass?"

Laughing, Mattie nodded, heading toward her desk with Clancy all but nipping at her heels.

"Fortunately, I do, Clancy." She patted her backpack where the drawings she'd been working on the past month—as well as all the sketch pads she'd used since she'd started drawing—were safely tucked away. "But it's a good thing I kept my sketch pads in my backpack and not my car."

"Why is that, lassie?" he asked with a frown, pausing at her desk.

"My car was stolen this morning."

"Nay!" His eyes rounded and he cocked his head to look at her. "I'm sorry, lass, but 'tis a surprise is all." Banking a smile, he shook his bald head. "Who on earth would want to risk prison for that rusted bucket of old bolts?"

She laughed, tugging the ponytail holder out of her hair, and running her fingers through the loose strands. "I'm not sure, but apparently they've got more problems than an old, rusted car."

"Aye for sure," he said with a nod, eyeing her backpack. "Well, lassie, are you going to let me see, or make me stand here waiting and wondering?"

"Clancy, I'm not at all sure they're any good—"

"Aye, lass, so you've told me." He rocked on his heels, eyes twinkling. "Every single day since I asked you for them."

With a sigh, Mattie dragged her backpack off and unzipped it, extracting four sketch pads and hesitantly handing them to Clancy.

"This is everything I have," she admitted. Except the sketch of Joe. She was having it framed right now, and since she would be having dinner with him and his family on Sunday, she thought that would be the perfect day to give it to him. But it wasn't going to be a gift from her, but from the boys, to thank Joe for all his time and attention.

"All the sketches I've done since I was in high school." Reluctantly, Mattie watched Clancy take control of the sketch pads. She felt very possessive about her work, and since she'd never shown anyone else her sketches before, she also felt a serious bit of trepidation.

"Feel like you've just handed over your firstborn?" Clancy asked with a knowing smile and a nod when he saw her face. "Felt the same way myself when your aunt first asked me to show her my portfolio. 'Twasn't something I did with ease, lass, well, certainly no more ease than you have right now." Chuckling, he began flipping pages, studying the sketches, cocking his head this way and that, humming softly as he absorbed everything.

"By the way, lass," he said as he flipped through the fourth and final book. "I've a business proposition for you."

"For me?" She frowned. "What kind of business proposition?"

Eyes twinkling, he glanced up at her. "Well, if you've a mind to sell one of your sketches, I've got a buyer." Maureen had been thrilled to learn about Mattie's artistic secret, and then truly stunned when he'd shown her Mattie's drawings, immediately deciding she wanted to showcase Mattie's work in the gallery. But knowing her niece as well as she did, Maureen was sure that Mattie would never believe she had true talent, but would think Maureen was merely being…kind.

So Maureen had decided that she would buy Mattie's art outright, then she'd be free to display Mattie's work in the gallery without fearing Mattie would think it was simply nepotism. It was, in fact, merely good business.

Astonishment had Mattie gaping at him. "Someone wants to buy one of *my* sketches?"

"Aye, lass, that's what I said." Clancy's eyebrows drew together.

"Why?" she asked, still stunned. She'd never even considered, never allowed herself to hope that one day she could actually sell her work. It was a dream she'd let go of a long,

long time ago, certain she had neither the talent nor the time or tenacity to make a go of it as an artist.

She knew that some artists—most artists—spent a lifetime without ever selling anything. Taking on another profession simply to pay the bills, while their quest for the art world's holy grail of sales and a devoted following consumed them.

But now, Clancy was offering her the one thing—the one dream—she'd long ago stopped dreaming of, and she could hardly contain her joy.

Clancy laughed at her response. "Why, indeed. I believe, lass, because like me, the buyer thinks you have a great deal of talent, not to mention potential."

His words made her heart dance with pride and pleasure. "Clancy, are you sure someone wants to pay money for one of my sketches?" Disbelief tinged her words. "Real money?"

"Aye, Mattie, I believe money was the currency we're discussing."

She shook her head, trying desperately to take it all in. "Who? I mean why? Which sketch?" A million thoughts crowded her mind, and came tumbling out of her mouth, making Clancy laugh.

"Aye, lass, I think you'd best sit down before shock knocks you down." He pulled out her desk chair and gently eased her into it. "Now," he began, kneeling beside her so they were eye level. "The who, I'm afraid is going to have to remain anonymous. The buyer prefers not to be known for right now. I'm acting as the…agent in this matter."

"Okay," she said slowly. After working in the gallery for almost five months now, she was aware of the many idiosyncrasies that both artists and buyers possessed. Idiosyncrasies as well as superstitions.

"And as for which sketch, 'tis the one of your aunt. You know, the one of her in the garden?"

"Yes, yes, I remember that one." And she remembered, too, how Clancy had admired it. She reached for his hand. "Oh, Clancy, thank you, but you don't have to buy that sketch. I'll give it to you."

He chuckled. "Well, lass, I wish I would have known that *before* I agreed to speak to you on the buyer's behalf."

"You're not the buyer?" she asked in surprise.

He shook his head. "Nay, lass, I'm sorry to disappoint you, but I'm not. Although if the truth be told, I wish I were. But the buyer has asked me to offer a sum that I think is both fair and reasonable." He named a figure that had Mattie goggling at him. It was a good thing she was sitting down, because if she hadn't been, surely she would have fallen down.

"Oh my word, Clancy, I can't accept that kind of money."

"Shh, lass, shh," he muttered, pressing a finger to her lips to shush her. He rolled his eyes, shook his head, then glanced around to make certain Mattie's words hadn't been overheard. "Aye, lassie, never, ever turn down a princely sum for your work, you'll ruin it for the lot of us." He sniffed, then flashed her a charming grin. "You must always make the buyer think they've gotten themselves a bargain, lass. And in this case, they truly have."

"But Clancy—"

"No buts about it, Mattie girl. I've made you an offer fair and square. If the sum's not agreeable to you, I can try to get the buyer higher."

"Oh my word, that's not necessary, Clancy. Truly." She hesitated for a moment. To even consider not accepting the initial offer, generous as it was, would be both foolish on her part and an insult to the buyer. "Clancy!" Her eyes gleamed suddenly. "If I sell my sketch I can afford to buy a car."

"Aye, lass, I imagine you can. A car and a whole lot more, I venture," he added, watching as pleasure pure and simple flooded her face, her eyes. It made his own heart swell, for he knew what it was to make a dream come true for a budding artist. Nothing gave as much pleasure, except, of course, selling one of his own paintings for a princely sum.

"Does the buyer know this is my first work?" Mattie asked, wanting to make certain she wasn't taking advantage of anyone.

He nodded. "Aye, the buyer is well aware of that. And I might add, interested in your other pieces." He held up the sketch pads. "That's why I needed to see these." Grinning, Clancy winked at her.

"You mean they're interested in seeing more of my work?" The possibility was dazzling, dizzying, and Mattie felt as if she'd just guzzled a whole bottle of champagne.

"Aye, lass, they are. Unless, of course, you have a problem with that?"

"A problem?" Mattie jumped to her feet, grabbing him up in a hug and doing her own version of an Irish jig around the gallery with him. "No problem at all, Clancy. None at all."

"Aye, lass," Clancy said with a laugh, trying to keep up with her. "Then I guess we have a deal."

Her first thought—the only coherent thought that slipped through her haze of joy—was that she couldn't wait to tell Joe, to share this wonderful news with him.

Excitement was still humming within Mattie when the school bus dropped the boys off promptly at three. Standing at the door, she frowned as she watched them look both ways, then barrel across the street toward her, nearly knocking each other over in an effort to get to her first.

"Mom! Mom! Guess what?" Connor beat Cody to the door by a hair. "Guess what happened in school today?"

"She'll never guess," Cody said, skidding to a halt and trying to catch his breath. "Let's just tell her."

Mattie held up her hand. "Wait a minute. Before you tell me what happened at school today, Cody, I'd like you to tell me where your shoe is?"

"My shoe?" Cody repeated innocently, glancing down at his feet. He had one school shoe on. His other foot was clad only in a dark blue sock—with a hole over the big toe. He wiggled his toes as he brought his perplexed glance up to hers and gave her a shrug. "Dunno."

She wasn't going to laugh. She really wasn't. But she did, wondering how on earth this child could still delight her while he also frustrated her so. "Cody, how on earth could you not know where your shoe is?"

Cody scratched his head, looking up at her wide-eyed. "Ma,

I don't understand what you just said.'' He shrugged his skinny shoulders. "I dunno what happened to my shoe. We had gym class right before we came home, and I put my shoes in my locker, but when I went in it after gym, my shoe was gone.''

"Gone?'' she repeated with a lift of her eyebrow. "And did you ask your teacher about it?''

"No, Ma, 'cuz I don't think Mrs. O'Malley needed my shoe.''

Ruffling his hair, Mattie gave in to the urge to laugh. Her babies simply delighted her. "Cody, what on earth am I going to do with you?''

"Ma, I don't know what that means, either,'' he complained. "Now, can we tell you what happened at school?'' he asked impatiently.

"Yes, of course,'' she said, corralling both boys and leading them toward her desk, where she had their after-school snacks waiting.

"There's gonna be a play at school,'' Cody announced, bouncing up and down in excitement.

"Yeah, for the end-of-the-semester celebration.''

"A play?'' she said, pulling off their backpacks and setting them atop her desk.

"Yep.'' Cody grinned at his brother. "And me and Connor, we both are gonna be in it.''

"You are?'' Pleased, she grinned at them both. "That's wonderful. What play are you doing?''

"Charlotte's Web,'' they said almost in unison.

"It's about a stupid girl spider. But I get to play a runt pig named Wilbur,'' Cody announced with a giggle.

"Yeah, and I get to play an even bigger pig named Uncle.''

"Ma, what's a runt?'' Cody wanted to know.

"A runt? Well, that's a word that's generally used to describe the smallest animal in a litter. Like the smallest cat or dog, or in this case, pig.''

"Uncle and Wilbur meet at the fair,'' Connor informed her.

"They do, do they?'' Mattie cocked her head to look at her

sons. "Do either of you remember me reading that story to you when you were younger?"

The boys exchanged glances, then looked at her and shrugged their shoulders. "Nope."

"Well, I did." She smiled at them, then opened the refrigerator and pulled out two cans of soda. "And you both loved it," she said, handing each one a soft drink.

The boys merely stared at her. "This is soda," Cody said unnecessarily.

"Yes, I know."

"But we never get to have soda after school," Connor said, just as confused as his brother.

"Well, today is a special day and I thought we'd celebrate."

"Cool." Cody popped the aluminum top on his can and tipped it back to take a long drink, gulping noisily. "What are we celebrating?"

"Oh, lots of things. My car got stolen this morning—"

"Are we supposed to celebrate that?" Connor wanted to know with a frown of worry.

"Well, not usually, but I also sold one of my sketches today. And for enough money that we can buy a new car."

"Cool."

"And Coach Joe invited us to have dinner with him and his family on Sunday."

Both boys exchanged glances again, then grinned. "Can we go?" they both asked, and Mattie laughed.

"Of course." She brushed Connor's hair out of his eyes. "And I'll be making brownies to take with us as well. You'll get to meet all of Coach Joe's brothers and sisters."

"All of them?" Cody wanted to know.

"As far as I know," Mattie said.

"Can we talk to them, Ma?" Connor asked. "Coach Joe's brothers and sisters, I mean." They still hadn't been able to find out about Coach Joe and 'rithmetic, so maybe they could ask one of his brothers or sisters.

"Of course, honey," she said absently. "Now, since I don't have a car, Coach Joe is going to loan me his until I can buy a new one, so he'll be picking us up in a little bit. I thought since today was such a special day, we might take Coach Joe out for pizza tonight to celebrate. What do you say?''

''Awesome, Ma, awesome. Then we can tell him about the play and how we got parts and everything.'' Cody took another gulp of his soda.

''Yeah, and maybe he could even help us with our lines. We have to learn our lines and then remember them, Ma.'' Connor pushed his glasses up his sweaty nose.

''We gotta memorize stuff,'' Cody added, pleased that he remembered the word Mrs. O'Malley had used.

''I imagine you do, honey.''

''So can we ask Coach Joe to help us?'' Connor asked.

''We gotta remember all of our lines,'' Cody specified in case she wasn't clear.

''Well, you can ask him, honey,'' Mattie said hesitantly, not wanting them to be disappointed. ''But I don't know that he's going to have the time, with baseball practice and all. But I'll be glad to help you.''

''Well, can we ask him to come to our play, then?'' Cody wanted to know.

''Of course you can.'' Mattie smiled. ''But right now, Cody, the only thing I'd like you to remember is *where* you left your shoe.''

Chapter Eight

"Ma, how come we gotta get dressed up?" Cody asked Sunday morning as Mattie gave her sons one last visual inspection.

"Yeah, Ma, and how come we gotta wear stupid ties?" Connor added, flipping the end of the navy-and-red tie he wore up and down like a flag.

"Because we're going to have dinner with Joe's family and it's important that you look nice."

"Can't we look nice without ties?" Cody asked, earning a look from her.

Mattie blew out a breath and shooed them out of her bedroom. "Go on downstairs now and wait for me. Joe should be here any minute. I'll be right down."

After checking herself in the mirror one last time, Mattie grabbed their sweaters off her bed and then remembered something. "Oh, and Cody," she called down the stairs before she forgot, "don't you dare take your shoes off today."

She'd already had to buy him one new pair of school shoes this week, since the one he lost on Monday remained MIA.

She still couldn't understand how the kid could lose a shoe, and worse, not notice or remember where on earth he'd lost it.

"I won't," he grumbled, glumly following his brother down the stairs and flopping into one of the Queen Anne chairs facing the front window in the living-room. "Do ya' think Mrs. O'Malley will be there?" he asked Connor, who had plopped onto the sofa.

"Probably. She's Coach Joe's sister, Ma said."

"Then how come she's got a different name?"

"Because when a woman gets married, boys, she takes her husband's name," Mattie said as she shifted her small clutch purse from one hand to the other and came down the stairs. In her arms she carried a sweater for each of them, as well as the gift-wrapped sketch of Joe the boys were going to give him today.

"Then how come her name isn't Mrs. Joe?" Cody wanted to know, making Mattie laugh.

"Sweetheart, Joe is her brother, but if he wasn't and she married him, her name wouldn't be Mrs. Joe, but Mrs. Marino. Which is Joe's last name. A wife takes her husband's last name when they marry." At the confused look on his face, she explained further. "Before I married your dad, my name was Mattie McBride."

"Like Aunt Maureen, right?" Connor said with a grin.

"That's right, honey. But your dad's name was Maguire, so when we got married, I took his name and became Mattie Maguire. Does that make sense?"

"Nah," Cody said with a shake of his head. "But that's okay."

"It just means if Ma marries Coach Joe her name will be Mattie Marino, right, Ma?"

Uh-oh. Mattie glanced from one of her sons to the other, wondering what on earth was going on. Connor's comment had triggered her mother's early-warning alarm system, and right now it was on full-scale alert.

"Yes," Mattie said carefully. "That's right, honey."

"But what would our names be?" Cody wanted to know.

"That depends," she said carefully. She hesitated a moment, wondering if she was about to step on a land mine. "What's all this about me marrying Coach Joe?" she asked, her gaze going from one to the other. She wanted to groan. They were up to something. Again. "Okay, boys, fess up. What's all this about?"

"Nuthin'," Cody said, hunching his shoulders defensively and glancing out the window to see if Coach Joe had arrived yet.

"We was just wondering," Connor said.

"Wondering," Mattie repeated, setting the sweaters and the package on the cocktail table. "Come here, boys." She held out her arms, waiting while they exchanged another silent glance before they walked over to her.

"I want you to listen to me very carefully." She draped an arm around both of their shoulders, then gave them a comforting smile. "Coach Joe and I are just friends. Now, I know that we've been spending a lot of time with him, and you both like him very much—"

"Lots," Connor said.

"*Real* lots," Cody confirmed, making Mattie smile.

"I know, sweetheart, and he likes you two a lot as well, but just because we spend a lot of time together and just because Coach Joe and I are friends doesn't mean I'm going to marry him."

"But you said you liked him," Cody protested.

"You're right. I did," she admitted. "But I like Mr. Clancy, too. That doesn't mean I'm going to marry him."

"Yeah, Ma, but Mr. Clancy's old."

"Real old."

"Like Grandpa."

"And you never kissed Mr. Clancy, Ma."

Well, Mattie thought, the kid had her there.

"But you kissed Coach Joe," Cody thought it necessary to point out. "You kiss him a lot."

"Yes," she admitted hesitantly, feeling herself flush a bit. She had become so comfortable with Joe, she hadn't realized how much they'd been kissing. In front of the boys, which she realized had given them the wrong idea. "I have kissed Coach Joe, but that doesn't mean I'm going to marry him." She grinned. "And for the record, boys. I have kissed Mr. Clancy, too." On the cheek, numerous times, but she didn't think it necessary to point that out.

"Why'd ya kiss him?" Cody asked.

"Because we're friends," she said, straightening Cody's tie.

"I'm sure glad we don't gotta kiss our friends," Connor said in relief.

"Yeah, I wouldn't ever wanna hafta kiss Bobby Dawson." Cody made gagging noises to show his disgust.

"Or Amy Bartlett," Connor interjected, clutching at his stomach and making gagging noises as well. "She might puke on you," he said, laughing.

"Yuck." Cody clamped a hand over his own mouth as if to protect it from any offending female kisses.

"Okay, boys, that's enough," Mattie scolded gently, wanting to make sure she'd handled this situation so they understood it. "So, now do you understand? Coach Joe and I are friends." She looked from one to the other. "*Just* friends," she specified, wondering why, for the first time in her life, she felt as if she wasn't being totally honest with her children. "And sometimes friends…kiss, or hug, or do nice things for one another. That doesn't mean they're going to get married. Do you understand?"

Cody and Connor exchanged silent glances. "Yeah, we understand, Ma," Connor said glumly, realizing they were going to have to figure out another way to convince Coach Joe to be their dad.

They thought because he liked their mom, maybe he could marry her and then he'd hafta be their dad. That *was* a rule, Bobby Dawson had told them. So, they figured if they could just get Coach Joe to marry their mom, well, their problem would be solved.

Finding a dad wasn't as easy as they thought it would be. But they'd better hurry up, or else their grandma was going to make their grandpa be their dad 'cause she said they really *needed* one. Another one of those rules, Connor thought dejectedly.

But they wanted a dad of their own, one who could do all the things they liked to do. One who could run and play baseball and maybe even knew 'rithmetic. And they hadn't had a chance to ask yet, but he and Cody were pretty sure their grandpa didn't know nuthin' 'bout doing 'rithmetic.

Connor sighed, wondering what they were going to do next.

"Joe's here," Mattie said, unable to stop her grin as she watched him pull up to the curb. Her heart began a quick two-step just at the sight of him.

"Can we give him his present now?" Cody asked, reaching for it.

"Not yet," Mattie laughed. "Let him get in the door first."

After smoothing down the skirt of her summer dress, Mattie took a deep breath and answered the doorbell.

"Hi," she said as she pulled open the door.

"Hi, yourself," he said with a grin. "You look gorgeous." She was wearing a white summer shift, sleeveless. It skimmed her knees, leaving her long legs tan and bare. On her feet she wore a pair of sinfully sexy strappy sandals that made his mouth water.

Trying not to drool, he leaned forward and brushed his lips against hers, aware that both boys were standing behind them, watching intently in wide-eyed fascination.

Joe drew back and his eyebrows lifted. "Ties, Mattie?" His gaze shifted from the boys to her and he tried not to smile. "You made the boys wear ties?"

"She said we gotta look nice," Cody muttered, giving his tie another flip.

"Do you guys want to wear ties today?" Joe asked as Mattie stepped back to let him enter.

"Uh-uh," Cody said with a wild shake of his head.

Grinning, Joe motioned toward the boys. "Come here." Both marched obediently toward him. "Let's get rid of these nooses, okay?"

"Okay!" Thrilled to have a comrade who apparently didn't

like ties either, the boys beamed as Joe helped both of them off with their ties, tossing them carelessly atop the television.

"Now, is that better?"

The boys beamed at him. "Yeah. Much."

"Good."

"We got a present for you, Coach Joe," Cody said, bouncing up and down and almost dropping the heavy frame he had clutched in both hands.

"Yeah, it's just for you. Ma made it."

"She did, did she?" Joe's gaze shifted to Mattie's and he grinned. "Well, that was very nice of your mom, wasn't it?"

"Our mom's nice," Cody pointed out, earning a surprised look from both Joe and his mother. "*Real* nice," he added.

"And she reads good stories, too," Connor added.

"Cody," Mattie cautioned in a voice her sons knew well. "Connor." She waited until they both looked at her. "I don't think Joe needs a laundry list of my...niceness," she said, trying not to laugh. She knew what the twins were doing, but still, it embarrassed her to think her boys had to point out her assets to Joe.

"We helped Ma wrap it." Cody held out the gaily wrapped package. There was enough scotch tape to hold a battleship together, and almost enough paper to wrap one in as well, but it was the most beautiful gift Joe had ever seen.

"Wow, you did this?" He took the package. "I'm impressed. It's beautiful. The best wrapping I've ever seen. Maybe you guys could help me at Christmastime. I've got tons of presents to wrap every year."

"We'd love to, Coach Joe," Connor said, beaming.

"Can I open my present now?" Joe asked.

"Yeah, open it."

"Open it."

Slowly, Joe unwrapped the present, his eyes softening in surprise when he saw the framed picture of himself, the one Mattie had sketched. "It's beautiful, Mattie," he said, more touched than he'd been in a long time. "Just...beautiful."

"You like it, Coach Joe?" Connor asked.

He grabbed both boys up in a quick hug. "I love it, guys.

And I really loved the wrapping paper, too. I'm going to hang this in my house and one day I'll be saying, 'Oh, that's an original Mattie Maguire, personally drawn for me before she became famous.'" His confidence in her and her abilities filled Mattie's heart with joy. "Thanks, Mattie. This means a lot to me." He leaned over and gave her a kiss, aware that the boys were wide-eyed, watching.

"Are we ready?" Mattie asked.

"In a minute." Joe hesitated. "Mattie, I came early because there's something I want to talk to you about. You and the boys," he said, glancing at them.

"Okay, Joe," Mattie said, wondering what on earth was going on. Joe rarely, if ever, seemed this serious. "Come sit down. Do you want something to drink?"

"No, no, I'm fine," he said as he sat on the couch and set the package back down on the cocktail table. Both boys scrambled to sit next to him, one on either side, and Joe absently draped an arm around each of them.

"Whatcha' wanna talk to us about?" Cody asked.

"Well, son, I wanted to talk to you about Johnny."

"Who's Johnny?" Connor asked.

Joe took a slow, careful breath, aware that Mattie was watching him carefully. "Johnny is my twin brother."

Cody's eyes rounded in excitement. "You gotta twin brother, too?" At Joe's nod, Cody grinned at his own twin. "Cool."

"Yeah," Joe said with a laugh. "It is cool. But my twin, Johnny, is just a little bit different than I am." In his experience, kids could understand and accept anything as long as it was explained to them.

"How come?" Connor asked. "Doesn't he look like you? I look like Cody and he looks like me and we're twins."

"I know," Joe said with a smile. "Johnny looks just like me, too. And I look just like him. We've always looked identical." Joe hesitated for a moment, wanting to make sure he explained this so that the boys could understand. "But we're not exactly alike," Joe added, taking each of the boys' hands in his. "A long time ago, when Johnny and I were about twelve years old, he had an accident."

He heard Mattie's quick intake of breath and glanced up. Eyes wide, her slender hand was pressed to her throat and he could see the empathy in her eyes. Some of the frost that had surrounded his fragile heart for so many years seemed to begin melting.

"What kind of accident?" Connor asked.

"Johnny and I were riding our bikes to the park. It was summer and we went to the park every day to play baseball."

"Johnny likes baseball, too?" Cody asked in excitement.

Joe nodded. "Loves it, and in fact, he's a better player than I ever was."

"What kind of accident did he have?" Cody asked, and Joe sighed. A bad one, he wanted to say, but didn't. The memory of that day had remained fresh in his mind, in his heart, as if it had just happened yesterday. As did his guilt.

He'd never stopped blaming himself for Johnny's accident. If he hadn't suggested they race to the park that day... Deliberately, Joe forced the thought away and continued.

"Johnny and I always used to race our bikes, to see who could get to the park faster." Joe managed to smile a bit at the memory. "That day, I was beating him. I'd crossed Main Street first simply because Johnny slowed to avoid hitting a stray dog. He didn't look before he pedaled into the street. He was still worried about the dog, and had turned back to make sure the dog was all right."

"Oh, God. Joe." Mattie's heart was racing and she had a horrible premonition of what was coming.

"There was a car coming. Johnny didn't look before he raced into the street, and the driver wasn't watching where he was going. He had just glanced down to change the station on the radio, and his car was going faster than it should have when Johnny darted in front of him and the man hit Johnny with his car."

"Did he get hurt?" Connor asked solemnly, and Joe nodded.

"Yes, Connor, he did." He looked down at the boy. "Some

of Johnny's injuries were physical." He rushed on to explain at the look on the boy's face. "That means his body was hurt."

"You mean like a broken leg or something?" Cody asked, eyes wide.

"Exactly. Johnny had a lot of broken bones, but he also had some injuries that weren't on his body, but…in his brain where you couldn't see them or fix them."

"Oh, Joe." It was all Mattie could do not to get up and wrap her arms around him. She could see the anguish in his face and it tore at her heart.

"Anyway, Johnny stayed in the hospital for a long, long time. Most of the injuries to his body finally healed, but the injuries to his brain didn't." Joe took a deep breath, then looked at the boys carefully, trying to judge how much of what he was saying they understood.

"How come?" Cody asked.

"Because sometimes, Cody, when you injure your brain, there's no way to fix it."

"So what happens when you can't fix your brain?" Cody wondered.

"Well, even though Johnny looks exactly like me, and is as tall and as big as me, inside where his brain was injured, he's still like a little boy."

"You mean kinda like us?" Connor asked, and Joe nodded.

"Yes, that's exactly what I mean. He's kinda like you boys. But because Johnny looks big, and is big—"

"Like a grown-up person?" Cody said, surprising him.

"Yeah, Cody, because Johnny looks like a grown-up person on the outside but is really just a little boy on the inside, it sometimes frightens people and they don't like Johnny or want to be around him." Joe hesitated. "And sometimes they even call Johnny mean names."

"That's stupid," Cody said with a scowl, making Joe smile.

"You're right, Cody, that's very stupid. But sometimes people can be stupid even when they don't try to be."

"Bobby Dawson." Cody glanced up at Joe. "Sometimes Bobby Dawson is stupid and he doesn't even try."

"Or mean," Connor added solemnly, playing with a button on his shirt. "Sometimes Bobby Dawson is mean to me." He lifted stricken eyes to Joe. "Sometimes," he added quietly, hoping his mom wouldn't hear 'cuz she'd get all worried, "he makes fun of me."

"Connor, why does Bobby make fun of you?" Joe asked softly. This was the first he'd heard of this, and from the look on Mattie's face, the first she'd heard of it as well.

"'Cuz I can't run as fast as the other boys." He hesitated a moment. "And because I wear glasses," he added, pushing his dreaded glasses up his sweaty nose.

"I see," Joe said quietly.

Embarrassed, Connor continued to stare at the button on his shirt. "And sometimes Bobby calls me...a retard," he whispered so only Joe could hear.

"That's a very mean word, Connor," Joe said. "And a very mean and stupid thing to say to someone. You know that, don't you? And just because someone says something about you, mean or not, it doesn't make it so."

"I know," he said glumly, trying to blink back tears. "But I hate when he calls me that."

"Coach Joe?" Cody tugged on his shirt, and pulled Joe down so he could whisper in his ear. "When Bobby calls Connor that, I sock him." Not certain if he was going to get scolded or not for the admission, since he wasn't supposed to be fighting, ever, Cody flashed a guilty glance at his mother, who, sitting across the room, couldn't hear what he was whispering.

Joe ruffled Cody's hair, proud as a peacock of the kid, but one glance at Mattie told him he probably shouldn't express that opinion at the moment, so he tempered his words a bit.

"While I don't think it's a good idea to just go around hitting people, Cody, I think it's wonderful that you stick up for and defend your brother." Joe grinned. "Johnny always stuck up for me and I always stick up for him."

"'Cuz that's what brothers do, right, Coach Joe?"

"That's right." Joe smiled, making a mental note to have a little chat with Bobby Dawson *and* his father. "Then you understand what I mean about people calling Johnny names because he's different?'' He glanced at both boys and they nodded in unison.

"It's mean and it makes you feel bad," Connor said. "And sometimes it makes you cry," he added.

"You're right," Joe responded, tightening his arm around Connor and drawing him closer in comfort and support. "That's why it's important to accept everyone for who they are and what they can do. And not call them names or hurt them just because they're different."

"Coach Joe, does Johnny live with you?" Cody asked, and Joe shook his head.

"No, son. Johnny has to live in a very special place where there are people who know how to take very good care of him. That's where we're going today, to the place where Johnny lives."

"How come Johnny can't live with you?" Cody wanted to know.

"Well, son, remember I told you that Johnny had some injuries to his body?"

Both boys nodded.

"Well, because of that, Johnny needs to have special nurses to take care of him and make sure he stays healthy." Joe held his hand out, palms up. "And unfortunately, I'm a certified nursing idiot," he admitted, making both boys giggle.

"Does he like it at that place?" Connor asked and Joe grinned.

"He loves it, Connor. Johnny has his own bedroom, and his own television, and all of his favorite things around him." Joe leaned down to whisper, "He even has his own dog."

"A dog?" Excitement had Cody and Connor bouncing up and down on the couch. "Johnny's got a dog, really?" They turned to their mom. "Ma, Johnny's got a dog. A real live dog of his very own."

"I know, honey. I heard," Mattie said with a smile. She hadn't been able to take her eyes off Joe. Now she understood so much more about him. So very much more. And what she understood only made her feelings for him stronger.

"What kinda dog does Johnny got?" Cody wanted to know.

"It's a little sheltie. You know what Lassie looks like?" Joe waited for their nods. "Well, Johnny's dog, his name is Clumsy—"

"Clumsy?" Cody repeated with a laugh. "That's funny."

"How come that's his name?" Connor wanted to know.

"Because when we first bought him for Johnny, the dog was just a puppy, and he was always falling down or tripping over his own legs. So Johnny decided to call him Clumsy. Anyway, Clumsy looks like a little baby Lassie."

"Can we see him?"

Joe laughed. "Of course you can. Where Johnny goes, Clumsy isn't far behind."

"Do you think Johnny would let us play with his dog?" Cody asked hopefully.

"Absolutely," Joe assured them.

"Coach Joe?"

"Yes, Cody?"

"Can he still play baseball?" Cody asked. "Not Clumsy," he clarified. "But Johnny?"

"Oh yeah," Joe said with a laugh. "Johnny can still play baseball better than anyone I've ever seen."

"Cool."

"Every Sunday, everyone in our family, all my other brothers and sisters, go to see Johnny, and we all have dinner together at the home where Johnny lives, and we generally end up playing a few innings of baseball after dinner."

"Does Johnny like that? I mean, you going to see him?" Cody asked.

"He loves it," Joe said, glancing at Mattie as she wiped a tear from her cheek. "Our family is very, very close, boys, and when my father died—"

"Our father died, too," Connor said solemnly. "Before we was even born."

"I know, son. I know. Sometimes it's very hard not to have a father, isn't it?" The boys exchanged glances, then both nodded their heads. "Before my father died, I promised him I would always take care of Johnny."

"Like Ma takes care of us?"

"Exactly," Joe said. He hesitated for a moment, then lifted his gaze to Mattie's. "Do you understand?" he asked quietly. He was talking to the boys but looking at Mattie, and suddenly all the pieces of the puzzle about Joe finally clicked into place.

He had responsibilities. Every word he'd said to her that first night at the pizzeria, when he'd told her he never wanted to get married or have a family of his own because he already had responsibilities, suddenly took on new meaning.

The deathbed promise he'd made to his dad: to always take care of Johnny. *Oh, Joe!* Now she understood why he never wanted to marry. Because he wanted to honor his promise to his father and take care of his brother. But she didn't understand what had made him think he couldn't do both.

"We understand," Connor said, glancing at his own brother.

"Do you think Johnny will like us?" Cody asked hesitantly, making Joe grin.

"I'm sure of it," Joe assured the young boy. "But you have to remember, boys. Because of Johnny's accident, he doesn't talk like I do, or walk like I do, and he sometimes forgets things."

"We don't care about that," Cody said, nearly melting Joe's heart.

"Yeah, we don't care about stupid stuff like that," Connor added.

"Even though Johnny looks just like me, a grown-up, there're lots of things Johnny can't do that I can," Joe explained.

"Like what?"

"Well…" Joe was thoughtful. "Johnny can't drive."

"We can't drive, either," Cody informed him, in case there was any question about the matter. "We're too little."

"Sometimes Johnny gets tired and can't walk or run without falling."

"I fall all the time," Connor pointed out. "And sometimes I'm not even tired."

"Sometimes Johnny doesn't remember things, even things you just told him, so you'll have to be patient—"

"Couldn't we just tell him again the stuff he forgets?" Cody asked.

"Works for me," Joe said with a grin, wondering why he'd thought this was going to be so difficult.

"What *can* Johnny do?" Cody asked, making Joe smile.

"Well, like I told you, he can play baseball. He can bat better than anyone I've ever seen, but he can't run the bases very well. He gets tired and then his legs don't work right. But he can draw and color. He loves to color pictures, boys, and he loves to watch movies. *The Lion King* is his favorite."

Connor brightened. "We like to color, too. Could we bring our crayons and coloring books with us when we go to see Johnny, Ma?"

"Of course," Mattie said with a smile, loving her sons more with each passing minute.

"Maybe he'll let us watch *The Lion King* with him." Connor grinned, rubbing a scab on his elbow. "We like that movie a lot."

"I'm sure of it," Joe said.

"And do you think maybe he'll let us play baseball with him? We can play real good now 'cuz you taught us," Connor said.

"I'm sure he'd love to play baseball with you."

"Coach Joe?" Connor said hesitantly.

"Yes, son?"

Wide-eyed with innocence, Connor glanced up at him. "Do you think Johnny...do you think he might wanna be our friend?"

Emotions flooded Joe's heart and he swept up both boys in a fierce one-armed hug, knowing that these two little boys, mischief-makers they may be, had completely and totally stolen his heart. "Of course, son." He let out a sigh of relief and met Mattie's gaze. His heart, empty for so long, so very, very long, seemed to fill and then overflow, nearly making him weak. First he kissed the top of Connor's head, and then Cody's. "Of course."

* * *

"Cody Maguire, if you take the lid off those brownies and sniff them one more time, you're going to leave nose prints all over them," Mattie said, making the boys giggle. She glanced in the back seat where the boys were sitting, just to make sure Cody hadn't snuck another brownie.

"But I'm hungry, Ma," Cody complained, rubbing his stomach and juggling the plastic container of brownies that was sitting on his lap. "When we gonna eat?"

Joe laughed as he made the turn into the long, winding driveway of the rehabilitation home where Johnny lived. "Soon, Cody. I promise. We're here."

"We're here. We're here," Connor and Cody caroled, bouncing up and down as far as their seat belts would let them. Cody craned his neck to see out the window. "It's all green," he said. "Everywhere. And look, Connor, there's a swimming pool."

Connor tried to see out Cody's window. "They even got a swing set, and a baseball field."

"Mattie," Joe began. He'd been holding her hand like a lifeline from the moment they'd gotten into the car. He had no idea why he was so nervous about bringing her and the boys here, but maybe it was because he had no idea how she'd react. "This is a special facility, primarily for adolescents and young adults. Johnny's been here since he was released from the hospital. It's a wonderful place, handpicked by my folks. They take wonderful care of Johnny."

"It looks beautiful," Mattie said, doing a little glancing around herself. "It's so huge, though," she said. "I didn't expect it to be quite so big."

"That it is," Joe agreed. "But my dad wanted to make sure there was plenty of land around, and greenery. He didn't want Johnny to feel penned in."

"Where's Johnny's house?" Connor wanted to know, craning his neck to see.

Joe pointed out the windshield. "You see that row of pretty white buildings right over there?"

Squinting, Connor looked where Joe pointed. "Yeah?"

"Well, the second one on the right is where Johnny lives." Joe turned down the lane leading to Johnny's residence hall. "Ah, Sal's here already." He turned to Mattie. "See that little black sports car there, the vintage Porsche? That's Sal's."

Mattie laughed. It was exactly the kind of car she'd expected of a gorgeous heartthrob.

"What?" Joe glanced at her. "What's so funny?"

"Nothing, really," she said with a shake of her head. "It's just, you've told me so many stories about gorgeous Sal, the female heartthrob, I can't wait to meet him."

Joe laughed. "Well, your wait's about over." He pulled in to a parking spot, then shut off the engine. "Okay, boys, now listen carefully. Before we get out, make sure we've got everything. Connor, have you got your crayons and coloring books?"

"Got 'em." He held up the pile of books and a plastic container of crayons so Joe could see them.

"Cody, have you got the brownies?"

"What's left of them," Mattie interjected with a grin, turning to wink at her son.

"Got 'em."

"Okay, now, boys, I want you to make sure that you don't go wandering off by yourselves. There're woods back there, far behind the buildings, and I don't want you guys wandering off and getting lost. Make sure you stay with an adult or Johnny at all times, okay?"

"'Kay," they caroled.

"Okay, let's hit it, then." Joe threw open his car door and climbed out, opening the back door for the boys to slide out. He went around the front and helped Mattie from the car, then took her hand. The boys walked side by side behind them.

"Coach Joe?"

"Yes, Cody?"

"Does Johnny know we're coming?"

"I told him I was bringing some new friends to meet him today, but I'm not sure if he'll remember. You remember what I said about that, don't you?"

"Yep." Cody shrugged. "So if he doesn't remember, we'll remind him again."

Joe reached out and ruffled his hair. "Good idea, sport." Taking a deep breath, Joe climbed the four steps that led to Johnny's residence hall and pulled open the door, letting Mattie and the twins in.

"Afternoon, Sheriff, good to see you." A nurse, pushing sixty, with bottle-brown hair and big blue eyes, winked at him. She was manning the visitor's desk right inside the door. "I see you've brought us some new visitors."

"Hi, Stella," Joe said as he signed in. "Stella, this is Mattie Maguire and her sons, Connor and Cody."

"You guys are twins, I bet," she said with a wink.

"Yep, we are," Connor confirmed with a grin.

"Well, we're always glad to have such fine, handsome upstanding men come visit, aren't we, Sheriff?" she asked with another wink.

"She called us men," Cody repeated with a giggle, clamping a hand over his mouth.

"How's he doing today, Stella?" Joe asked.

"Doing fine, Sheriff. Right as rain and as excited as all get out knowing you all were coming." She glanced down the hall toward Johnny's room. "Sal's already here. He took Clumsy out for a walk, but Johnny's in his room. You all can go on back if you like."

"Thanks, Stella, we'll do that." Taking Mattie by the hand, Joe glanced at her. "Ready?"

She nodded.

"Good, come on, then. Boys, follow me." Joe led them down the hall and knocked gently on one of the end doors. "Johnny, it's me. Joe." He knocked gently again, glancing down at the boys.

The door was opened slowly and Mattie found herself staring at an identical version of Joe. Dressed in loose-fitting jeans and a short-sleeve polo-style shirt, he was the mirror image of Joe. Same hair. Same beautiful brown eyes. And same beautiful smile.

"Joey." Grinning, Johnny took a step forward and hugged his brother tightly. "I missed you."

"I missed you, too, bro. How you doing, Johnny?" Joe asked, hugging his brother back.

"Fine, Joey." Johnny drew back and looked at the boys curiously. "I'm fine. Are these your new friends, Joey? The ones you said you were bringing to see me?"

"Yep. This is Cody and this is Connor."

"We're twins," Cody said, taking a step forward and making Johnny grin.

"I'm a twin, too." Johnny glanced at his brother. "With Joey. He's my twin." He angled his body so he could stand right next to Joe, shoulder to shoulder. "See. We look alike."

Connor angled his body so he was standing right next to Cody. "And we're twins, too." He giggled. "Cody's my twin. And we look alike."

"Nice," Johnny said. "Two sets of twins."

"We brought our coloring books and our crayons," Connor said, showing them to Johnny, whose face brightened.

"I like to color," Johnny said. "And I have lots of crayons. The nurses put my pictures up on the walls so everyone could see them."

"Our ma does the same thing," Connor said. "But she puts them on the refrigerator."

"Could we color together sometime. Maybe?" Johnny asked hesitantly, making the boys grin.

"Sure," Cody said.

"We'd like that." Connor looked up at Johnny.

"Do you want to come in and see my room?" Johnny asked, stepping back to let them enter. "You can put your stuff on my bed if you want. I don't mind."

Joe entered first, followed by Mattie and the boys, who grew wide-eyed when they saw Johnny's room. It was almost as large and spacious as the whole downstairs of their little house.

"Your room is so cool," Cody said with a roll of his eyes. He dumped everything in his arms on the bed, brownies forgotten as he glanced around. "Ma, look at all these model cars."

"Don't touch, Cody, " Mattie cautioned as Cody began to roam the large room, looking at all the toys, games and books on display on open shelves.

"It's okay," Johnny said. "He could touch. I don't mind. I like model cars," he told Cody, getting one down off the shelf and handing it to the young boy. "And my brothers sometimes bring me new ones." He pointed to a shelf that was only half-full. "This is the new shelf. It's for all the new model cars." He grinned. "I still have lots of room for more."

"Cool." Awed, Cody fingered the model car and stared at everything in fascination, trying to take it all in. Johnny's room was better than a toy store.

Johnny smiled at Mattie. "You're pretty," he said.

"Johnny, you've still got great taste," Joe said with a laugh, patting his brother on the back. "This is my friend Mattie. Mattie, this is my twin brother, Johnny."

"Hi, Johnny." Mattie held out her hand to him and Johnny took it, shaking it solemnly. "It's very nice to meet you."

"Hi, Mattie. Thank you for coming to see me today and for bringing me two new friends." He glanced at Cody and Connor with a smile. "I like new friends who like to color."

"You're welcome, Johnny. Thank you for inviting us."

"You're Joe's special friend, aren't you?" Johnny asked with a smile. "The one he always talks about." Joe flushed crimson as Johnny leaned forward to whisper to her. "He thinks I don't remember, and sometimes I don't remember so good. But I remember he likes you and likes to talk about you." There was a gleam in Johnny's eye and Mattie couldn't help it, she laughed, realizing that Johnny had the same sense of humor as Joe as well. "A lot," Johnny said with a roll of his eyes that reminded her of her boys. "He said you were real pretty and you are. Right, Joey?" he asked with a mischievous grin that reminded Mattie so much of Joe she couldn't believe it.

"Thanks, bro," Joe said, giving Mattie a sheepish shrug.

"You're welcome," Johnny said, his eyes twinkling in amusement.

"Johnny, are those real baseballs?" Connor was standing

by one wall shelf, pointing where several glass display cases protected baseballs.

"Yes." He moved over to where Connor was standing. "Those are real autographed baseballs. My dad and brothers bought them for me."

"No kidding?" Eyes wide, Cody and Connor stared at the displays in awe.

"I wouldn't kid you," Johnny said solemnly. "Here, you can look at them." He reached up and removed the glass case on one of the balls, then handed it to Cody.

"Be careful, Cody," Mattie cautioned. "Don't drop it."

"It's okay if he does," Johnny said with a smile. "I sometimes drop it."

He reached up and removed another ball for Connor, then handed it to him. "This ball is from the Chicago Cubs." He grinned. "From the 1969 pennant race. My dad bought it for me."

"Wow." Connor's eyes rounded as he read the signatures on the ball.

"And the one you have, Cody," Johnny said, surprising the boys by remembering who was who, since no one else ever did, "has Babe Ruth's signature. He was a real good baseball player a long, long time ago. Before even I was born. My brother Joey bought that for me." Johnny scratched his head. "But I can't remember when." He looked at Joe, then shrugged.

"Don't look at me," Joe said with a laugh. "I can't remember, either."

"We love baseball," Cody said, examining the ball carefully.

"Me too," Johnny said.

"Maybe later we could play baseball together," Connor said hopefully.

"Yes." Johnny beamed. "I would like to play baseball with my new friends."

"But I can't run so fast," Connor admitted, glancing down at the baseball he still held in his hand.

Johnny laughed. "Neither can I, Connor. So maybe we could not run so fast together."

"Johnny, this mutt is a menace. He fell or slid or tripped into every patch of mud, sticks and stones and debris he could find. Then he fell all over himself in his excitement." Laughing, Sal Marino pushed open the door with his elbow, then stopped when he realized Johnny had more company.

"Sal, Clumsy always trips and falls." Johnny said with a grin. "Like me sometimes. That's why I named him Clumsy."

"Yeah, it was a good choice." Carrying Clumsy in his arms, Sal pushed the door open farther, stepped into the room and grinned at everyone.

"Well, hi there," he said to the boys. "I'm Sal, Joe's brother." Sal set Clumsy down and the dog immediately tripped over his own feet and slid across the room as he tried to make a beeline for the boys, sniffing and jumping on them, making them giggle. "This is Clumsy, Johnny's dog."

"I'm Cody."

"I'm Connor." Both boys bent over to play with the dog.

"He likes you," Johnny said to the boys. "He won't bite even if he jumps a lot. Do you want to go outside and play with Clumsy? He likes to play outside."

"Can we, Ma?" Both boys implored. Mattie nodded her head, unable to speak. She was still standing there staring at Sal in speechless surprise, her mouth hanging open like a gaping guppy. Again.

She'd had the same reaction the first time she'd laid eyes on Joe, she remembered, but this was different.

"We'll behave and listen to Johnny," Cody assured her, wondering why his ma had a funny look on her face.

"It's fine." Joe said to Johnny. "Just keep an eye on them."

"I will, Joey." Johnny looked at the puppy. "Come on, Clumsy, let's go outside and play with our new friends." Waiting for Clumsy to follow—after he'd given Mattie a thorough sniffing—Johnny and the boys trooped out the door, holding hands, while Clumsy slipped and slid behind them, occasionally adding a bark or two. "Maybe later we can watch a movie…" Johnny's voice trailed softly down the hallway.

"Uh, Mattie?" Joe said, trying not to grin as he gave her a gentle poke with his elbow. "You all right?"

"All right?" she repeated numbly, realizing she was still just standing here staring at Sal Marino with her mouth hanging open like a twitless teenager.

"Yeah, are you all right?" Joe asked again, giving her another gentle poke. "Because I want you to meet my brother Sal."

With a smile, Sal extended his hand toward her. "Hi, Mattie. It's nice to meet you. I've heard quite a lot about you."

"And I've heard a lot about you," she managed to say once she found her voice.

"Ah, so my brother's been telling tales from our illustrious youth again, right?"

"Something like that," she said, somehow managing a smile for him.

Amused, Sal reached up and scratched his forehead. "But I gather from the look on your face, he apparently didn't tell you…uh…everything?"

"Uh, no. Apparently he forgot to mention a few things." Mattie glared at Joe.

"What? What?" Joe said innocently, and Mattie couldn't help it, she gave him a whack on the arm.

"What? *What!*" She whacked his arm again. "Don't act innocent. You told me just about everything about Sal and your family, but you didn't think it was important to tell me your gorgeous brother Sal, the Marino family heartthrob, was a *priest?*"

"Mattie, come on, you still can't be ticked about Sal?" With her hand tucked in his, Joe and Mattie walked around the expansive grounds of the home.

Dusk was just settling in, dinner was over, several innings of baseball had been played, and now, Johnny, Cody and Connor, along with Clumsy, were in Johnny's room watching a movie. Stella had made them some popcorn right before Gina and her brood had to leave, so the boys were quite content to have Johnny all to themselves again.

With a laugh, Mattie shook her head. "I'd say stunned would be more like it." She glanced at Joe. "You really didn't think it was important to tell me Sal was a priest?"

Joe shrugged his shoulders. "Not unless you were having erotic fantasies about him." He turned to her, amusement shimmering in his eyes. "You weren't, were you?"

Laughing, she tried not to blush. "You loved this, didn't you? Simply loved seeing me almost drop my teeth when I laid eyes on Sal."

"Well, you have to admit, it was pretty funny." Joe bent and picked up a stick, then sent it sailing into a bank of trees that surrounded the grounds.

"Joe?"

"Hmm?"

"Why…why didn't you tell me about Johnny before today?" she asked softly, trying not to let it hurt, but on some level it did.

Joe shrugged. "I don't know," he hedged.

"Did you think I wouldn't understand or be able to accept him?" The mere thought made her heart ache. That he might think so little of her, even after all this time.

Stunned, Joe came to a stop, then turned to stare into her eyes. "Mattie, I swear, that never crossed my mind." He laid his hands on her shoulders, enjoying the feel of her. He hadn't touched her all day, not since he'd kissed her when he arrived at her door, not since their drive up, and he was feeling a bit deprived, needing her touch. "Truly."

Laying her hands to his chest, Mattie studied his face carefully. "Joe, is this the reason you said you never wanted to get married, never wanted a family of your own? Because of Johnny?" she asked softly.

He was quiet for a long moment, taking her hand and walking toward the bank of trees that surrounded the grounds. Finally, he sighed deeply, then turned to her.

"Yeah." He hesitated. "And his circumstances, of course." He hesitated again. "You know how I feel about family?"

"Of course, Joe." It was one of the things she admired so much about him.

"Well, I'd never walk away from my responsibilities. Not ever. I made a promise to my father on his deathbed, Mattie, and that's something I take very seriously." He hesitated, then went on. "If it wasn't for me, Johnny wouldn't have had that accident." The guilt had always felt like a lead weight on his chest, his shoulders.

"Oh, Joe, you can't believe that."

"Of course I do, because it's true. If I hadn't suggested we race to the park that day, Johnny would never have had that accident." He'd replayed that day over and over in his mind for years, desperately wanting to change the outcome. "From the day it happened, I knew that no matter what, I'd always take care of him." He looked at her. "Always. No matter what." He hesitated for a moment, a shadow passing over his eyes. "I was engaged once, I think I told you that."

She nodded. "But you said you realized you were making a mistake and broke it off."

"Well, that's not quite the truth. Or the whole truth." Blowing out a breath, Joe glanced around, then took Mattie's hand and pulled her over to a concrete bench that bordered the lavish lawn. "Have a seat." She did, and pulled him down next to her. He draped his arm around her and drew her close.

"I met Gloria when she was living in Healing Harbor, attending university. I was a lot younger and it was all heat and fire at first," he admitted with a sad smile. "We thought we were in love. I asked her to marry me and she said yes." Joe glanced off into the distance. "She knew about my family, of course, and about Johnny, but to tell you the truth, she wasn't very comfortable around him."

"Why?" Mattie asked in genuine surprise.

He smiled sadly, bringing his gaze back to hers. "I guess she'd never been around anyone like him, and claimed she didn't know how to act. I brought her out here a few times, but to tell you the truth, being here made her visibly uncomfortable. I actually think she was afraid of Johnny, although I can't possibly imagine why. Anyway, she was also so weird around Johnny that it made him uncomfortable and very self-conscious. He's not an idiot, Mattie, he can see and hear fine, and he still has feelings."

"Oh, Joe." Her heart melting and aching, Mattie reached for his hand, brought it to her lips for a kiss of comfort, then held it tight. "Of course Johnny's not an idiot. That word would be reserved for your former fiancée." Wanting to soothe, to comfort him, Mattie kissed his hand again, wishing she could do more. "That must have been terribly difficult for you."

"Yeah, it was. At first I thought she was just uncomfortable with Johnny, and that was bad enough, since I had no clue what I was going to do about it. But soon it became very clear that she resented the time and attention I gave to him." He sighed, clinging tighter to her hand. "Anyway, Gloria finally told me that since she was going to be my wife, my first responsibility was to her, not to Johnny."

"I'm so sorry." She would never understand such desperately deliberate cruelty. She would give anything to erase the pain and anguish in his eyes, on his face.

"Yeah, well, so was I, especially when she went on to tell me that she thought it was time I 'cut the apron strings' with Johnny and move back to the city with her. She'd just gotten her degree and wanted to pursue a career in the city, where she'd have more opportunities, at least more than she'd have here." He glanced at Mattie, then shrugged.

"I realized then this was a marriage that just wasn't going to work. It simply wasn't fair of me to expect Gloria to make all the sacrifices. Staying in Healing Harbor, having me put Johnny first. It just wasn't fair to her. I guess I was being selfish and I realized it then."

She couldn't believe what he was saying, it was so not Joe. Clearly he was reciting what his former fiancée had told him, believing it to be fact.

"Marriage isn't about what's fair, Joe, but about what works best for both people, as a couple. That's where compromise comes in. If she loved you, truly loved you, these things wouldn't have been sacrifices but simply accommoda-

tions and acceptance of what she needed to do to be with the
man she loved. That should have been more important to her
than anything else. Just being with you.''

"Should have been, but it wasn't. She couldn't get past the
fact that I wouldn't leave Johnny. Gave me an ultimatum.''

"Her or Johnny?'' Mattie guessed correctly, and he nodded.

"That's about it. She told me that I had no right to expect
her to live in this one-horse town, as she put it, wasting away,
nor did she think it was fair of me to put Johnny's needs ahead
of her desires.''

"Selfish brat,'' Mattie muttered, making him laugh.

"No, Mattie, I've got to tell you, I could see her point and
really couldn't blame her. She was right on a lot of issues. My
wife—any woman—should expect to come first in her husband's life. I knew that I would never be able to do that, put
a woman ahead of my brother and my responsibilities.''

"So that's why you said you'd never marry?'' Mattie said
softly, finally understanding Joe's declaration. His desire not
to marry had nothing to do with his being selfish, but more to
do with his desire to take care of Johnny.

"Yep, that's when I realized that I couldn't in all good
conscience ever get married, knowing it wouldn't be fair to
any woman.''

"But Joe,'' Mattie protested, wondering why his words
made her heart ache so. "Not all women would feel the way
Gloria did. And if a couple is truly in love, they both make
sacrifices, compromises that they can both live with. You don't
just issue declarations or ultimatums. Now *that's* selfish.''

His smile was wan when he turned to her. "Love conquers
all? You can't honestly still believe that.''

"Yes,'' she said firmly. "I do.'' And she did, had for as
long as she could remember. But the key was to have the love
in the first place, something she'd never had with Gary.

"I wish I could believe it, Mattie.''

"But you don't,'' she said, knowing his answer was going
to hurt, and knowing, too, there was no way to stop it.

"Mattie, can you honestly say that a woman shouldn't have
the right to feel that she comes first in her husband's life?''

He had her there, and she struggled to find the right words to explain to him how wrong he was.

"Mattie," he went on before she could come up with a response. "My responsibilities to my family are mine, not someone else's. Especially a woman's."

"But—"

"No, let me finish. Any woman I married would rightfully expect to come first in my life, before my family." He blew out a breath, weary now after the emotions of the long day. "But that's not possible, Mattie, not for me. I knew full well what I was promising my father, and it's not something I resent, but something I feel honored to be able to do."

"But Joe—"

"So that's why I will never get married, Mattie, or have a family of my own." Pain and sadness radiated from him. "It wouldn't be fair, nor would it be fair to ask a woman to share this responsibility with me, because that would only lead to resentment in the long run, like with Gloria. So, rather than hurt someone else, or get hurt myself, I decided that it's best that I never marry." His gaze met hers, his eyes dark and very determined. "And it's not something I ever expect to change my mind about."

Mattie merely stared at him in the darkness, her heart aching in a way that left her wanting to weep.

For herself. And for Joe.

He'd never lied to her, she realized. He'd told her from the beginning that he never wanted to get married. The reasons didn't change the reality.

So why did the knowledge ache so much? she wondered, blinking back tears as she glanced into the darkness.

And in that instant, the answer was clear, and devastating. The knowledge hurt so very much because until today, until this moment, she hadn't realized she'd done the unthinkable.

She'd fallen hopelessly, helplessly…in love with Joe.

She'd fallen in love with another man who didn't want a wife or a family—no matter what the reasons—the reality didn't change. She'd made the same mistake once again.

Looking at Joe now, his beautiful features shadowed in the

moonlight, Mattie felt an ache deep in her battered, scarred heart. And she knew she couldn't let things go on like this; she couldn't continue to allow Joe access in her life, because she'd simply get more and more attached to him, emotionally and every other way. And what was the point? He'd already told her, he'd never marry. Not her. Not anyone.

So even if she loved him, loved him in a way she had never loved anyone else, it didn't make any difference. She had no hope for a future with him. None. He'd made that clear.

So she had no choice but to put some distance between them. The thought brought more tears to her eyes, but she knew for everyone's sake, it was the only sensible thing to do.

Chapter Nine

She'd been avoiding him.

It had been ten days since Joe had taken Mattie and the boys to dinner with his family, ten days since he'd introduced them to Johnny, and since then, Mattie had been deliberately...avoiding him.

Oh, it had been nothing overt, or rude, nothing he could call her on, but he *knew* it, just as he knew instinctively that something had changed in her and their relationship.

And it was hard, real hard not to imagine the worst.

Mattie still attended daily baseball practice, she just didn't bother to make a point of talking to him—before or after—practice. She'd turned down his offer to go out for pizza after one practice, citing the fact that she had to help the boys study their lines for the end-of-year school play.

He'd even stopped in the gallery a few times, hoping to catch a few free moments alone with her, but each time he'd stopped by, she'd been supposedly too busy to talk. And if she wasn't busy when he arrived, she made sure she became busy. Very busy while he was there.

While she was polite, helpful and all the other things she'd always been, it was clear something had changed between them.

And Joe couldn't help but feel hurt. Desperately, deeply hurt. He had no idea what had happened, but he didn't want to believe or conceive that, like Gloria, Mattie had found herself uncomfortable with his family situation, including Johnny, and had decided to just keep him at arm's length.

On this Monday morning, as he poured himself his first cup of coffee, frustration had him in a foul mood, something that rarely happened to him. Easygoing was his middle name, but in the past ten days he'd found that his heart ached in a way it hadn't for a long, long time. The heart he'd vowed to always protect.

Some job he'd done, he thought with disgust. If he didn't know better, he'd swear he'd fallen in love with Mattie. And of course with her boys as well. But he couldn't really have been that foolish, he kept telling himself, knowing how dangerous that could be. He simply couldn't have been that foolish.

Still, he found himself daydreaming about what it would be like to be married to Mattie, to be able to call Cody and Connor his own. He wondered what it would be like to have a child with Mattie, a girl maybe, just to round things out.

He'd also found himself daydreaming about making love to her, daydreams that were now particularly torturous, knowing she was deliberately trying to put distance between them.

He hadn't touched her, kissed her, since that beautiful Sunday when they'd last spent the day together, and he found himself going through something akin to withdrawal. His body ached, longed for her. His hands itched to touch her, stroke her, to hold her hand or touch her cheek. But he hadn't so much as brushed against her, not in ten days. And it was killing him.

Worse, he had no idea what was going on, and if the truth be told, he was almost afraid to ask, fearing he'd hear something he didn't want to hear. Not from Mattie.

But Joe realized without any other explanation, based simply on his own observations and experience with her the past ten days, he had no choice but to believe the worst.

And it almost broke his heart.

This morning, early as it was, he resolved to finish the paperwork he'd put off on Friday. The weather had stayed warm throughout the second, and now this third, week of May, hovering in the mid eighties. Everyone, including him, had a very bad case of spring fever and very little ambition.

Sipping his coffee, Joe sat down behind his desk, prepared to put Mattie out of his mind as he dug into the first of several stacks of reports he had yet to complete. When the phone rang, he was busily filling out an expense report that had to go to the town council for approval.

"Sheriff's office," he said absently, "Marino speaking."

"Coach Joe?"

He frowned. "Connor?"

"No, it's Cody."

Surprised, Joe glanced at the clock on his desk. It was barely 7:00 a.m. "Cody, where are you?"

"On a chair."

"What?" Frowning, Joe rubbed his stubbled chin. It was too early for him to solve riddles. "Cody, where's your mom? And what are you doing on a chair?"

"In bed," Cody said. "My mom's in bed, Coach Joe. And me and Connor, we think something's wrong with her. She always gets us up for school and makes our breakfast and lunch. But we can't get her up. We can't get her up, Coach Joe. She's still sleeping, and me and Connor are gonna be late for school." He could hear the tears trembling in the boy's voice and that, more than anything, had panic settling in.

Joe shot to his feet so quickly he knocked his chair over backward. He couldn't even imagine Mattie not being up to care for the boys unless something was desperately wrong with her.

His heart jumped in his chest and his hands grew clammy, but he knew he couldn't let Cody know he was concerned. He didn't want to scare the boy any further.

"Cody, listen to me very, very carefully. Okay, son?"

"'Kay."

"Where are you. Exactly?"

"On a chair."

Joe's eyes slid closed. He'd forgotten that kids took things literally. "On a chair," he repeated. "Okay, I got that. Why are you on a chair? And where's the chair at?"

"I couldn't reach the phone, so Connor and I pushed a kitchen chair over to the phone and I climbed on it. Then I called you."

"That was a very smart thing to do, Cody. So you're in the kitchen, right?"

"Right."

"Now, is your aunt Maureen home?"

"Nah, I heard her tell my ma that she had to go to another town or something. She won't be back until Sunday."

Joe was already searching his desk for his car keys. "Okay, Cody, listen to me. I want you to do everything I tell you, exactly as I tell you, okay?"

"'Kay."

"First, I want you to hang up the phone. Wait—Cody, not yet. Don't hang up on me yet. Wait until I'm done. I'll tell you when."

"'Kay."

"After you hang up the phone—"

"When you tell me, right?" Cody asked with a sniffle.

"Right. After you hang up the phone, I want you to very, very carefully and very slowly climb down off that chair. Do you understand me?" Visions of Cody falling backward off the chair and tumbling headfirst to the floor nearly made Joe's legs buckle. He couldn't bear the thought of anything happening to those boys. Not now. Not ever.

"Yeah, I understand."

"Then I want you and Connor to go sit on the chairs in the living room and watch out the front window for me. When you see me pull up, and only me, Cody, no one else, I want you to go to the front door and unlock it. Do you understand?"

"Yep."

"Now, Cody, do *not* open the door for anyone else, and

don't let anyone else into the house except me. Do you understand?''

''Yep. Are you gonna help my ma?''

''Yes, son, I promise. I'm on my way right now. Now you can hang up the phone, Cody, and remember what I said, carefully and slowly get down from the chair, then you and Connor go sit in the chairs in the living-room and watch for me.''

'''Kay. Goodbye.''

Joe dropped the receiver back onto the cradle, dug his keys out of the mess on his desk and called to Clarence. ''I've got an emergency, Clarence. Can you keep a handle on things here for a while?''

''Will do, Sheriff. Need any help?''

''Not that I know of,'' he called, already heading out the door. ''I'll check in with you later. Just call my cell phone if you need me.''

''Will do.''

Someone had stuffed lead weights inside her head, Mattie was almost certain of it. Why else would her head be throbbing so violently? And if that wasn't enough, someone had set those lead weights to clanging, because she could hear them ringing, echoing loudly in her ears.

Trying to stop the cacophony in her head, Mattie tried to turn over, and groaned when her body responded by sending a river of aches and pains up and down every joint and nerve ending.

''Is our ma going to die?'' Connor whispered, his lower lip trembling in fear.

''No, son, she's not.'' Standing in the doorway, Joe kept an eagle eye on Mattie—who'd finally begun stirring, much to his relief—and draped one arm around each of the boys. ''But she may feel like it. She's got the flu, boys. Just a very bad case of the flu. Remember I explained that to you the other day when I first got here?''

''I remember,'' Cody said. ''We sometimes get the flu, but Ma never gets sick. She's never been sick before.'' He glanced up at Joe, still a little scared. He'd never seen his mom in bed during the day before, and never for lots of days. "I didn't know moms could get sick. I thought it was a rule or something that they couldn't."

"Well, it probably should be a rule, Cody," Joe said with a smile. "But it's not."

"Connor?" Mattie's voice was barely a whisper. "Cody?" Her throat felt as if someone had been running a lit stick of dynamite up and down it. She tried to swallow, and found the motion had her moaning in pain. Pressing a hand to her throat, she desperately tried to sit up, while trying to keep the covers close because she was so cold.

"Ma?" Wide-eyed in fear, Connor took a step into the room, watching his mother shiver. "Are you awake?"

"Yeah, I think so." She hesitated, trying to get her bearings. She glanced down at herself, realizing she was wearing a short-sleeved cotton nightgown, which might account for why her arms were so cold. "Give me a minute and I'll get up and get you guys ready for school." She could do it, she was almost certain. All she had to do was manage to lift her head from the pillow, sit up, make her legs swing over the bed and then set her feet on the floor.

Cody giggled. "Ma, we don't gotta go to school until morning."

Mattie blinked, trying to focus. "Morning? It *is* morning." With some effort she turned her head, saw darkness shimmering beyond her bedroom drapes, and Joe and the boys standing in the doorway, watching her intently. "Where did the morning go?"

"Which one?" Joe asked with a smile as he moved into the room and gingerly sat down on the bed next to her. The rush of relief he'd felt when he'd realized she was finally awake made him realize he'd better sit down before he fell down.

He couldn't ever remember being this scared before, but then again, he'd never seen Mattie sick like this before.

And he was quite sure he never wanted to see her this sick again.

He felt her forehead. She was still warm, but nothing like

she'd been the past couple of days. The worst of it was finally over.

"Joe?" She blinked, wondering if he was a mirage, or a vision from one of her fantasies. She'd been thinking of him so much, dreaming about him so much, maybe he'd simply materialized out of her dreams. "W-what are you doing here?"

"Taking care of you and the boys," he said, plumping the pillow behind her head. When she looked at him wildly, he laughed, and drew the blanket up higher, tucking it under her chin. "You've got the flu—"

"I do not!" she protested vehemently, trying to lift her aching head again. With a moan, she gave up and simply lay still, moving nothing but her eyes, and even that was some effort. "I never get the flu," she insisted. "And I never get sick."

"Well, then, you've done a pretty good imitation the past few days." He lifted her hand, held it in his, feeling a rush of gratitude that she was finally up and able to talk.

"Who...who got the boys ready for school this morning?" If she lay still, and only moved her mouth and opened her eyes for a little bit of time, she could handle the pain and the clanging. She was almost sure of it.

"I did," Joe said, brushing her hair off her face with his hands. "This morning, yesterday morning and Monday morning."

"It is Monday morning," she whispered, blinking at him. "Isn't it?"

"Ma, it's Wednesday," Cody said with a laugh, moving closer to the bed. "Wednesday night. Coach Joe and us, we've been having a slumber party while you was sick. Coach Joe slept over. We watched movies together and he let us bring our pillows and blankets downstairs so we could sleep in front of the television."

"Tattletale," Joe said in amusement, swiping a finger down Cody's nose.

"And we had pizza for dinner, too," Connor added with a grin. "Twice. And Coach Joe, he let us stay up late. Real late," he added, making Joe wince. "Then he got us ready for school in the morning and even made us breakfast—well, cereal anyway, and then he took us to school, too.'' Connor rubbed his nose and inched closer to his mother, not so afraid, now that her eyes were open and she was talking again. ''We was only late once. Well,'' Connor added with a frown, ''twice if you count today.''

''Yeah,'' Cody said, bravely inching closer to the bed as well. ''And Coach Joe even helped us with our lines for the play. Now we remember them real good.''

''Wednesday.'' Wildly, Mattie looked at Joe, a million thoughts zooming through her aching head. ''It's *Wednesday?*''

''All day,'' Joe confirmed with a grin.

''Oh Lord,'' Mattie muttered, trying to gather enough strength to push the covers off so she could get out of bed. ''The gallery. I've got to get to the gallery. Aunt Maureen is in Milwaukee for the week and I promised—''

''You're not going anywhere but back to sleep, Mattie,'' Joe said, covering her hands with his and effectively stopping her struggle to get up. ''I've got everything covered, so relax.''

When she just lifted an eyebrow, he sighed, then went on, just to assure her that he indeed did have everything covered and she could relax and concentrate on getting well.

''The gallery is being handled. Since Annie's finished her last final, she's been covering your shift for you, going in every afternoon to relieve Colleen.'' He couldn't help but grin at the shock on Mattie's face. ''She's even sold a couple of pieces for you,'' he added. ''And my sister Sophie, the boys' kindergarten teacher, has taken over your stint at baseball practice, coming straight after school and bringing the boys with her. So you're covered there, too. And as for the boys, as you can tell by looking at them, they're none the worse for wear. As soon as Gina heard you were sick, she started sending over full-course meals for me and the boys.'' He straightened the edge of the blanket, needing something to do with his hands. She looked so fragile, pale and small, he just wanted to scoop her up in his arms and hold and protect her. Instead, he flashed her a smile. ''So you see, there's absolutely nothing for you to do. Or worry about,'' he said, giving her hands a gentle squeeze. "We've got everything under control, truly. So just lie back and relax until you feel better."

Bewildered, and more touched than she could ever remember, Mattie merely stared at him. "Why?" she whispered, blinking back tears. "Why on earth would your family do all that for me?"

"Why not?" he responded with a smile and a shrug. "I told you, Mattie, this is a small town. People help other people. Everyone's part of the community and we help one another out. And you know how my family is. You've met most of my sisters, and once they heard you were sick, they simply jumped in to help. It's really no big deal. You'd do the same for them, wouldn't you?"

"Of course." Sniffling, she blinked quickly to clear the tears from her eyes. "But it's a *very* big deal, Joe." Especially to someone who'd never been able to depend on anyone to help her do anything, not since she was eighteen. Especially not her husband or her in-laws. But Joe's family had pitched in and helped her, without thought or without looking for anything in return. "I...I don't know what to say."

"Thank you will suffice," he said, running a finger down her nose.

"Oh, Joe, thank you," she managed to whisper, reaching out a hand and laying it on his chest.

Her mind could barely function or comprehend that his entire family had pitched in to help her and her boys, taking care of her and her responsibilities without missing a beat.

She'd never experienced such overwhelming kindness or support before. Never. But now that she had, she realized just how wonderful it was to have a supportive, loving family, and she realized with a pang just how much she'd missed and how much her boys were going to miss by not having that family.

"You're welcome." He laid a hand to her cheek. It was flushed and still warm, but at least she wasn't burning up as she had been. "Your aunt called this morning."

"What did she say?"

"She said you're not to worry about anything. She and

Clancy will be back late Sunday, but if you need anything in the meantime to call her. She gave me the number of her hotel, but I told her we had things covered.''

"Clancy and Aunt Maureen are together?'' Mattie asked in surprise, remembering the pact she and Clancy had made.

"Apparently,'' Joe said with a grin, "although I don't think I'm old enough to want to know the details.'' He straightened her blanket. "Now, think you could handle a little something to eat?''

"We got some pepperoni pizza left, Ma,'' Cody offered, and Mattie almost turned green at the thought.

"I was thinking more along the lines of some soup,'' Joe said, trying not to grin. "Gina sent over some homemade chicken broth with baby pastina. Generations of Italian kids have grown up on it. It's guaranteed to make you feel better.''

"I…could try a…little,'' Mattie managed to say, putting a hand to her head, hoping to stop the pain. She wasn't hungry, but she was so weak, she knew if she didn't eat something, she wouldn't be able to get her strength back.

"Okay, boys. Let's go down and warm up some soup for your mother.'' Joe stood up. "I'll bring some aspirin up for you as well, Mattie. That should take care of the marching band in your head,'' he added with a smile.

"Have we been taking good care of you, Ma?'' Cody asked, hesitantly stepping closer to the bed.

With a weak smile, Mattie reached out to her sons. "Come here, guys.'' After glancing at Joe to see if it was okay, both boys moved closer to the bed. "You've been doing a wonderful job taking care of me. That's why I'm almost all better.'' She could see the fear shimmering in her sons' eyes, reminding her once again that she was their sole stability and security. A wave of guilt rolled over her for scaring them. "I'm sorry if I scared you.''

"We wasn't scared,'' Cody fibbed. "Coach Joe was here and he said you'd be okay 'cuz we was all gonna take real good care of you.''

"He did, did he?'' Mattie managed a smile for Joe. "Well, he was right. Her lids were getting heavy again and the clanging was starting to get louder, but she didn't want her sons to know that. "I should be up and about in another day or so."

Joe just lifted his eyebrows, and then smiled, realizing she was merely trying to soothe the boys.

Sensing Mattie had expended what little energy she had, Joe motioned the twins toward the door. "All right, guys, let's go down and let your mom rest until her food's ready." Joe leaned over and kissed Mattie on the cheek. She clutched a hand on his shirt, wanting to feel him close if only for just a minute. "We'll be back in a few," he said, giving her another quick kiss before leading the boys out the door and down the stairs.

With a sniffle, Mattie turned her head into the pillow and let the tears come, feeling sorry for herself. Everything ached, but especially her heart. Seeing Joe again was just a reminder of how much she loved him. But it didn't matter, she realized. He would simply never allow himself to love her in return.

Joe overslept Thursday morning. And then again on Friday. After pulling on a pair of ragged jeans and barely taking time to zip them all the way, he raced around barefoot and shirtless getting the boys up, dressed, fed and out the door to the school bus so they wouldn't be late, feeling more like one of the Keystone Kops every minute.

Since this was the last Friday of school before the last week of school, the boys only had half a day. Gina was picking them up and taking them to her house for a celebratory sleepover with her own kids.

He'd gotten Mattie to agree to it simply because he'd convinced her it would be good for the boys—which was true. He couldn't believe how excited they'd been, whispering and talking excitedly into the night, keeping him up—hence he didn't hear the alarm and woke up half an hour later than he should have.

Plus, he'd told Mattie she really needed to rest for another day. Although she was better yesterday, and had even managed to sit up and get up for a little while, he still wasn't confident she was completely well.

So tonight would be a well-deserved night off for both of them.

Standing at the window in the living room, watching the boys wave goodbye, Joe dragged a hand through his hair and turned to scowl at the mess in Mattie's living room. He'd seen disaster areas that looked better.

The boys' sleeping bags and blankets—from their impromptu slumber party the past few days—were strewn all over the previously immaculate living room. An empty pizza container, several empty bowls with remnants of popcorn and an assortment of candy wrappers decorated the tabletops.

Pillows, sheets and blankets were strewn from one end of the living room to the other.

He knew he was going to have to tackle this mess before Mattie saw it, but right now he needed some coffee, and he needed to go check on her.

He went into the kitchen and poured them both a cup of fresh coffee, setting them on a tray he'd found stashed in one of the overhead cabinets.

Whistling softly he headed up to her room, realizing with a jolt this is what his life would be like if he and Mattie were…married. Quickly, he shook the thought away, knowing he couldn't even allow himself to let his thoughts go in that direction. No point to it.

Her door was open so he could hear her during the night in case she needed anything. She was still sleeping, her face in such quiet repose, he merely stood there for a moment, staring at her in silence, his heart aching with love.

She was so beautiful, he thought. Just so beautiful. Inside and out. And she deserved all the wonderful things that a woman like her needed and wanted. All the things a man like him could never hope to offer.

Shaking his thoughts away, Joe quietly walked into the room, setting the tray on the nightstand.

"Joe?" Mattie's voice was whisper soft as her eyes fluttered open slowly, bringing him into full view. There was something so gentle, so tender in his face, she found her throat closing up.

Then she shifted her gaze and almost goggled.

Dressed, Joe was a mighty fine sight to behold.

Half-naked, he was more than enough to set a woman's heart and hormones racing, sick with the flu or not.

He had on a pair of jeans.

And nothing else.

His feet were bare, as was his chest, and the sight of it— all burnished gold and copper covering bare, chiseled muscles, had her mouth going dry and her hands itching to reach out and touch him.

Sick or not, she wasn't dead or blind, and the sight of the man she loved, barely dressed, and looking so dangerously sexy, had Mattie's muddled mind clearing quickly as every fantasy she'd ever had about him vividly sprang to life.

"Oh my," was all she managed to whisper, lifting a hand to her suddenly dry throat. Need, desire and lust—plain and pure—grabbed at her and hung on, nearly made her moan with wanting. She couldn't ever remember wanting a man with the intensity she wanted Joe.

Nor could she ever remember *feeling* this strongly for someone. The needing and the wanting, coupled with the desire and her own feelings for him, left her weak and dizzy, and the feelings had nothing to do with her illness and everything to do with her heart.

The sight of all that beautiful golden burnished skin made her hands itch to touch him, to feel his skin warm from the heat of hers, to have her own skin pressed against his, feeling his heart beat in time against hers.

She was delirious, she mused. Had to be. Why else would she be sitting here gaping at the man, with these dangerously erotic thoughts parading through her mind?

But what a man, she thought with a sigh.

"I brought you some coffee."

The scent of fresh-brewed coffee filled the room and Mattie almost swooned, not certain if it was from the coffee or the sight of him.

"My hero," she said, reaching out a shaky hand for a cup

and taking a sip. She couldn't take her eyes off Joe. Or his body. "Did the boys get off to school all right?"

He nodded. "They got off just fine." Apparently unaware of her stare, or the impact he was having on her, he picked up his own cup, took a sip, then gingerly sat on the bed next to her, letting his gaze take her in. "How you feeling this morning?" She wasn't quite as pale as she'd been yesterday or the day before that. There was finally some color back in her cheeks, although she was still looking far too weak for his peace of mind.

"Better," she said, taking another sip of coffee and letting her eyes slide closed in pleasure as the caffeine poured into her empty system. With him sitting so close, if she didn't close her eyes, weak or not, she just might...jump him. "Much better," she managed to get out.

"Well, I've got some aspirin on the table here somewhere, just in case you need them." She'd still had that horrible headache for most of the day yesterday.

She managed a smile for him. "I don't think I'll need them today." No, what she needed didn't come in a bottle or in pill form. What she needed was *him*. All of him. Mind. Body. Heart. "I really do feel much better."

"Yeah, well, you might change your mind when you see the...downstairs." Dragging a hand through his hair, he gave her a weary smile. "The boys and I, well, we aren't exactly what you'd call...neat freaks."

She actually found the strength to laugh. "Now, why doesn't that surprise me?" she asked with a grin. "It doesn't matter, Joe. I'm just so grateful for everything you've done, I don't even know how to begin to thank you."

Feeling ashamed for the way she'd treated him recently deliberately keeping him at a distance—Mattie realized she had no idea what she would have done without him the past few days.

"Grateful?" Joe repeated with a lift of his eyebrow, feeling slightly affronted. He was quite sure grateful was not at all what he'd hoped Mattie felt for him. "Gratitude is not necessary, Mattie," he said a bit stiffly.

"Perhaps not, but I feel it nonetheless. I don't know what I would have done without you the past week, Joe. And that's the truth."

"I'm just glad you're feeling better."

"I am, a lot better."

"That doesn't mean you're well, Mattie. Far from it. You're still going to need a few days to get your full strength back."

Mattie sighed, knowing he was right. "Well, Joe, well or not, I want to take a shower."

They'd had this conversation yesterday morning as well. Fortunately, the moment she'd tried to get out of bed, she realized he'd been right; she hadn't been quite strong enough yet.

"You're not strong enough to take a shower by yourself," he repeated, just as he had yesterday. He had visions of her collapsing in the shower, hitting her head on the tile, slipping on the wet floor.

The mere thought was enough to send him into a panic again.

"Joe, I *need* a shower, and unless you want to come in and hold my hand, I don't have a choice but to take a shower by myself."

He grinned at her. "Take a shower with you?" He wiggled his eyebrows as he took another sip of coffee, contemplating. "Now, why didn't I think of that? If that's an invitation, I accept."

Laughing, Mattie shook her head, more than seriously tempted. But this wasn't the right time. "You'll have to settle for a rain check, I'm afraid. I'm not sure after being sick for four days even *I* want to be in the shower with me."

"Mattie, really, your shower can wait until you're feeling a little stronger. I don't think you should push—"

"I want to kiss you, Joe," she said simply, shocking him into silence "And I can't and won't do that until I've taken a shower and cleaned up a bit."

He merely blinked at her and she almost laughed at the confusion and shock on his face.

"You...you want to kiss me?" he repeated as if he couldn't

quite believe he heard her right. First she avoided him, now she wanted to kiss him?

Maybe he was the one who was delirious.

Mattie laughed. "Yes," she murmured with a smile. "Among other…things." Not having him in her life the past ten days had made her realize how much she'd come to depend on him, to need him, to want him. And it had taught her how much she missed him.

She'd seen what her life would be like if he wasn't in it, and she didn't like it. At all.

If this was all she could have of him, well, then, she'd rather have this than nothing. It was certainly far more than she'd ever had before.

"You're serious, aren't you?" he asked, and she slowly nodded her head, a sly, sexy smile on her face. More than a bit flustered, Joe set his coffee cup down. "Well then, by all means, let me help you up so you can take a shower." Joe pulled back her covers and scooped her up in his arms, grateful to just be able to touch her again.

"Joe," she laughed, wrapping her arms around his neck and hanging on. His masculine scent lingered on his bare skin, teasing her, tempting her. "You don't have to carry me."

Unable to resist, she pressed a kiss to the curve of his jaw and saw him swallow. Hard. Intrigued, she pressed more kisses along his jawline, murmuring softly as she stroked a hand over his bare chest, letting her finger encircle his nipple, nearly buried in the whorls of dark hair on his chest.

"I can walk, Joe, honestly," she murmured, still stroking him with her hand and letting her lips trail down his neck, gently lapping at the skin with her tongue. She loved the taste of him, she thought as she felt a shudder race through him.

"No, no, it's all right." His steps faltered. He could feel the warmth of her body, the curve of her breasts pressing against his bare chest through the thin cotton of her gown, and it was driving him mad. "I…don't mind…" He had to swallow. Again. "Carrying you," he finally managed to get out.

"Well, good, then, because I like being in your arms," she admitted in a soft whisper. Her warm breath fluttered softly against his jaw, his chin, his mouth, and it was all he could do not to crush her to him and take her. But she was right; this wasn't the time.

She was weak and worn down, and he was feeling far too needy.

His heart was pounding, his body was aching, hardening in a way that was wreaking havoc with his self-imposed control, leaving him feeling weak.

He'd kept a tight rein of control over himself, knowing how scared and distrustful Mattie was with men. He never wanted to do anything that would scare or spook her, especially now, when he felt he was finally making some progress in the trust department. Well, he thought he'd *been* making some progress, at least until she'd started avoiding him.

It was a good thing they'd reached the bathroom. He wasn't certain how long he could last.

"I'm going to set you down, Mattie. You sit while I start your shower and let it get warm. I'll get you some fresh towels."

"Fine," she said as he set her down, reaching over to close the cover on the commode. She sat, watching him. If she didn't know better, she'd swear he was…flustered. For some reason, the thought amused her. Gorgeous Joe flustered by a few kisses and caresses. His reaction was both endearing and amusing.

Patiently, she sat while he turned on the shower, tested it with his hand, then headed out to the hall linen closet to get some fresh towels.

When he returned, carrying several large fluffy towels, he set them on top of the tank, then held out a hand to help her up. "I think the water should be ready about now."

"Good." She kept her gaze on his as she slowly reached down and lifted the hem of her cotton gown, slipping it over her head. It was the most brazen act she'd ever done, and surprisingly, she didn't feel the least bit nervous or self-conscious.

When his mouth dropped open and his eyes all but bugged out of his head at the sight of her naked body, she simply felt…wonderful. And giddy. And incredibly, wonderfully lovely.

"Uh…Mattie."

"Yes, Joe," she said with a smile, taking her time folding her cotton gown.

"You're…you're…uh…naked." The words came out a strangled moan.

"Mmm, yes, I know."

"Mattie."

"Yes, Joe." Smiling at him, she found she was enjoying this. This was just the tonic she needed, and was far better than aspirin or any other medicine to make her feel better.

"Get in the shower," he ordered, his voice harsh and deep. He closed his eyes and clenched his fists tightly together, fearing if he didn't, he'd do something rash. Like grab her and take her. Here and now. Need for her was building with the intensity of a volcano, and any minute he feared it just might…blow.

"Please, Mattie," he all but whimpered, sliding the shower door open so hard it bounced against the wall and came sliding back.

"Okay, Joe." Still smiling, she held out her hand to him. She could see the dark dash of desire in his eyes, in his body, and it made her feel sexier and more feminine than she ever had in her life. But then again, she reasoned, she'd never felt so bold or so brazen with a man before. Not ever. But something about Joe brought out all the feelings, physical feelings that she'd always just assumed she'd been lacking. Now she knew differently.

He took her hand, helping her step over the tub and into the shower. "Thanks," she said with one of those wonderfully sexy female smiles that had his eyes darkening even more.

He had to clear his throat. "You're…welcome," he managed to get out. "I'll wait right here until you're done. So, if you start feeling weak or anything, just call me."

"I will." Mattie stepped into the spray of warm water and let out a heartfelt sigh. It felt heavenly. Closing her eyes, she turned, and tipped her head back, letting the warm water slide through and over her head, her hair, and then run down her back.

The moment the door closed, and he knew she was safely in the shower, Joe sank back against the wall, desperately needing something to hold him up.

His legs were weak, his body shaky. If she was trying to drive him crazy, she was doing a very good job of it.

How on earth was he supposed to keep himself under control when she looked at him with those damn sexy eyes?

Or when she dropped all her defenses, along with her clothes, and stood before him naked and vulnerable. And oh so trusting.

He supposed that's what got to him more than anything, humbling him. She trusted him. She had to or she would never have stood naked in front of him.

The thought that Mattie had given *him* her trust made him want to do everything possible, everything in his power, never, ever to abuse that trust.

He wanted her, yes. And if he wasn't mistaken, she wanted him as well. But Mattie wasn't the type of woman to go in for one-night stands, any more than he was the kind of man who was interested in something like that, either.

It simply wasn't his style.

But there was no reason that they couldn't…want each other, and make love with each other, knowing that they had mutual respect, caring, kindness and love.

Love.

There it was, he realized, the crux of his problem. All along he had known that Mattie was different, known too that he had to be particularly careful with her and her feelings. Getting her to trust him had taken Herculean effort, and while he had been trying so hard to get her to trust him, he'd apparently missed the fact that somehow he'd fallen in love with her— whether he wanted to or not.

"You all right in there?" he asked, straightening his frame and shaking off his thoughts.

"Fine, Joe," she called over the rush of water. "Just fine."

He heard the faint peal of the doorbell. "Mattie, someone's

at the door. Will you be all right while I run down and answer it? It's probably just one of my sisters stopping by to see how you are. I shouldn't be more than a minute.''

"Joe, go. I'm fine," she said as the doorbell pealed again. After giving her one final glance to make sure she was all right, Joe raced out of the bathroom, then through the bedroom and down the stairs.

"I'm coming, I'm coming," he yelled as the bell pealed urgently again. He got to the door and yanked it open without bothering to look to see who the visitor was, and found himself staring at a stranger.

"Can I help you?"

The woman, whom he guessed to be somewhere close to seventy, had a severe cap of silver-blue hair and frown lines etched around dull gray eyes. She was sturdily built and wore a dress of unrelieved brown, with matching, sensible shoes.

"I'm Evelyn Maguire," she said coldly. "And who might you be?" she asked, taking in his attire. Or rather lack of it, with an expressive lift of her eyebrow.

So this was Mattie's mother-in-law, Joe thought, absently leaning against the doorjamb. She looked almost exactly as he'd expected her to look. Pinched and pursed lips, cool, disdainful eyes, and an attitude that really required some adjustment.

"Joe Marino," he said formally, extending his hand. "Sheriff Joe Marino."

She glanced at his hand and pointedly ignored it, clutching her purse tighter to her ample frame with both hands. "You're the sheriff?" she said with such disdain Joe simply flashed her a charming smile.

"I am."

"What are you doing here this early in the morning?" Her glance of disapproval was clear. "And half-naked at that?" She sniffed as she deliberately lifted her gaze from his chest to stare somewhere over his shoulder. "And where is my daughter-in-law?"

Joe glanced down at himself. If this woman thought she could rattle and intimidate him the way she did to Mattie, she had another guess coming. She had no hold over him, nor did he have to worry about her feelings in the same way Mattie apparently did.

He gave her a smile just to annoy her, then crossed his arms over his chest. "I prefer to think of myself as half-dressed, Mrs. Maguire. And as for Mattie, she's taking a shower."

"A shower?" She made a sound of disgust. "If it's not too much trouble, I'd appreciate it if you'd tell my daughter-in-law I'm here to talk to her about the children." Her glance swept over him again, then over his shoulder to the mess in the living room. "And I can see by the looks of things, it's not a moment too soon, either."

Chapter Ten

Wrapped in a warm, terry-cloth robe, Mattie was curled up on the couch, trying to hold on to her temper and her patience as she listened to her former mother-in-law rage at her.

Joe had slipped into the kitchen to clean up, not wanting to intrude and not wanting to give Evelyn an easy target.

"Really, Mattie. Having a man spend the night in your home—a man you're not married to or related by blood—while my grandsons are in the house, why, it's a disgrace." Purse in her lap, legs crossed at the ankles, Evelyn had a disapproving scowl on her face. "I mean, what were you thinking?" she demanded. "Is this why you wanted to move from Chicago? So you could carry on and carouse with men?"

"Evelyn," Mattie said again, "I have not been carrying on or carousing with men, and I resent your even thinking such a thing, let alone saying it." Mattie sighed. "I've told you several times already. I've been sick. I had the flu. Joe is a friend. He came over to take care of the boys while I was sick." She was beginning to feel as if she was reciting a speech, the same explanation over and over again, and it still didn't get through to the woman.

"You would rather have a stranger care for the boys than his own grandparents?" Evelyn demanded, clearly offended.

"Evelyn, you and Bob weren't here, and I really didn't have a choice in the matter." Mattie met the older woman's gaze. "Joe is not a stranger, but our friend."

"I can just imagine what kind of friend he is," Evelyn said with a sniff. "Be that as it may, I want you to know we don't approve of these kinds of goings-on, and especially not when my grandchildren are around. I would think you'd have more sense. You could have picked up the phone and called. We would have been happy to come and get the boys."

"Exactly," Mattie snapped. "You would have done what you always do, what's best for *you,* not the boys. They're in school, Evelyn, in case you've forgotten, and they're involved in community activities, and they have friends and a life here. They can't just up and take off for a week. And besides that, they were scared. I've never been sick before. They wanted, needed to be here, to see for themselves that it was just the flu I had, and I was going to get well."

"Still, it would have been far better to have the children with us than having your half-naked lover prancing around in front of my grandchildren."

That did it.

Mattie shot to her feet, her heart pounding in anger. She was not about to tell this woman that Joe was not her lover, simply because it was none of her business, and more importantly, with any luck, Mattie was hoping Joe *would* be her lover. Soon. But she wasn't about to lie about it, not to anyone, for it certainly wasn't anything she was ashamed of.

Taking a deep breath, Mattie decided the time had come to put her former mother-in-law in her place. "Evelyn, I've gotten more help and support from Joe in the past week than I have from you since I got pregnant with the twins. You have no right to pass judgment on me or what I do with my life. You've never been here, Evelyn," Mattie finally snapped, realizing she didn't mean just the past week, but from the moment she'd met the woman. ''Not ever. From the moment I got pregnant, you and Bob, as well as Gary, abandoned me.'' Mattie swallowed hard, clenching her fists so tightly her nails bit into her palm. She would not cry over this, she told herself. She simply wouldn't. They weren't worth it. None of them.

''That's ridiculous,'' the older woman snapped. ''That was your decision. Not mine. You have only yourself to blame.''

''Myself?'' Mattie's voice rose. ''I was carrying your son's children. Didn't that mean anything to you?'' Mattie cried. ''I never got to make a decision, Evelyn. What I was given was an ultimatum, an ultimatum you had no right to issue. This was between Gary and I, and if you would have stayed out of it, maybe—'' Mattie's voice broke off, and she was appalled by what she'd almost said.

''Then maybe what?'' Evelyn's eyes glittered with anger and tears. ''Then maybe my son would still be alive?'' Evelyn got to her feet, clutching her purse tightly. ''How dare you?'' she breathed. ''How dare you say such a thing to me!'' Her chin lifted. ''If our son hadn't met you, he'd still be alive. You're the cause of his death, not me.''

Mattie's eyes slid closed and she realized this was the crux of the problem with the Maguires. They were still blaming her for their son's death.

Mattie crossed the room until she was standing in front of her former mother-in-law. She could take the insults about her parenting ability, but she was not, under any circumstances, going to let Evelyn blame her for Gary's death, nor was she going to allow this woman to impugn Joe or his character. She'd never met a decent, finer man, and to have this woman attack his character after the way she'd behaved over the past five years was outrageous. Totally outrageous.

''Evelyn.'' Mattie took a deep breath and slid her hands into her robe pockets. ''For the past five years I have listened to you criticize and berate me and everything I've ever done to or for my boys. I've allowed it because I never wanted to deprive the twins of grandparents. I felt I owed my children that much since they were already growing up without a father.

I thought having you in their lives was worth whatever abuse I had to take and put up with from you."

"Abuse?" Evelyn scoffed. "That's ridiculous. We've never said anything but the truth."

"No, Evelyn," Mattie said coolly. "You wouldn't know the truth if it bit you on the...nose. You're so busy finding fault that you can't see beyond it. Can't see beyond your own selfish pain and needs. But you've gone too far now. Much too far." Mattie's voice was far too calm and quiet. Anyone who knew her knew that was more dangerous than if she'd been yelling and screaming.

Evelyn looked up at her coldly, confusion etched in her features. "I don't know what you're talking about," she insisted, glaring at Mattie. "We only wanted what was best for our grandsons."

"Exactly, Evelyn. What *you* thought was best." Mattie's fists clenched tighter inside her pockets as she stared at the woman who'd made her life and her sons' lives a living hell. "You never ever considered what was best for the boys, but only what *you* wanted, needed, not what they wanted or needed." Inhaling deeply, Mattie knew she had to get all this out now before she exploded. "You're not the boys' mother, Evelyn. I am, something you've totally disregarded and never taken seriously."

"But—"

"No, Evelyn, for once you're going to *listen.* I have stayed quiet and let you insult me, berate me and terrorize me for the past five years. I really thought I was doing it for the boys, but I realize now I was simply doing it out of guilt. But you know what? I don't have any reason to feel guilty. Not for you or your loss. It wasn't my fault, Evelyn," Mattie said with a weary sigh. "I didn't kill Gary, nor did I have anything to do with his death. His own irresponsibility and selfishness are to blame. Not me, and I'm not going to feel guilty about it any longer. Nor am I going to allow you to make me feel guilty about it." Taking a deep breath, Mattie studied her former mother-in-law. "You profess to love the boys—"

"We do," she snapped. "More than anything else in the

world. But I don't expect someone like you to understand that.''

"You don't scare or frighten someone if you love them, Evelyn, and that's something you've done repeatedly to the boys and they don't deserve it. Now," Mattie said, taking another deep breath, "I'd like you to leave my home."

"What!"

"You heard me," Mattie said. "I'd like you to leave. And from this day forward, unless you can refrain from scaring the boys by talking about things that are none of your business, and unless you can refrain from criticizing my parental abilities whether you agree with me or not, you're no longer welcome in my home or *in our lives.*"

Evelyn's eyes went wide and her lower lip began to tremble. "Y-you you can't mean that," she sputtered.

Determination slid through Mattie and she folded her arms across her chest. "I do mean it," she insisted. "Until you can conduct yourself like normal grandparents—and that means putting the boys needs and feelings ahead of your own, and not upsetting them—you're not welcome here." Mattie walked to the front door and opened it wide. "Or in my children's lives. Now, please leave."

"I…this is wrong. You have no right," Evelyn said. "You can't do this."

"I can and I will. *This* decision is up to you, Evelyn."

"But you can't forbid us from seeing our grandchildren."

"Goodbye, Evelyn," Mattie said, holding the door open and waiting.

"You haven't heard the last of me."

"No, I didn't imagine so," Mattie muttered as Evelyn stormed out the door. "Goodbye, Evelyn," Mattie said quietly to the woman's retreating back.

Taking a slow, deep breath, Mattie watched the woman climb into her car, and then peel away, before she slowly closed the front door, leaning wearily against it.

"I never knew I could prance," Joe said with a smile, coming in from the kitchen. He'd tossed on a rumpled sweatshirt, but was still barefoot, with a dish cloth tossed over his shoulder from the scrubbing he'd just given the kitchen.

"Half-naked, as well," he said with a smile, walking straight to Mattie and slipping his arms around her. She was pale as the moon and clearly shaken. "Must have been some sight," he said quietly. His gaze met hers. "You okay?" he asked softly, and Mattie nodded, blinking back tears. She wasn't going to waste any more tears on any of those people.

"Yeah, I'm fine," she whispered, glancing down, not wanting him to see the tears that were already forming in her eyes.

He hated to see her like this, hurting and upset. She didn't deserve it. "Come here," he said quietly, drawing Mattie closer until she was pressed against him. Her whole body was trembling and it nearly broke his heart. "For what it's worth, you did the right thing, Mattie. She was wrong. Dead wrong."

"I guess when she started making derogatory remarks about you, I just…lost it." Weary, Mattie rested her head on his shoulder, slipping her arms around his waist, needing to feel his warmth, his closeness.

She sighed, allowing herself to rest against him, feeling the hard length of him pressed against the length of her and savoring the feeling. "I've taken so much from them, Joe, that this was just the final straw, especially after everything you've done for us this past week." Mattie lifted her head to look at Joe. He was such a beautiful person, she thought, wondering what on earth she would do without him. So beautiful. Inside and out. She'd never met a finer man.

He smiled at her. "I'm proud of you, Mattie, for standing up to her, and for making her leave. She was wrong, and had no right saying those things to you." He drew back. "You don't blame yourself for Gary's death, do you?"

Mattie shook her head. "No, I never did, and I think that bothered her more than anything."

"Because they *did* blame you?"

"Yeah." She blew out a breath, still unbearably shaken. "I guess that's why they've treated me this way all this time. They blamed me," she said, still unable to believe or comprehend it. "I just didn't realize it until now."

"And yet they never considered their own culpability?" Joe shook his head, unable to believe people could be so blind. "It's amazing how blind people can be when it comes to seeing their own failures and problems." He kissed her forehead. "Come on, Mattie, I think it's time for you to rest." She was far too pale for his liking.

"Joe—"

"At least lie down for a while. You're still weak, and this certainly didn't help." He kissed her again. "And if I'm not mistaken, you've got another headache."

She smiled, hooking her arm through his as he led her toward the stairs. "You're right, there." She pressed her free hand to her temple, trying to ease the ache.

"You take some aspirin, then a nap. And I promise I'll have a surprise for you when you wake up."

They'd just reached the top of the stairs and she looked at him wildly. "Surprise? What? Are you going to blow the house up?"

After taking one look at the chaos in the living room, blowing the joint up might be easier than cleaning it after a week of mainly males inhabiting it.

He laughed, taking her hand as he led her into the bedroom. "Nothing quite that drastic." He nudged her toward the bed, pulling the covers down so she could climb in. "You'll find out when you wake up. Now, in you go."

He held the covers out while she slid into bed. It wasn't that she was feeling ill any longer, no, now, she was just plain weary and tired from five years of nonsense with her in-laws, but now, finally, it was over, and all Mattie wanted to do was put it behind her.

"I never got to kiss you," she complained as he shook two aspirin out of the bottle and handed them to her, along with a glass of water.

He chuckled. "I know, but believe me, I intend to take you up on that as soon as you're better."

"I don't suppose you'd believe I'm better right now?" she teased, reaching out a hand to him. Torn, he looked at her for a long moment. "Joe," she said quietly, "I don't need aspirin. I don't need rest. I need...you."

He swallowed. "Mattie, uh...are you sure?"

She tugged on his hand to bring him closer. "I've never been surer of anything in my life." Her gaze remained steady on his, all the love inside fueling her feelings. "Stay with me, Joe. Please?" Her gaze wide and open and full of trust searched his. "Make love to me, Joe," she whispered quietly. "Please."

"Mattie..." His voice trailed off as his thoughts tangled. He wanted this, desperately, wanted Mattie, but he wanted to be certain it was what she wanted. "I...I...I...don't want your gratitude," he said, and she laughed.

"Joe, is that why you think I want you to make love to me? Out of gratitude?" He looked at her, not answering. "Joe, I love you," she said simply, laying her heart open. "And it has nothing to do with gratitude," she added softly. "I know you probably aren't happy to hear that, but—"

"Mattie." The one word stopped her cold and she looked at him. He captured her hand, lifting it to his mouth to tenderly kiss each and every fingertip. "I love you, too," he said gently, knowing in that instant it was true. "But loving each other, Mattie, it isn't—"

"Joe, it's enough for now," she said, not letting him finish. She was fully aware of how he felt, fully aware that they'd never marry, but it didn't change how she felt about him, or how much she wanted him. Perhaps she couldn't have the marriage, but she still wanted the man.

"Please just make love to me." She lifted her face toward him, praying he couldn't tell how scared or nervous she was.

He sat down beside her, framing her face with his hands, letting all the love he felt inside for her wash over him.

"You are so beautiful," he whispered, kissing her eyes, her cheeks, her nose, and finally her lips, letting his mouth linger to tease and seduce. "So beautiful," he whispered again. His warm breath fluttered over her lips and Mattie shivered, reaching for him, wrapping her arms tightly around his neck as they fell backward together on the bed.

He continued to kiss her, trailing his lips softly, gently, across her face, her lips, then sliding lower to light a fiery path of passion down the slim column of her neck.

Mattie moaned softly, shifting her body so she could feel his, wanting this flaming ache inside relieved.

''Mattie.'' Her name came out a low groan as desire whipped into him, blurring his mind, awakening his senses. He wanted—needed to touch her, to feel her body, soft and ready for him, wanting with the same kind of need and desire that lashed through him.

His hand slid from her slender waist upward to cup her breast through the thin cotton of her gown. Her low moan heated his blood, desperately urging him on.

He felt her fingers clutch in his sweatshirt, her small, sharp gasp as he cupped her small breast in his hand, caressing it slowly, gently, until she was arching against him, moaning softly, driving him nearly mad.

He took them deeper, slowly, inch by inch he gave her all the passion and desire that had built inside for her. He slipped off her gown, sliding over each inch of exposed skin with his lips, his tongue, making her shudder and moan, and reach for him.

Her body was pale white and slender as a young girl's, with little trace that she'd ever given birth. Her legs were long and shapely, legs that he'd drooled over on more than one occasion.

Her breasts were high and firm, small, they fit her body structure to perfection, and fit his hands as if they were made for him. Only him.

She was the most beautiful creature he had ever seen. Just the sight of her, naked, and wanting him was enough to nearly send him over the edge.

His own desire became a fierce, breathing animal bearing fire. All heat and warmth, he couldn't seem to get enough of her. Couldn't seem to fill his hands, his mouth, his heart.

His mouth went to her breast, her nipple, and she cried out, arching again, her eyes glazed with desire, passion. Gently, his other hand caressed the silk of her skin, her thighs, then higher, until she was whimpering softly, the sound only fueling his own desire.

His own body hardened and ached in a way that had his breath nearly ripping from his lungs. He couldn't wait, not an instant longer. He needed to be inside her, to be one with her, in body, and in heart. He'd never needed like this, never loved like this, and surely had never wanted like this.

He rose over her, pinning her hands with his. He paused, met her gaze, and looked deep into her eyes.

"I love you, Mattie," he whispered, watching her eyes glaze as he slowly entered her. "I love you."

She clung to him, whispering words of love in his ear as he began to move inside her. Slowly at first, drawing out moans and whimpers that were more beautiful to him than the greatest symphonies.

"Joe, please." Her voice was husky with passion, her body pliant with desire as he moved faster, bringing them both higher and higher. He never released her hands, needing something solid and steady to hold on to. He never drew his gaze from hers, watching all the emotions streak across her face, watching as love filled her eyes and desire fueled her body, higher and higher.

When she hit the first peak, he heard her gasps of breath, the short, muffled scream as she clung to him, dazed. He didn't stop, but drove her back up again until she was clinging to him, moaning softly.

Gasping for breath, Mattie reached for his hips, urging him on, faster, faster, until they both fell off the cliff—together.

Dazed, Joe shifted his weight, fearing he was hurting her. He'd never felt so complete, as if the final puzzle piece in his life had finally slid home.

"No, don't move," Mattie whispered against his chest. "I like having you here."

"I'm too heavy for you," he said, glancing down at her. They lay side by side, his arm around her, their hearts beating in rhythm. "I don't want to hurt you."

She laughed, pressed her lips to his chest, still savoring the taste and touch of him. "You won't." She hesitated. "Joe?" Her gaze searched his when he turned his head to look at her. Feeling suddenly shy, she glanced away. "I'm...I don't...I don't have a lot of experience at this, and I know I'm probably not very good at—"

He burst out laughing, then hugged her closer, pressing kisses atop her head. "Not any good?" He laughed. "Mattie, if you'd have been any better, you'd have probably killed me." He kissed her again, then sighed deeply in contentment, crossing his ankles.

"It's never been like this before, Joe." She toyed with the hair on his chest. "Not with anyone." She tilted her head so she could see his face, then smiled. "I never knew it could be like this." She was far too embarrassed to tell him she'd never been with anyone but Gary, and even then it had been a rather rushed, ridiculous affair.

"It's never been like that for me, either, Mattie." Joe smiled at her. "Not with anyone else, either." He stroked a hand down her hair, still a bit dazed and thoroughly delighted. "It was...incredible."

"Joe—"

"You're worrying, again, Mattie," he said with a knowing smile. "I can see it by your eyebrows. Tell me, what are you worrying about now?"

She hesitated for a moment, then a seductively feminine smile slid across her face as she lifted herself to slide the length of his body. His eyes widened in surprise, but he adjusted himself. Quickly.

She slid her fingers through his hair, lifting the back of his head so she could reach his mouth. "I was just worried that maybe you wouldn't want to do this again." Laughing, she pressed her mouth to his, lapping gently at the corners with her tongue.

Desire hit him hard and fast again, making him reach for her as she began to undulate on top of him.

"Uh...Mattie," he all but moaned, his eyes almost sliding back in his head at the teasing pleasure radiating through him. "I'd say you've got nothing...to worry about."

"No?" She lifted herself and then gently, slowly, impaled herself on top of him. When his breath caught, she smiled and lowered herself still farther on him. "Good." She pressed her hands to his chest, then slid her fingers to his nipples in a slow, circular motion that caused him to mutter an oath. "That's what I was hoping you'd say."

Clutching her waist, Joe held on as she slowly began to move up and down. "Mattie?" The word hitched out on a jagged breath.

"Mmm, yes, Joe?" she murmured, watching him in fascination as the wild flare of desire she felt was reflected in his eyes.

"At this rate, you just might…kill me," he all but moaned as she pressed her lips to his neck and began to nibble. "But I can't think of a better way to go."

By Monday, Mattie's world was back to normal. She was fully recovered from the flu, the boys were back in school and more excited than she'd ever seen them to be starting the last week of this semester. Tomorrow evening was their play, and she and Joe had promised to go over the boys' lines one more time with them tonight.

Her aunt had returned from Milwaukee, very excited about the prospects of holding a showing for a new artist she'd discovered. She and Mattie had a meeting set up right after lunch to work out the details.

Since Mattie was out of school now, and had her mornings free, she'd started going in to the gallery to help Colleen out. With summer going full force, tourists had been arriving in droves, creating a great deal more foot traffic.

This morning, as she consulted with a buyer about one of Clancy's paintings—the one he'd been working on for the past few weeks—Mattie kept an eagle eye out the window, hoping to catch a glimpse of Joe.

They'd spent the rest of Friday together, more in bed than out, she thought with a blush now. And she couldn't ever remembering having a more wonderful evening.

Sated and satisfied, about midnight, they realized they were hungry, so they'd warmed up some of the leftovers from all the dinners Gina had sent over. And they'd talked. About everything except the obvious. Their relationship.

She'd finally explained to him why she'd been avoiding him, shocked when he'd told her he'd been afraid it was because of Johnny and his family. It had hurt, she remembered now, to have him think that of her. So she'd quietly explained that she knew on the day they had visited Johnny that she was in love with him, a day he'd reiterated his intention never to get married. So she'd thought it best to put some distance between them, if only to keep her heart from being broken.

Her confession seemed to clear the air between them, but they'd both deliberately avoided talking about the future. Or their relationship. Content to just…let it be for now.

It was enough for her to know he did love her. It would have to be enough, Mattie had rationalized. He'd been honest with her from the beginning, and she would never want to force him into doing something he didn't want to.

"How soon can you ship it then?" the buyer asked, bringing Mattie out of her reverie. She shook her head to clear it.

"I'm sorry, what did you say?"

He smiled. "How soon can you ship this piece?" He glanced at Clancy's painting, displayed under soft light on a full easel. "I'd like to have it in and up in time for my wife's birthday party."

"If I ship today, you should have it by the end of the week. No later," she assured him.

"That will be fine." He smiled and extended his hand to her. "I'll leave the details in your capable hands. It's been a pleasure."

After putting a small Sold sign on the painting, Mattie gathered the paperwork to give to Colleen to handle. She'd take care of the shipping herself, later this afternoon, since she had other pieces to ship as well.

Mattie had just reached her desk when the bell over the door tinkled. She turned with a smile and froze.

Standing inside the doorway was Evelyn Maguire, looking very out of place and uncomfortable. Quickly, Mattie glanced around the gallery to see how many patrons were there. The last thing she wanted was a scene in the gallery.

She rushed forward, hoping to head Evelyn off. The last thing she wanted was to air her family problems in public.

"Evelyn," she said, keeping her voice deliberately cool. "I'm surprised to see you."

The older woman hesitated, glancing down at her hands, which had a death grip on her purse. "I imagine you are," she said quietly. She met Mattie's gaze. "Is there somewhere we can talk?"

Mattie started to shake her head. "This is my aunt's place of business, Evelyn. I'd prefer not to cause a scene here. And if I recall, we both said everything we needed to at my house last week."

"That…that's why I'm here, Mattie. Because I think there are a few more things I need to say. I've done a lot of thinking since I left your house, and there are some things I simply must say."

Realizing the woman wasn't going to leave until she had her say, and her way, which was par for the course, Mattie sighed, then pointed toward the back of the gallery.

"There's a small workroom in the back. It's empty right now, so we can probably use it for a few minutes."

Evelyn nodded, then followed Mattie toward the back of the gallery. "Colleen," Mattie said, pausing at her desk. "I'll be in the workroom for a few minutes. Can you handle things until then?"

Colleen's gaze went from Evelyn to Mattie, then she grinned brightly. "Sure, Mattie. No problem."

Mattie glanced at her watch. "And if Joe comes in to pick me up for lunch, tell him I'll be right with him." He was supposed to be here in fifteen minutes and she had no idea how long this was going to take.

"Will do."

Mattie continued toward the back of the gallery, knowing Evelyn was behind her, and knowing, too, that Evelyn had heard her conversation about Joe. But Mattie wasn't ashamed of her relationship with him, nor was she about to hide it.

Once inside the workroom, Mattie slid the door closed and turned to face the woman. "You've obviously got something on your mind." She was not in the mood for this today.

"Mattie, I've come to apologize to you." Evelyn smiled when Mattie's face registered shock and her mouth all but dropped open. "I know, you probably never expected to hear those words from my lips."

"No, I must admit I didn't," Mattie said, still not entirely sure what was going on. Mattie tried not to notice how tired, and suddenly, how very, very old Evelyn looked. Why hadn't she noticed it before? she wondered, feeling a strong bout of sympathy for the woman.

"After I left your house, I admit I was angry. Very, very angry." Evelyn hesitated, licking her lips and glancing away for a moment. "Then I realized exactly what I was so angry about. It wasn't with you, Mattie. I realize that now. It was just easier to blame someone else than to have to look at my own failings." Tears spilled slowly down the woman's cheeks. "All this time, I've been trying to avoid taking the blame for my son's death." She managed a weak smile. "I knew I'd spoiled Gary. I know that we hadn't helped him by giving in to him all the time, by giving him all the things he wanted." She shrugged. "But we loved him so much. He was our miracle. We never thought we'd have a child, and when he came along…" Evelyn's words trailed off and she sniffled, opening her bag to dig for a handkerchief. "We thought we were doing the right thing by giving him anything and everything he wanted. I realize now that was exactly the wrong thing." With a wan smile, she wiped her nose, then her eyes. "But sometimes parents don't realize the truth until it's too late."

"Evelyn, I'm sorry," Mattie said softly, meaning it. She couldn't imagine the burden of guilt this woman had to carry, feeling as if she was responsible for her own child's death. Nor the grief that went along with it. Losing a child was not something any parent should have to go through, nor probably would ever get over.

"I know you are, Mattie. But you've got nothing to be sorry for. You are the only person who's acted with any integrity or common sense since this whole mess began. Once Gary died, it was like I'd lost everything. I literally almost went mad with grief.'' She shook her head, then took a slow, deep breath. ''And then when you had the boys…it was like we'd been given a second chance.''

''But they're *my* children,'' Mattie reminded her gently.

''I know.'' Evelyn sniffled. ''And we certainly didn't make things any easier for you. Not then. Not now. And I truly am sorry about that.'' She hesitated, studying Mattie's face. ''I think you're a wonderful mother, Mattie. You're raising your children with rules and goals and discipline so that when they grow up, they'll be responsible young men, capable of dealing with whatever life hands them.'' Her eyes grew sad. ''Something that I'm afraid Gary never learned to do.''

There was nothing for Mattie to say because Evelyn spoke the truth, so she merely stood there, listening.

''The last thing I want, Mattie, is to lose my grandsons. I don't know how much time I have left, but I know enough to know that those are the only grandchildren I will ever have and it's important that Bob and I are a part of their lives.''

''There's no reason for you not to be part of the boys' lives, Evelyn, and I've never objected to it—''

''No, you haven't, Mattie, even perhaps when you should have. I realize now that what you said was true. I put my own selfishness ahead of the twins, and that's not right.'' She took a slow deep breath. ''I'm repeating the same mistakes with my grandsons as I did with my son.'' She smiled. ''Fortunately, this time I realized it before it was too late. I can't change what's happened in the past, but I can apologize to you for it, and promise that it won't happen in the future.'' Evelyn took a step closer to Mattie and reached for her hand. It was the first time in memory, Mattie could remember the woman ever touching her or showing any affection.

''Mattie,'' she began hesitantly, ''Bob and I promise not to criticize you or interfere with your life or the boys' lives…we promise to be merely indulgent grandparents.''

Mattie stood there for a moment, taking everything in, trying to understand. The look on the older woman's face spoke volumes. There was hope, yes, but there was grief as well. Fresh and fierce. And Mattie knew that whatever this woman had done to her or the boys had come out of someplace in that grief, a grief that was simply unimaginable. Mattie put herself in the other woman's place, and realized what a heavy burden Evelyn had been carrying.

Mattie was neither mean nor spiteful, and even if she wasn't ready to forgive or forget so easily—the hurt went too deep, the pain cut too far—she wasn't about to deprive her sons of the opportunity to finally have a real, normal set of grandparents.

"Evelyn," Mattie finally said, "tomorrow night the boys are in a play at school. It's *Charlotte's Web,* and they each have a part. My aunt and a few of our friends are going to see the play, and I was wondering if you and Bob would like to join us." Mattie smiled. "I think the boys would like that."

Hope brightened the older woman's eyes and she smiled. "Oh, Mattie, yes, we'd like that very much, too."

"Good." Blowing out a breath, Mattie glanced at her watch. "The play starts at six, and everyone is meeting at my house around five-thirty."

"We'll be there," Evelyn said, giving Mattie's hand a squeeze. "Thank you, dear. You will never know how much this means to me. I can't wait to get back to the hotel to tell Bob."

"You're welcome, Evelyn. All I will ever ask or expect of you is to always put the boys' needs and feelings first."

"We will from now on, dear, honest." When Mattie glanced at her watch again, Evelyn must have realized how busy she was. "I'd better go, Mattie. I've taken up enough of your time." Wiping her nose one last time, she gave Mattie a smile. "We'll see you tomorrow." She patted Mattie's hand. "And thank you, dear. Thank you."

Mattie waited until she heard the overhead bell tinkle before she walked out of the workroom. She was still stunned, still in a bit of shock, and not certain if Evelyn was to be believed, but for now, she'd give her the benefit of the doubt.

For her children's sake.

Chapter Eleven

On Tuesday evening, with the boys' play scheduled to begin in less than fifteen minutes, Mattie paced the sidewalk in front of the school, wondering what on earth had happened to Joe.

She was nearly frantic now, knowing this wasn't like him. He wasn't irresponsible, nor would he just not show up to something he'd long ago promised the boys he'd attend.

She hadn't seen him since last night, when he'd helped her go over the boys' lines with them again after practice. He'd stayed, helped her put the twins to bed, and then the two of them had gone out and sat in the backyard, just talking and enjoying having some quiet time alone together.

Everything had been fine.

Until today.

She'd started calling him around noon when he didn't show up for lunch as planned. She'd called the sheriff's office, but Clarence had informed her he hadn't seen Joe all day. But he had had a rather hasty phone message from him, telling him to handle the store for a while. If Clarence thought that particularly odd, he didn't mention it to her.

She'd repeatedly called Joe's house and his cell phone, but there was no answer at either phone, leaving her simply to worry and wonder.

As the minutes ticked by, Mattie realized she couldn't wait out here any longer. The play was about to begin, and she wasn't about to miss it.

It was almost midnight by the time Mattie finally got the overexcited boys down to sleep. They'd been extremely disappointed when they learned that Joe had not made the play, but Mattie had smoothed things over by telling them that something very, very important must have come up for Joe to miss it. She reminded the boys that Joe never made promises he didn't keep. This was an exception.

If the boys were disappointed, they'd been thrilled to know that Johnny had attended the performance. Mattie had called the residential facility last week and invited Johnny to the play. She'd even driven out to pick him up this afternoon after work. It was supposed to have been a surprise for the boys as well as Joe.

Johnny had been thrilled to be invited and included, and happy to watch Cody and Connor perform. After the play—which she'd assured them they'd been brilliant in—the Maguires had invited everyone over to the ice-cream parlor for sodas and malts to celebrate.

With the twins nearly falling asleep in their ice cream, she had driven Johnny back to the home, then she'd brought her own boys home, anxious to get them down for the night.

Now, walking through her darkened house alone, Mattie rubbed her chilled arms and wondered what on earth could have happened to Joe.

She'd checked her telephone messages as soon as she got in, but there weren't any. Nor were there any messages for her at the gallery.

With another glance out the front window, scanning the darkened street, Mattie knew she had to get to bed, or she'd never be able to get up in the morning. With a sigh, she curled up on the couch and tried not to worry about all the horrible things that might have happened to Joe.

Someone was knocking on the front door.

Bleary with sleep, Mattie unfolded herself from the couch, glanced at the mantel clock and frowned when she realized it was just after 3:00 a.m.

She tossed the throw cover off her and struggled to her feet, hoping to get to the door before the boys awoke. Using the peephole, she checked it to see who was on the other side before opening the door.

With a rush of relief, she saw Joe and scrambled to get the door unlocked.

"Joe, my God, I was so worried." She threw her arms around him, grateful that he was here and in one piece.

His arms slid around her and he held her tight. "I know, I'm sorry. I tried calling but I was in Chicago and my cell doesn't have a roaming feature."

"Chicago?" She drew back and finally noticed his clothes were rumpled, his hair mussed and he looked as if he hadn't slept in days. There were worry lines around his eyes and mouth. "What happened, Joe? What's wrong?" She took his hand and drew him to the couch, fearing he'd fall down if he didn't sit down.

Scrubbing his hands over his face, Joe blew out a breath. "It's Angie."

"Angie, my God, what happened, is she all right?"

He nodded. "She's fine. For the moment," he added, leaning back against the couch and letting his aching muscles release some of the tension they'd been holding. "Late this morning I stopped by to check on her. I found her collapsed on the floor."

"Oh, Joe." Mattie sat down next to him, wanting to soothe, to comfort him.

"I called 911. The Healing Harbor ambulance came, of course, but the paramedics took one look at her and said she probably was going to have to be transferred to a larger, metropolitan hospital that had a neonatal intensive-care unit."

"She was in labor?" Mattie asked, and Joe nodded.

"By this time, yes, but she'd collapsed because her blood pressure had gone so high. They were afraid they were going to lose her and the babies."

"Joe, why didn't you call me?" Fear and worry made her voice sharper than she intended. "I'm sorry," she said quickly. "I didn't mean it to sound like that. I'm sure you had your hands full."

"You're not kidding. And I tried calling you, Mattie. I tried the gallery this afternoon but the line was busy for almost an hour, and then I couldn't leave Angie."

She patted his hand. "I understand, Joe, what happened next?"

"Once we got to the hospital, the doctors tried to stabilize her, but they recommended she be sent by air ambulance to Loyola University Medical Center in Chicago. They have a top-notch neonatal wing as well as high-risk obstetrical specialists on staff. So they transferred her there. We had to wait a couple of hours for the air ambulance, and by the time we finally got to Loyola, she had gone into labor." Joe shook his head. "This whole day seems like one long nightmare."

"Did she have the babies?"

His smile was grim. "She still had about five weeks to go, but fortunately, both babies are strong, healthy and are doing well." He managed a smile. "My two new nieces are just fine. They'll be in intensive care for a few weeks, but the doctors are pretty confident they're going to be just fine."

"Oh, Joe." She leaned over and kissed his cheek. "I'm so glad, I was so worried."

"Mattie." The tone of his voice had her looking at him curiously. He took her hand in his. "I missed the boys' play."

"I know, Joe, it's okay. They understand."

"No," he said simply. "*You* don't understand. You know I'd never do anything deliberately to hurt the boys."

"Of course. I know that, Joe."

"And you also know how much I love them, and you."

"Yes, I do," she said, wondering where he was going with this.

"I love you guys, Mattie, with all my heart, and you know I'd never deliberately let you down, but I did, Mattie, tonight. I let you and the boys down by not being there."

"Joe, that's not the way it is. They understand—"

"But they shouldn't *have* to understand, Mattie, that's my point. I disappointed both you and the boys tonight because my family—my sister needed me. And Mattie, I can't see that changing anytime in the future." He blew out a breath.

"What are you saying, Joe?"

"I love you and I love the boys, Mattie, but I have no right to. I can't and won't marry you because you have a right to expect to come first in your husband's life, ahead of everything, and I can't ever promise that."

"I don't recall ever asking you to," she said quietly. She got up from the sofa and went to the television set, picking something up off it. "Do you see this, Joe?"

He nodded. "Yeah, it's a video camera."

"Joe, I probably understand about family responsibilities coming first more than anyone. Haven't my boys always come first in my life?" She didn't give him a chance to answer. "While I understand the responsibility you feel toward Johnny and admire it," she added, "and love you for it as well, I don't think you truly understand the meaning of family."

"What on earth are you talking about, Mattie?" He was doing this for her own good. And the boys. He never wanted to hurt any of them. He loved them all too much and simply couldn't bear disappointing them.

"You see this camera? When I realized you might not make it to the boys' play, I brought it with me and taped the whole performance so you wouldn't miss anything."

For the first time since he'd arrived, Joe smiled. "You're kidding. That's great. Thanks, Mattie."

"You're welcome."

"I don't understand what taping the play has to do with me not really understanding the meaning of family, though."

Mattie smiled. "Joe, you and I are always going to have responsibilities. To our children. To our individual families and family members, but we also have a responsibility to ourselves and the love we have for one another. Because we love each other, we have a responsibility to be as happy as we can and to share our lives, our loves and all our responsibilities with each other. That's what a real family does. They share their family and their responsibilities with the person they love. That's what makes a family, Joe. Sharing of all these things.''

''What are you saying, Mattie?'' he asked carefully.

''I'm saying, Joe, that if we love each other, truly love each other and want to be together, do you really think Johnny or your responsibility toward him should be the reason we can't be together?'' Cocking her head, she looked at him. ''How do you think he'd feel if he knew that's what you thought? He wouldn't like it, would he?''

''Of course not, but Mattie, do you have any idea what you're saying?''

''Of course I do. I've done everything on my own for so long, I don't even know what it's like to have a family.''

''And are you saying you'd like to find out?''

''Yep.'' She grinned. ''I would.''

''Mattie, but what about Johnny?'' he asked softly, making her grin spread. ''You know I take my responsibility toward him seriously. It comes first, it always has, it always will. Can you live with that?''

''Well, let me put it this way, Joe.'' She grinned. ''I love Johnny, truly, and apparently the feeling is mutual.'' Her grin widened and she rocked back on her heels. ''In fact, if you don't want to marry me, I've got a standing offer from him.''

''Johnny?'' Surprised, Joe merely stared at her. ''What— how did that come about?''

''At the play tonight—''

''Johnny was at the play?'' He shook his head. ''When— how—'' He shook his head again, too exhausted to think. ''I don't understand.''

''The boys wanted to invite him, so I offered to go get him. I called the home and got permission to take him out for the evening. Johnny was thrilled to go with us.'' She shrugged.

"We all went to the play, out for ice cream, and then the boys and I drove him home."

"And you're all right with that, Mattie? Having Johnny as part of our lives?" He held his breath, unable to dream, to hope.

"He's part of our family, Joe, why wouldn't I be comfortable or all right with that?" She laughed. "The boys love him so much they want to go live with him." She pushed her hair back. "I told them that still needed a great deal of discussion. But maybe, Joe, we could have Johnny live with us at some point. Even if it's just a night or two a week. I think it would be good for everyone."

All the fears and doubts he'd carried around inside evaporated like a misty fog, and his heart swelled with love. "Mattie, you are incredible."

"No," she said with a laugh. "Just practical. I figured if you wouldn't marry me, hey, Johnny would."

Joe reached for her. "He's going to have to get his own girl." He kissed her full and hard on the mouth. "You're mine."

"Does this mean you're going to marry me?"

Joe held her tight, then let all the empty hopes and dreams he'd carried around in his heart for so long…go.

"I am, Mattie, if you and the boys will have me."

"We'll have you," Cody and Connor yelled from their perch on the steps were they'd been eavesdropping for the past five minutes. "We'll have you." Jumping up, the boys scurried down the stairs, raced across the living room and jumped in Joe's lap.

"Does this mean you're going to marry our ma?" Cody asked, snuggling closer to Joe.

"Indeed it does," Joe responded, ruffling his hair.

"Then it's a rule that you gotta be our father, right?" Connor asked, snuggling to get closer as well.

Joe and Mattie exchanged glances. He'd been around the boys long enough now to know when they were up to something. But at the moment, he was too tired to try to figure out what.

"A rule?" He shook his head. "Well, I don't know what those rules are you're talking about, but I would like very much to be your father. That is if you boys want me." Joe looked from one impish face to the other then relaxed as both boys grinned.

"Yes, yes, we want you," they both shouted, making him wince. "Can we tell Bobby Dawson tomorrow?" Cody asked. "I can't wait to tell him we got our own dad now."

"Yeah, and our dad can play baseball and run fast."

"He likes us and—" Cody stopped abruptly, turning to face Joe. "Coach Joe, do you know how to do arithmetic?"

Joe's eyebrows went up. "Arithmetic?" He glanced at Mattie, remembering they'd already had a conversation about this. Several, in fact.

"Well, yeah, I guess you could say I know how to do arithmetic." He frowned. "Why, is it required to be your dad?" he asked skeptically. Another thought followed that one. "Does this have something to do with Bobby Dawson?"

He had a feeling that Bobby Dawson had a lot to do with a lot of things the twins got mixed-up in. And mixed-up about, he realized with a smile.

Both boys exchanged mischievous glances. "Well, Bobby said that we get arithmetic problems in school and we'll have to bring them home to do."

"Yeah, and I said that was stupid," Cody explained.

"So…let me see if I'm getting this," Joe said, realizing he just might be following the maze of the boys' minds. It was a scary thought. "So you wanted a dad who knew how to do arithmetic so he could help you when you had to bring problems home, right?"

"Yep." Twin strawberry-blond heads bobbed up and down. "You got it."

"That's what I was afraid of," Joe said with a laugh. He wrapped his free arm around Mattie and drew her close. "Well, Mattie, I guess it's a done deal. You're stuck with me."

"And you with me." She kissed him, her heart soaring as she looked at the man she loved holding the children she loved. She'd never seen anything more beautiful or perfect. "Okay, boys, it's time to get back to bed. You have school tomorrow."

"Aw, do we have to?" they complained as she shooed them off Joe's lap and toward the steps.

"Hey, Connor?"

"Yeah, Cody?"

"We got us a dad, right?"

"Right?"

"And a new friend, Johnny."

"Yeah."

Cody turned and flashed his parents a mischievous smile. "I wonder how Coach Joe feels about…dogs." With a laugh, both boys bounded upstairs.

"I'm going to love being a father," Joe said. "Mischievous or not."

"You know they're going to drive you nuts now until you let them get a dog."

"Hey, not me. That's a family issue. And we're a family, remember?"

Mattie pressed her lips to Joe's and sighed. "I remember." A family, she thought warmly. It was what they had wanted and needed all along.

Epilogue

One year later

"Cody, if you take that tie off, your mom's going to skin us both alive," Joe said as he glanced around the gallery, trying to make sure Mattie wasn't within sight. Or earshot.

"How come I gotta wear a tie?" Cody asked.

"Because this is your mom's first solo showing of her artwork. It's very important to her that we all look nice." Joe fiddled with his own tie, wishing he could take it off. "And now that she's bought the gallery from Aunt Maureen, it's important to your mom that everything run smoothly."

"Dad, do you think anyone's gonna buy Mom's pictures?" Connor asked, looking up at him.

"I'm sure of it," Joe said proudly. "Remember how Aunt Maureen explained that she'd already sold five sketches? She's taking some of your mom's sketches with her to Europe as well."

"When's Aunt Maureen leaving?" Cody wanted to know, making Joe smile.

"Well, Aunt Maureen and Clancy are leaving on their honeymoon sometime tomorrow."

"Honeymoon?" Cody giggled. "What's that?"

Uh-oh. Joe's frantic gaze searched for Mattie. This was not a question or a subject he wanted to get into, at least not now, not with the boys. He didn't think he was old enough to talk about this with them yet.

"Mattie?" He waved toward her, then smiled when she turned and started walking toward them.

"Thank goodness," he murmured, grabbing her arm and pulling her close. "Cody wants to know what a honeymoon is."

Mattie saw the look on Joe's face and burst out laughing. "If I didn't know better, I'd think you were scared," she teased, making him run a nervous hand around his collar.

"Scared?" He shook his head. "Terrified is more like it. You explain it to them."

"Fine." Mattie bent down so she could see both boys' faces. "A honeymoon, boys, is when a man and woman who've just gotten married go away together on a vacation, just them two alone."

"How could they have any fun alone?" Cody wanted to know, almost making Joe choke. "Can't they bring any friends?"

"No," Mattie said. "No friends."

"What about toys?" Connor asked, and Joe almost lost it.

"No, no toys," Mattie said, smothering a smile of her own.

"Boring," Cody complained. "Can me and Connor go sit outside with Johnny and Clumsy?" he asked. "It's hot in here."

"Sure," Mattie said, placing a gentle, loving hand on his cheek. "Just stay right in front, and stay with Johnny."

"We will."

Mattie waited until the boys were outside before turning to her husband. "Well, I think you handled that…well."

"Hey, hey, you've got years more experience than I have with this parenting stuff. I've only got a year."

"Yeah, well, let's hope that's enough experience for what's coming."

He drew back and gave her a suspicious look. "What? What's coming now?" He had to admit, there was never a dull moment in his house.

"A baby," she said softly, meeting his gaze. "We're having a baby, Joe."

He merely stood there, staring at her for a moment. "A real-live baby?" he stammered, not certain it had registered yet.

"As opposed to a fake-doll baby? Yes, Joe, a real live one."

His gaze went to her belly. It was still flat as a pancake. "Are you sure?"

"Positive."

"When? When are we having this baby?"

She grinned. "In about six months or so, Joe."

"A baby," he breathed softly, lifting her off her feet with a whoop. "We're having a baby," Joe repeated loud enough to make Mattie roll her eyes. She was almost positive everyone in the gallery knew her news now.

"Joe, please, put me down." She grabbed his shoulders.

"We're having a baby," Joe said to Maureen and Clancy who walked up to them wearing identical grins.

"So we've heard," Maureen said, lifting her glass of champagne in the air. "A toast." Her gaze shifted to Mattie. "To my beautiful niece, her beautiful husband and her beautiful, expanding family. May she always know the joy of love."

"Hear, hear," Clancy said, draining his glass, before turning to Mattie. "Well, lassie, my money's on another set of lads."

"Set?" Mattie repeated with a shake of her head. "I don't think so, Clancy."

"No?" He grinned, and held out his glass for a waiter to refill. "I've got good money that says it's a matched set of lads identical to the ones you've got."

Joe almost shuddered at the thought of another pair of mischievous male twins. "I've got ten bucks that says it's a single, female."

"You're on," Clancy said, touching his champagne glass to Joe's before taking his bride by the arm to spirit her away. "Come on, love, our honeymoon awaits." Clancy gave Mattie a kiss on the cheek, and with a wink, he and Maureen were gone.

Six months later both Joe and Clancy lost their respective bets when Mattie gave birth to female triplets.

* * * * *

SPECIAL EDITION™

Three small-town women have their lives turned
upside down by a sudden inheritance.
Change is good, but change this big?

by Arlene James

BEAUTICIAN GETS MILLION-DOLLAR TIP!

(Silhouette Special Edition #1589,
available January 2004)

A sexy commitment-shy fire marshal meets his match
in a beautician with big...bucks?

FORTUNE FINDS FLORIST

(Silhouette Special Edition #1596,
available February 2004)

It's time to get down and dirty when a beautiful
florist teams up with a sexy farmer....

TYCOON MEETS TEXAN!

(Silhouette Special Edition #1601,
available March 2004)

The trip of a lifetime turns into something more
when a widow is swept off her feet by someone
tall, dark and wealthy....

Available at your favorite retail outlet.

COMING NEXT MONTH